"I have a favor t[...]

Heather held her purse in her hands. "I'm not going to..."

"Please hear me out," he interrupted before she could walk out on him. No matter how much he probably deserved it, he wasn't up to having her leave him again. The first time had pretty much killed him.

Killed the old him, anyway. Leaving him with a shadow of a man who lived to make amends— not to be happy.

"It's not for me."

"Of course it's for you. Couched in a client's need, perhaps, but it's about your win. I'm not going back down that road, Cedar."

He swallowed. Pursed his lips so they wouldn't open until he had himself in check. He wasn't going to pour out his truths. Couldn't play with her emotions that way. The turns his life had taken were personal. His alone. They weren't to get her back. Or even to show her that he'd become a better man. He was a man who'd lost his way, and that was a shadow he would carry forever.

Dear Reader,

On one hand this letter is very, very difficult to write. After twenty-five years writing for Superromance, this is my very last one. One of the very last that will ever be printed. I'm so, so thankful to all of you for your years of faithful support and following. *A Defender's Heart* is everything that is TTQ and Superromance. It's full of intense emotion—and a situation that is seemingly hopeless. And yet...there's hope. Because that's the bottom-line truth. Hope. It's what I, and Superromance, have spent decades giving to you and what I pray you will take with you from our immense body of work.

A Defender's Heart stole my heart. It's a story of imperfect people making mistakes that aren't just going to go away. It's about choices. And the will to fight for what matters most, even when fighting for right might mean giving up. We're giving up Supers; we aren't giving up story. Love. Or hope.

And because I don't just write fiction for entertainment, but believe wholeheartedly in the hope and love we portray in our books, I've got hope to leave with you! My stories are going to continue to be available to entertain you into the foreseeable future. I'll still be right here at Harlequin, writing for Special Edition. And more great news—it looks like while Superromance is ending, The Lemonade Stand and Where Secrets are Safe are not. Stay tuned!

Tara

TARA TAYLOR QUINN

A Defender's Heart

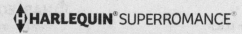

Recycling programs
for this product may
not exist in your area.

ISBN-13: 978-1-335-44926-9

A Defender's Heart

Copyright © 2018 by TTQ Books, LLC

Printed in U.S.A.

Having written over eighty-five novels, **Tara Taylor Quinn** is a *USA TODAY* bestselling author with more than seven million copies sold. She is known for delivering intense, emotional fiction. Tara is a past president of Romance Writers of America. She has won a Readers' Choice Award and is a seven-time finalist for an RWA RITA® Award. She has also appeared on TV across the country, including *CBS Sunday Morning*. She supports the National Domestic Violence Hotline. If you or someone you know might be a victim of domestic violence in the United States, please contact 1-800-799-7233.

Books by Tara Taylor Quinn

HARLEQUIN SUPERROMANCE

Where Secrets are Safe

Wife by Design
Once a Family
Husband by Choice
Child by Chance
Mother by Fate
The Good Father
Love by Association
His First Choice
The Promise He Made Her
Her Secret Life
The Fireman's Son
For Joy's Sake

A Family for Christmas
Falling for the Brother

Shelter Valley Stories

Sophie's Secret
Full Contact

HARLEQUIN HEARTWARMING

Family Secrets

For Love or Money
Her Soldier's Baby
The Cowboy's Twins

MIRA BOOKS

The Friendship Pact
In Plain Sight

Visit the Author Profile page at Harlequin.com for more titles.

For Paula Eykelhof, Jane Robson, Victoria Curran and Piya Campana—I am the only one left here, and yet I take each of you, every day, into every story I write. God gave me talent, I have the will, but you made me the writer I am. Thank you from the depths of my soul. I love and miss you all.

CHAPTER ONE

THE PARTY WAS in full swing. Vehicles, mostly expensive ones, lined both sides of the street. Slowing his SUV out front, Cedar could see the shadows of people milling around behind the sheer drapes that covered the massive windows. Men, women…indeterminate ages.

He could almost hear the laughter and the conversation. Figured most of it would be sincere.

Heather wouldn't surround herself with fakes.

In black jeans and a new button-down, black-and-white striped shirt, he started to feel underdressed. Thought about taking off.

Judging by the quiet surrounding him outside, there were no other late arrivals. His entrance could cause a stir.

She'd invited him to her engagement party.

As someone who paid attention to people—although, admittedly, he'd used what he got to his own advantage—he was curious why his ex-lover and, he privately suspected, the one woman he'd ever loved, had issued that invitation. Curious enough to maneuver into a spot between two sparkling-clean SUVs and pocket his keys.

He'd have stayed anyway, curious or not. His goal was atonement.

It didn't come easy.

"YOU LOOK BEAUTIFUL…"

In a figure-hugging, short black dress and matching wedge heels, with her blond hair in a sophisticated updo, Heather smiled as yet another of her parents' friends spoke to her as she passed by on her way to somewhere else. She'd occasionally worn the dress clubbing in LA, but had little reason to put it on now that she was back in Santa Raquel full-time. She exchanged a few more pleasantries, acknowledging that, yes, her independent polygraph business of five years was thriving, and moved on.

She was looking for Charles. She'd seen him a total of five minutes max since they'd arrived at her parents' beachfront home, just down the road from Charles's house—and ten minutes from her own beachside bungalow.

Fifteen years her senior, her fiancé was handsome. Fit. A dentist who was actually popular with his patients. He had a way of putting people at ease. She'd known him since he'd moved into her parents' neighborhood after his divorce ten years before; she'd been home visiting while on break from college. And she'd started dating him the previous summer, when they hooked up at a neighborhood Fourth of July bash she'd attended with her folks.

Because she'd been too lame to have plans of her own.

Or a date.

She thought she saw his thick, slightly graying hair on the other side of the living room and moved in that direction, hoping she could make it to him without being waylaid again. The party had been her mother's idea. And the guest list pretty much comprised the people invited by her parents and by Charles.

Heather's friends had mostly faded into lives of their own when she'd started dating Charles— and before that, too, after the "big breakup." She'd been part of a couple for almost six years, and while mutual friends had stuck by her—and him—she'd been the one to pull away from the group.

She'd been the one to break things off with him.

Thinking she'd go through the kitchen and enter the living room from the other side, Heather slipped away from the party and walked into a much smaller gathering—the two guests she'd invited, Lianna, her closest friend from elementary school on, and Raine, her college roommate. They stopped talking the second she came in.

"What's going on?" she asked, wondering if there was a problem with the food. Not that they were in charge of it. Her mother'd had the party catered. But they were in the kitchen and...

"I've been looking for you two," she added, glancing from green eyes to blue, red hair to blond. "You're supposed to keep me sane here!" She was only half joking. She couldn't wait to marry Charles—sometime after the year engagement she'd insisted upon—but this gathering was not her favorite part of the festivities.

If it hadn't been for Charles's need to introduce her to his large circle of acquaintances, she never would've agreed to have the engagement party, no matter how much her mother nagged her about social etiquette and doing the right thing.

Lianna and Raine exchanged a glance, Raine cocking an eyebrow at Heather's closest childhood friend. Almost as though conceding best-friend status or something.

"What's going on?" she asked again. The two had met a few times, but didn't know each other well enough to be involved in some big heart-to-heart. If this was about which of them was going to be maid of honor...

Her mother had been after her to make a choice—strongly preferring Lianna, of course, since the redhead had been part of their family since grade school. But Raine had seen her through the best, and then the worst, times of her life. The ones that had defined the woman she was, and would be.

Still, she couldn't imagine getting married without Lianna, her rock, by her side. And Raine was her safety net...

It was all too much. She'd decide later. Right now, she had to get to Charles.

"We're worried about you," Lianna blurted when Raine gave her a far-too-obvious silent nudge.

Heather chuckled. "About me? Are you kidding? I'm finally at a place in my life where there's no need to worry." She looked from one to the other, knowing that what she said was true. "Seriously." And then, when they both looked unconvinced, she added, "A year ago, yes." She'd come close to the brink of despair, close to not caring if she lived or died, when she packed up and moved out of the home she'd shared with Cedar. "But I'm fine now. Great, even. Or I will be as soon as this party is over."

"This engagement is so sudden..."

"Charles and I have been dating for more than six months. I moved in with Cedar three weeks after I met him." The math was important to her. She wasn't jumping into love ever again. Hadn't figured herself for someone who'd ever have done so.

She'd allowed herself that mistake, with the promise that she'd learn everything she had to learn from it, so she wouldn't have to repeat the lesson.

"And I insisted on a yearlong engagement," she reminded them. And herself. Charles wanted to get to the justice of the peace as soon as possible and start a family together.

Understanding that he wanted to be young enough to play ball with his kids, to coach Little League and soccer teams or move stage sets for dance competitions, she'd shortened the engagement from two years to one, but because of the oh-so-painful past, a result of the three-week courtship, she was holding firm on that year.

"He's fifteen years older than you." Raine acted as if she was making some big announcement. Heather slowed down for a second and stared at her two best friends.

"Surely the two of you aren't having a problem with our age difference? My God, Raine, your stepfather is closer to your age than your mom's, and you love him to death. Because, for the first time in your life, she's happy. Truly happy."

In colorful leggings that hugged gorgeous legs and a black formfitting shirt that defined hips that were just about perfect, Raine withstood Heather's intent look without fidgeting. Or answering.

"And you…" She turned to Lianna. "Dexter's only five years younger than Charles."

"We fit each other," Lianna came back without a second's hesitation. She took a step closer. In black dress pants and a cream-colored silk blouse, she could command any room she entered. "Charles fits your parents, sweetie. Look at him in there. He's having the time of his life."

"And you're in here." Raine came closer, too. "Trudging through a party you didn't want and counting the seconds until it's over. Is that really how you want to spend the rest of your life? Counting the seconds away?"

So she'd been watching the clock. But she'd been counting minutes, not seconds. And only because she'd never been a big partier. She liked to spend time with people in small groups—not coming at her all at once.

"Charles is good with large groups of people," she explained. "It's a strength he has that counters my weakness in that area. He covers for me there, and I cover for him in other areas, where my strengths counteract his weaknesses."

"He has weaknesses?" Lianna's droll tone wasn't lost on her.

"Come on, you guys." Heather looked from one to the other, pleading unabashedly. "You just need to spend more time with him. Get to know him like I do."

Well, not quite in that way, but…

"Seriously," Lianna said. "What strength of yours counteracts a weakness of his?"

"He sucks at anything to do with aesthetics. I have a talent for creating beautiful spaces."

"Your greatest talent is your ability to read people." Raine's tone, softer than Lianna's, was no less compelling. "Does he even know that?"

"He knows what I do for a living."

"*Strangers* know what you do for a living, sweetie," Raine said. "Every time you appear in court, everyone there knows you're a polygraphist. One trip to your office would tell someone that you administer lie detector tests, are a certified criminologist and also have a degree in psychology. I'm talking about your gifts, not your training. You deserve to be with someone who respects your ability to see inside people *and* relies on it. Someone who needs you in particular for what you have to offer. Someone who values your specialness."

Like Cedar had? She felt the familiar sensation of lead falling in her stomach, and she quickly diverted her thoughts before she sank down with it. She'd gotten over all of that.

Was beyond it.

Had moved on.

Her friends were staring at her. Raine had once told her she believed Heather was empathic. Heather's take was that other people could see what she saw if they just slowed their own thoughts and feelings enough to hear and see those around them.

Which was why she'd failed so miserably where Cedar was concerned. She'd been unable to get beyond her own feelings for him when he was around. She could now. And was ready to prove it.

"Being used isn't my idea of happiness," she said, as if any of them needed a reminder.

She'd had her doubts about Cedar, had seen what he was becoming, but she'd let passion cloud her judgment.

"So why did you invite him here tonight?"

No one had said the name aloud. They hadn't needed to. It was as if the renowned defense attorney was standing there, in the room with them…

"He didn't show." So the *whys* didn't matter.

"But why did you invite him?" Lianna pressed.

"It'll be easier if we find a way to be friends. Because if we ever run into each other professionally…"

"That's weak, Heather." Lianna again. Sometimes Heather wondered how she'd remained friends with her for so long, but deep in her heart, she knew. Lianna understood her. Well enough to see when she was faltering—and to give her the hard truths when she needed them. Lianna had always been a source of strength.

Just as she'd been one of Lianna's few sources of unconditional love.

"I heard he's still in the area," she said now, in her own defense. He'd sold the house they'd bought together, had paid Heather her share of the proceeds, which she'd used to buy the little bungalow within walking distance of the beach. She'd assumed he'd moved back closer to LA, but when she'd had lunch with a mutual friend from the city the month before, she'd found out differently.

Apparently he'd given up the apartment they'd kept in LA, too, but she assumed he'd bought another one there. Probably twice as nice.

Back when they'd been together, they'd spent some days in the city and some in Santa Raquel every week. Since the breakup, she'd quit staying in the city, choosing to make the hour-plus commute on the days she had to be in court. Or to interview someone who couldn't come to her Santa Raquel office. She'd figured Cedar had done the opposite—left Santa Raquel, making the commute from LA for as long as he kept his Santa Raquel office. Apparently she'd been wrong on that one.

"Just being in the area doesn't explain why he'd be on your guest list." Lianna wasn't dropping this.

"Because I'm over him." The words sounded slightly pathetic. Her reasoning was not.

"Again, no reason to party with him."

Raine's hand was fidgeting against her thigh. A sign that her college friend was truly upset... and holding back. "What do you think?" Heather asked her.

"I don't know," Raine told her. "But I think it's important that you do. So far, I'm not sure that's the case."

"I'm over him." That was the reason. Period.

"Are you?"

"Of course!"

Raine, of all people, knew that.

"You said yourself that I'm a different person now than I was a year ago."

Raine nodded. Licked her lips. Another sign of agitation.

Lianna's gaze was softer than usual as she stood there, watching the two of them. Her silence was more telling in that moment than anything else. She clearly thought that this was bigger than frank talk was going to solve.

"He didn't show, and I'm not even upset. What does that tell you?"

"That you didn't expect to see him here."

She hadn't really. But she'd been prepared, just in case. And she would've been fine.

"I invited him because I *am* over him," she

said again. "Because I knew I could handle it. And because I'd like us to be able to be friendly. If he's still in town, we're bound to run into each other at some point." As Raine had said, she was a criminologist with an undergraduate degree in psychology. A polygraphist who used the test as one of various methods of assessing the truthfulness of the people she tested. One of the skills that made her different from the rest was that she didn't just use a predetermined set of questions. When something raised a dubious response, she listened to what *wasn't* being said and asked more questions until she got a response that gave the signs of being truthful. The scientifically based insights she offered, coupled with the opinions she wrote, made her unique—and valuable. In the state of California, because of the track record she'd quickly built, she was considered an expert witness.

And Cedar defended criminals.

"Charles was okay with you inviting him?" Lianna asked.

"Yes."

The girls exchanged another glance.

"Now what?"

"Don't you find it the least bit odd that a guy doesn't mind if his fiancée's ex is at their engagement party?"

"Charles trusts me." That part sounded a bit

weak, even to her, but... "And I think he wants Cedar to see that I've moved on. He wants him to know that I'm with another man now."

He hadn't actually said so, but she'd read that into the conversation that had taken place between them. When she'd asked if it bothered him that she wanted to invite Cedar, he'd lied to her. He blinked more rapidly when he lied—making him an easy man to read.

One of the many things she loved about him.

She'd continued talking to him until she got to a semblance of the truth.

"Listen, you two, I promise you, I'm over Cedar Wilson. Completely. I'll do whatever you need me to do to prove that to you."

Instead of looking convinced, or even somewhat placated, her two best friends suddenly looked stricken.

"I'm guessing turning around ought to do it." The voice came from behind her and Heather froze. If it was possible to live without a heartbeat, she was doing it.

She knew that voice. Had heard it in her dreams for months after he'd betrayed her.

And woken up with wet cheeks every time.

But no more. She'd cried her last tears for the man who'd purposely manipulated her, who'd used her skills to set a guilty man free.

CHAPTER TWO

I'm over Cedar. Completely.

There she was. Heather Michaels. His Heather. Standing right in front of him.

Saying she was over him completely.

"Cedar! You made it. How are you?"

She sounded like her mother. Or any of the other thirty or forty voices coming from the front room. Superficial. Yet not ten minutes earlier, he'd been certain that the voices emanating from the party had to be sincere. Because the Heather he knew wouldn't have been celebrating her engagement with her parent's crowd.

What had they done to her?

Rather, was this what *he'd* done to her?

"I'm well, and you?"

Raine stood just off to her left. He wanted to catch the other woman's eye. It was good to see her, too. She'd been Heather's roommate when he and Heather first met. Had been there through all of their ups and downs.

It wouldn't be good to be on the receiving end of one of those looks of disappointment he'd occasionally seen on her face in the past. When he'd shown up late. Or not at all. Without bothering to call and let Heather know.

He'd been all about saving his clients' quality of life. At least that was how he'd described it. The way he'd thought about it. When he'd thought about it. If he'd ever thought about it.

"She's great!" Lianna burst into the silence that had fallen, alerting him to the fact that he and Heather had been standing there, staring wordlessly at each other.

He could only imagine what she was getting from him. What "tells" he was sending.

"I'm glad to hear that," he said, instinctively sliding his hands into the pockets of his jeans. Feeling damned conspicuous because she'd read some kind of message into that, too. Figuring he had something to hide. He wanted to pull them back out, but if he did so, that would communicate another message he didn't want her to have.

He'd learned a lot from her. And not nearly enough.

"Um, can you two please leave us alone for a sec?" Heather's tone had changed. Her gaze was still locked with his, but she sounded more like the confident woman he'd been with for the best five years of his life.

Pretty pathetic that his best five years included debts he'd spend the rest of his life paying off—

debts of the soul. And he'd die without ever having paid them off. In spite of the millions he'd amassed and was successfully investing. This wasn't a matter of money...

His peripheral vision caught a movement. The two women slid closer to Heather.

"Please," she said to them. "Just for a sec. I'm fine."

No one moved for a long few seconds. He had the sense of stopped time, the kind that was filled with tension and you knew you were at a make-it-or-break-it point. His cue to move in for the kill. The witness on the stand was about to crack. To present him with the source of that shadow of a doubt he had to put in the minds of the jurors.

His jaw ached with the effort it took to keep his mouth shut, the muscles in his neck bearing the brunt of the tension as he remained locked on Heather, rather than turning his manipulative abilities on her friends to help her get them out of there.

He wanted her alone.

God, how he wanted her alone.

But whatever was going on between Heather and her friends—the choice to leave her with the wolf or not—was solely up to them. He could use his skills and probably get what he wanted—Heather alone. But he couldn't take on any more of that kind of debt.

There simply weren't enough years left in his life to pay for it all. Unless medical science found a way for a guy to live to a thousand. He figured that just might cover it, considering that a few of the worst criminals he'd put back on the street not only came with the current victim to atone for, but the future ones, as well…

More movement. Heather's deep blue eyes seemed to glisten as her friends quietly—and very slowly—backed up. They were still watching him when they exited the room opposite the side he'd come in.

Then he was alone with Heather. He'd hoped he'd have that moment, of course…but hadn't counted on it.

He had nothing prepared to say to her, although there was so much he needed to tell her. No way to do that with a throat tight enough to strangle him.

Strangling. No less than he deserved.

But not until he'd done one hell of a lot more work.

"I'm sorry."

She nodded. "That's all behind us now. I'm just glad you could come. I want you to meet Charles."

He had it coming—watching her with the guy she'd chosen. The man who'd treated her right.

"I'd like to meet him," he told her, speaking for his better side. A small side, to be sure, but there.

"I'm sorry about the girls," she said, nodding toward the door through which her friends had just left.

She'd made no move toward that door, which would lead back to the party and, he presumed, her fiancé. It occurred to him to wonder what the guy would think, knowing that the woman he was going to marry had skipped out of their party and was alone in the kitchen with the man she'd slept with for five years. Slept with. Vacationed with. Did laundry with—in the early days, when they'd done their own. Cooked with.

"They're looking out for you," he said, forgiving Lianna and Raine even as he wished they'd been a bit more supportive of his presence. He needed their approval if he had any hope of convincing Heather to help him.

The irony was not lost on him. The jerk he'd turned out to be had broken Heather's heart, and now, in order to redeem himself, he'd come to her.

"They're afraid you're going to hurt me again."

"By saying hello?"

She shrugged and smiled. "They seem to think you're a lot more irresistible than I do…"

The words stung. He deserved them. But they stung.

"Are you sure there isn't a tiny part of you that wonders if there's anything left?"

He felt like he should smack himself upside the

head as soon as the words were out. Coming on to Heather wasn't in the plan. It was the furthest thing from the plan.

But she'd asked her friends to leave and made no move away from him. On the other hand, she'd given no indication that she had anything in particular to say to him, either. She just stood there, so close, looking at him, taking him in, making it seem as though they were talking without saying a word.

As though they were still who they'd always been.

They weren't, of course. He knew that. Didn't even want them to be. He had no intention of being that man again.

Not that she'd be able to tell with him practically begging her to admit, on the night of her engagement party, that she still felt something for him.

"You're wearing my favorite dress," he said aloud, in spite of his best intentions. He'd noticed the second he'd come in through the kitchen door and seen her standing there.

Thankfully he'd made it that far without either of her parents catching sight of him. Obviously they'd be polite, and he did have an official invitation, but he doubted they'd have left him alone with their daughter.

He wouldn't have blamed them.

Still, she'd invited him to the party and then chosen to wear the dress that she knew turned him on more than any other she'd owned. Just thinking about the last night she'd worn it with him... They'd gone to a business dinner, and then, in a rare moment of relaxation, he'd asked her to go out to a club. To dance and have some fun, for a change from the constant pressures of work.

They'd closed the club and then, completely sober, had gone home to make love for the rest of the night. The way she'd touched him that night... and let him touch her...

Looking at her now, under the bright lights in her parents' kitchen, he knew she was remembering, too. Her eyes had darkened, the way they got when she was aroused. He might not be an expert at determining the truthfulness of a statement as she was, probably because, at some point, he'd forgotten to respect the truth, but he could sometimes match her in the reading of body language.

Hers in particular. It had been like that from the very beginning—the physical and mental combustion that had melded them into an almost-instantaneous partnership, one he'd taken for granted. One he'd believed couldn't be severed. He'd been confident. Cocky.

And wrong.

Why had she invited him tonight?

And worn that dress?

Heather didn't do anything without reason.

Clearly her two closest friends had been communicating a similar message to her just before he'd come in. She'd felt compelled to assure them that she was over him.

Swelling with a bit of…he didn't want to examine what…he momentarily liked the idea that they'd been talking about him.

At her engagement party.

Because she shouldn't be marrying another man.

They belonged together. They always had.

He stepped closer to her, his lips a couple of inches from hers, when the swinging door from the living room pushed open and a man he vaguely recognized stood there.

In black pants, a white shirt and a black-and-white silk tie, the man put Cedar on edge. It was his confidence, his wealth—judging by the quality of his clothes and the watch he wore—and the way he held himself.

He remembered where he'd seen this man before. At one of Heather's parents' parties. He was the dentist who lived down the street.

So why was Heather leaving Cedar and the kiss they'd almost shared to walk over and put an arm around this man?

"Cedar, I'd like you to meet Charles," she said.

If not for years of courtroom practice, Cedar

might have let it be known that his solar plexus had just taken a massive blow.

"The dentist," he said, reaching out a hand. "We've met."

He hadn't remembered the guy's name. Or had any inkling that this...this dentist was the man Heather planned to marry. He was closer to her parents' age than their own.

"At the Labor Day barbecue, year before last," he continued, feeling ornery and not happy with himself. "Heather and I had just returned from a trip to Egypt, and her parents insisted they see for themselves that she'd made it back unharmed."

They'd been travel-weary, wrinkled and could hardly manage to keep their hands off each other. The trip had been partially for business—he'd had to meet with a man who'd skipped the country, but had information that could exonerate a very important client of Cedar's. He and Heather had also had a lot of time alone. He'd been able to focus on her almost exclusively for three whole days.

Charles, the fiancé, nodded, seemingly not the least bit put out by Cedar's rudeness.

"Glad you could make it tonight," he said instead. "I know it meant a lot to Heather to have you here."

And the guy didn't find that discomfiting? Or odd?

"I told Charles the same thing I told the girls,"

she said, her free hand on the man's flat stomach, just above his belt. "I'd like us to be able to be friendly if we ever run into each other, and I'm glad to see you here with none of the old feelings between us. Good or bad."

Was that so?

What did you call the almost-kiss that would have happened if not for Charles's suspiciously timed entrance?

Lianna had sent the older man. Cedar knew it as surely as he knew he'd be getting drunk that night when he got home.

"I wanted you to meet Charles and hoped you'd wish us well," she continued now, sounding more like her mother than ever.

"I do wish you well," he said, including them both in his best courtroom smile.

Heather would see through it. But then he wasn't buying her stance, either.

Still, he'd play along.

Didn't have much choice, really.

He needed her help, or a young woman might die at the hands of a man Cedar had put back on the streets. The man he'd manipulated Heather into helping him set free.

He hadn't done it to serve justice, but to serve his own compulsion to win.

"Then I hope you'll come join us for our cele-bratory toast. The champagne's been poured and passed around. We were just missing my bride-to-be."

With a bow of his head, Cedar conceded defeat. Or compliance. Or whatever the hell he was doing. Because Heather had asked him to come to her party.

He stood beside the happy couple as they were toasted again and again. He sipped champagne. And tried his damndest to be okay with the fact that the woman he loved was about to marry another man.

CHAPTER THREE

SHE'D ALMOST KISSED HIM. Or let him kiss her.

It had been a conditioned response. She knew that. But she was still disappointed in herself. If she was going to be happy, to quit worrying about making poor choices and letting herself down, to stop being paranoid about people using her and about being unable to use her skills on a personal level, she had to manage to be around Cedar and not capitulate to whatever he wanted.

To *anything* he wanted.

He wanted her. The knowledge was a boost to the pride he'd injured when he'd put her low on his list of priorities. But she wasn't proud of herself for having felt a thrill of gratitude that at least she'd mattered to him for more than how she could help him reach his goals. For more than the asset she'd been to his career and his unending drive to win.

He hadn't won her, and he wasn't going to.

The only reason she'd agreed, before he'd left the other night, to see him again—to meet him for lunch to discuss some business matter he had—was to prove to herself, and to him, that the incident in the kitchen had been an anomaly. A natural reaction to seeing a lover again for the first time since their intensely painful split. The pain had faded, the hurt feelings and blame dissipated, leaving room for good memories to slip in. Good memories were healthy. She welcomed them.

However, she wouldn't be swayed by them. Because she knew that memories were all they were. A few good times in between all the bad. They weren't significant, didn't represent a way of life. Or possibilities. They were merely the bag that lined the trash can.

Trying to scroll through the bad memories, she faltered, finding far more good ones that outweighed the disappointments—regularly missed occasions, perennial lateness, a constant lack of returned phone calls... Until that last case, the last week, the last day.

While most of Cedar's clients were wealthy businessmen who were charged with white-collar crimes, during the last year they'd been together, he'd taken on two high-profile criminal cases. She'd never been completely sure why. He'd earned a reputation by then; Cedar Wilson commanded the highest price, but he did what it took to get the job done.

The change in him had been gradual, as winning began to matter more than justice. More than right and wrong. Or even his clients. Maybe that was why she hadn't seen it coming, because it had happened slowly, over time.

Or maybe because, at home, he was still the man who struggled with insecurities. A grown-up version of the young boy who'd never been good enough to deserve personal acknowledgment from his famous father, the singer Randy Cedar-Jones. He'd called him after every case, telling him—through voice mail—about every victory. Without taking offense when there was never a response.

At home, he was a man who touched her tenderly. One who cooked beside her, who slept beside her, who woke her with a smile and a cup of coffee every morning.

As she dressed for lunch on Monday, she reminded herself of all the hard-earned lessons of the past year. And of the happiness she'd felt the night Charles had proposed to her.

Something Cedar had never done—despite years of conversations about "someday."

He hated seeing her in leggings, so she wore a pair of pink ones with black cactus shapes on them, topping them with a figure-hugging black tunic and short black boots. Not the professional he'd be expecting to see.

Not even how she'd normally dressed. The leggings were a gift from Raine, who'd become an online distributor for them. Heather had never actually worn them before.

Cedar had left shortly after the toasts on Saturday night, but not without a word in her ear about that day's meeting. He'd said it was strictly business. And really important.

She felt he'd been telling the truth, so she'd agreed to see him.

She would let Charles know about the meeting just as soon as she knew what it was about. Then she could reassure him about her lack of involvement in this "business matter" before he had a chance to get nervous about the contact.

Cedar was already seated at a table by the window of a local eatery when she arrived. In one of his signature designer suits—this one in tones of gray, his put-at-ease choice—his thick dark hair a little longer than he used to wear it, he'd have stood out from the crowd even without the advantage of his six-foot-two height.

The restaurant was one they'd favored during their time together, not only because of the talented chef, but because of the ocean views. Heather couldn't get enough of the water that kept rolling to shore, century after century. She wasn't sure if Cedar had ever given the Pacific's grandeur a second thought.

Charles had. He respected the ocean's power.

Its unending energy. He'd engaged in long talks with her about it as they'd walked, hand in hand, along the beach, watching the tide come in and go out.

"New outfit," Cedar said, as he stood to pull out her chair and then, as she sat, took his seat again.

She knew he didn't like it and was satisfied with her choice. But then she said, "Raine gave it to me. I have to wear it so when she asks me if I did, I can tell her yes."

She was making excuses. Felt like she was sliding backward. She had no reason or need to please Cedar.

"I like it," he told her. "It looks good on you." The sexy grin on his face, the warmth in his straightforward dark brown gaze, didn't give even a hint of untruth.

She didn't like the outfit. That was the truth. She'd worn it to spite him. It hadn't worked; she didn't like that, either.

"But then, anything looks good on you," Cedar added, picking up his menu. "Or nothing."

Her feminine parts filled with heat.

And she was ashamed.

He was a damned fraud. A man who'd created situations to fit what he knew people needed so he could get what he wanted. He'd vowed to himself he'd stop. And here he was…still orchestrating the situation.

The gray dress pants, white shirt, gray jacket and gray-and-white tie were proof of that. Although he'd gotten rid of most of his closet full of hand-tailored dress clothes, like an alcoholic pouring his stash down the drain, he'd held on to a few things. And he'd deliberately worn some of them that morning because he knew they'd be what Heather would expect to see. They'd put her at ease. He'd worn them purposely, to manipulate her comfort level.

Like he was the same man who'd used his lover to get the information he needed to manipulate a win.

His last win.

He'd ordered her sweet tea and his own black coffee. She glanced at both as she sat down, but said nothing. She immediately went for the tea, though. Took a long sip.

Sweet tea was her weakness.

He used to be, too.

"You said you had business to discuss," she said, not even looking at the menu. He'd figured they'd order first. Maybe even wait to broach his discussion until after they'd eaten. She'd been on his mind pretty much nonstop since he'd left her parents' house two nights before.

She was making a mistake, marrying Charles.

Not because she wasn't marrying *him*—not that he'd ever asked—but because there was no passion between her and the dentist.

If anyone knew and would recognize Heather's passion, it was Cedar. He'd been prepared to see her sharing it with another man.

That hadn't happened. Which meant nothing in terms of him. It meant only that she was making a mistake with her dentist.

Probably not a conversation starter at the moment.

"I have a favor to ask," he said, looking around for Molly, the waitress who'd taken their drink orders.

Heather held her purse in her hands. "I'm not going to—"

"Please, hear me out," he interrupted before she could walk out on him. No matter how much he deserved it, he wasn't up to having her leave him again. The first time had just about killed him.

Killed the old him, anyway. It had left him a shadow of a man, one who lived to make amends—not to be happy.

"The favor, it isn't for me."

"Of course it's for you! Couched in a client's need, perhaps, but it's about your win. I'm not going back down that road, Cedar."

He swallowed. Pursed his lips so they wouldn't open until he had himself in check. He refused to share his truths; he couldn't play with her emotions that way. The turns his life had taken were personal. His alone. They weren't to get her back. Or even to show her that he'd become a better man. He was a man who'd lost his way, and that was a burden he would carry forever. Telling her he was trying to change could serve his own good and that was the old him—serving his own good.

He wanted to ask her how she'd been. To know that she really was over him. That she didn't still carry in the depths of her heart all the pain he'd caused her by putting his need to win above everything else. That there were no lasting consequences in her life because he'd lost sight of what mattered most.

And yet…he suspected her dentist was one of those consequences.

Suspected she was settling for safety because she couldn't bear the idea of being hurt so badly again.

He didn't want that to be the case.

Didn't have time for more amends at the moment.

But this was Heather. If his actions had pushed her into a passionless relationship, if he'd driven her to a passionless life, he'd have to do whatever it took to undo the damage.

He'd figure that out. Take appropriate action if necessary. But first…

"I'm convinced a young woman is in trouble, that she's protecting a man she thinks loves her. She might have done some things that could put her in prison, but…"

Heather shook her head. "I'm not helping you free another criminal who should be serving time. I understand that United States law allows everyone the right to a proper defense. I believe in and uphold our laws. But I will not be party to working the system in the name of preserving someone's rights. I won't be used again, Cedar. Thank you for the lunch invitation, but I won't be staying."

She stood, her purse slung over her shoulder.

"She's not my client." He had no clients.

Heather took one step and stopped. He stood up, too, facing her. "She's the victim of a former client. I need you to help me get her to tell us the truth, Heather. Help me nail this guy before he kills her."

"How exactly are you going to nail him?"

"I'm going to take whatever evidence we can get out of her and go straight to the police."

She dropped back into her seat, and he slowly lowered himself into his.

"Isn't that a conflict of interest?" She eyed him warily, and it stabbed him to know she didn't trust him at all. He wasn't surprised. He'd known. Like the ass he was, he'd betrayed her. But sitting there, seeing the evidence of the fallout…it hurt.

He'd never cheated on her. Never even wanted to. But he hadn't been trustworthy. He'd never out-and-out lied to her. He'd just manipulated the truth to get what he wanted.

"It would be a conflict of interest if he were still a client."

"Even a former client… He has protection under the law from anything he might have told you. You could lose your license, and any competent attorney will get him off…"

"Let me worry about my license." At the moment, it was little more than a piece of paper. One he'd gladly burn if it would make things right. He knew he'd put criminals back on the street to bolster his own reputation. And he knew he had so much to do before he could even think about practicing law again.

He wasn't sure he'd ever trust himself to do it.

Because while it was absolutely true that everyone deserved a good defense, in the end, he hadn't been about his client's rights. Or the spirit of the law. He'd become all about his own win. At almost any cost. Just like Heather had said the day she'd walked out on him.

The day she'd found out he'd used her to obtain testimony that would keep an abuser out of prison—knowing that her career choice was based on her own personal need to avenge the death of her aunt, her mother's sister, who'd lied to law-enforcement officials to protect the man she loved.

"The woman I'm trying now to help never testified for me. The prosecution called her. Not me. And my client wasn't up for abuse. I was defending him on unrelated charges, which means this is extraneous to anything my client said to me—or to client-attorney privilege. However, I think I could give you enough information to help you ask the right questions to get him on abuse."

He was a top-notch manipulator. And she had the gift of being able to tell when someone was lying to her. Unless she was blinded by emotion...

That was the reason she'd thrown at him to explain her inability to recognize his duplicity. The fact that he'd never actually lied to her was irrelevant.

To his immense shame, he'd deliberately misled her to get her to do things he'd known she wouldn't do if he'd asked.

"He's beating her. And, he might be involving her in his drug trade. I never found anything to prove that, but I wouldn't be surprised. She obviously feels indebted to him, in a subservient kind of way, and if we don't intervene, she could end up dead."

Heather watched him for too long. She ordered the Cobb salad he'd known she'd order when the waitress came to the table. And she waited patiently while he asked for his usual fish tacos without jalapeños.

"Why are you doing this?" she asked.

"I...know her."

"You dated her."

He hadn't, but didn't deny it. He couldn't pour his soul out to her. It could soften her toward him and that would serve his own selfish good.

"You slept with a client's woman."

"No! Of course I didn't." He couldn't let her erroneous negative assumptions go that far. He'd done a lot of things. Infidelity wasn't one of them. Not with her and not with any other man's woman, either.

"You'd like to."

Not at all.

"I don't want to sleep with her. Never did. I just need to do this, Heather. I need to make this right. Will you help me?"

"If you're playing some trick to get me to think you've changed, that you're some kind of new man...you might as well give it up, Cedar. I'm not getting back with you. Not for one kiss. One night. Or a lifetime of them. I cannot fathom even entertaining the thought."

Her words took away his appetite and a whole lot more. "I understand."

She watched him. He withstood the silent interrogation.

"She's at The Lemonade Stand, Heather."

He knew the mention of the unique, resort-like women's shelter in town would reel her in. She and her parents had been longtime supporters of the facility. But even as he spoke the truth, he cringed, too. Using that knowledge felt like a well-oiled tactic. Something he would've done deliberately in the past, simply because he knew it would work.

"She says her abuser is a family friend, and that she won't press charges. She wants help but is afraid of the repercussions—with good reason. My personal opinion is that she's using the Stand as a hideout to buy herself some time for her bruises to heal and to figure out what she wants to do. If things are left as is, I'd bet my life's earnings that she'll end up back with Dominic. This might be our only chance to help her."

"Dominic?"

The man he'd set free by tricking Heather into getting to a truth his client wouldn't give him. Dominic's alibi for phone calls to the police had to do with domestic violence, not the drug trafficking for which he'd been standing trial.

It was the case that had blown him and Heather apart.

She dropped the fork she'd been toying with and stood up.

"If I do this…it has nothing to do with you. It would be for the girl. And only if, after I speak with her, I think there's any merit to what you're saying."

"Fine."

"If, on the other hand, I find out you're working me…trying to get information that'll protect your privileged and far-too-rich client from some other crime, I will go after your license myself."

A year ago, the idea would have panicked him. He'd have protected his career at all costs. Had done exactly that.

And in the process, he'd lost something far more valuable. More vital than he'd ever known.

"Understood."

He understood another truth, as well. If he was going to help Heather, if he was going to save her from the emotional consequences he was responsible for, then this case was his chance to get close enough to her to do that. He was, one by one, going through his client list, following up with everyone he'd helped set free, and doing what he could to protect those who might be hurt because of his actions…

And it occurred to him that by getting her to

help him, he'd have a chance to help her. He had no idea how. The plan was just coming to him. But after seeing her again, seeing the lack of passion, hearing the superficial conversation the other night…knowing how much she'd changed… he had to do something.

He was walking a fine line here. Having other motives, while also telling her the truth—the worst kind of manipulation.

But if he saved Heather from a possible life of unhappiness caused by him, he'd choose to walk that line every time.

CHAPTER FOUR

HEATHER WENT STRAIGHT back to work. Her salad hadn't been delivered when she'd walked out on Cedar, but she didn't stop to pick up anything. Food would just choke her. Getting air past the lump in her throat was struggle enough.

She had to work. To focus outside of herself.

To quit shaking.

The drive back to her office was a blur. Pedestrians. Stoplights. Lanes. And…blur. Blur. Blur. Blur. She couldn't let anything else in. Couldn't let herself *feel* him.

He'd stolen her faith in herself.

It made sense that seeing him again would bring up the old pain. She'd miscalculated that point. The reality that she'd feel…something… based on a post-traumatic-stress kind of theory.

She didn't really *want* him.

Her body just remembered sexual reflexes where he was concerned.

He'd given her a chance to help him right one of the horrible wrongs he'd done.

That thought kept her driving. Got her past the

floor's shared receptionist to her private suite and in the door without dropping her keys.

Inside, she moved immediately to her desk and took a long sip from the water bottle she'd left there. Sinking into her chair, she reached for the closed file in front of her computer screen. Lorraine Donahue would be there in a little less than an hour. The divorced woman was being accused of abusing her twelve-year-old daughter—by her daughter's father, not by the daughter.

The family lived in Santa Barbara, and, at the request of Lorraine's defense attorney, Heather was looking for the truth. Her goal was to keep that twelve-year-old girl safe. She'd already done preliminary interviews, reading them over would put her mind firmly in the Donahue household. She'd made a list of questions she was going to ask while the woman was hooked up to the polygraph machine. She had other questions ready, depending on the results of the first round. Not the way the test was generally run, but she wasn't a typical polygraphist.

Her combination of skills had resulted in more confessions, acquittals and convictions in their region of the state than any other approach. She was good at ferreting out the truth. Or at least a meaningful portion of it.

That afternoon, she was hoping to find out if Lorraine was a decent parent or a horrible one.

After first sitting with the woman—and separately with the child—Heather had been fairly convinced that Lorraine was more a victim of her husband's divorce attorney than a child abuser. But she wasn't sure enough to form an opinion she was willing to write.

Criminal charges had been filed. Lorraine, who'd been the sole caregiver for her daughter, since her ex had traveled all the time, was now allowed only supervised visits. Mother and daughter both desperately wanted to be reunited, to the point that Lorraine had chosen to forgo a trial by jury.

Heather's opinion would likely have a huge impact on the judge's final decision.

The mother's and daughter's desires couldn't come into play. Children commonly fought to be with a parent who'd abused them. And Lorraine didn't want to go to jail.

The truth was needed and—

Heather jumped as a knock sounded on the solid wooden door of her two-room suite. She was in the front room and had rounded her desk as she glanced at the clock on the wall. Lorraine was early...

Pulling the door open, she felt the clenching inside, like a steel band around her rib cage, even before she consciously acknowledged that Cedar, not Lorraine, was standing in the hall in front of her.

"Sheila wasn't at her desk, so I came on back..."

He still had her security code to get from reception to the offices beyond. He'd just needed to type the numbers into the keypad on the wall...

He was the only one she'd ever given it to.

She could have changed it after they broke up. Should have. Had actually thought about it and hadn't done it.

Mouth slightly open, she stared up at him. Afraid of the erroneous conclusions he'd draw about why she hadn't changed her code.

Whatever they were...they'd be wrong. He couldn't possibly know why she hadn't done something when she didn't even know herself.

There'd been some vague feeling along the lines of...if he used the code, that would prove he was untrustworthy. And if he didn't, she'd know she hadn't been completely insane to trust him. Maybe he wouldn't care enough to try to surprise her with the little gifts he used to bring in an effort to win her back. But maybe he cared enough to respect her wishes and leave her completely alone. The whole thing was a little ambiguous. The choice had been made a year ago. So much had happened since then...

"I brought your lunch." Cedar held out the restaurant's to-go bag she'd failed to notice until then. "It's your favorite."

"Thank you." As she took the bag, his gaze met

hers. She continued to stare back at him. Like the proverbial deer in the headlights. She just stared. It was either that or flounder.

And then, with a quick nod, he was gone.

HER AFTERNOON SESSION was a clockwork example of why she did what she did. The truth wasn't always what it seemed. Asking the right questions, after building her way to them with questions whose answers led her down an unexpected path, Heather got the truth out of Lorraine Donahue. She wasn't hurting her daughter. Neither was her husband. The twelve-year-old was hurting herself, and Lorraine was afraid the courts would take the girl away from her. That they'd lock her up when she was certain that what the child needed more than anything was a stable, battle-free household, filled with the kind of love only a mother could give. That was the reason she'd filed for divorce from a man she still loved, but who argued about everything. She believed their relationship was at the root of their daughter's problems.

Lorraine could be right. The answers ahead weren't up to Heather. Writing her report was all she could do, but as she ushered Lorraine out, she wished she could give her a hug big enough to absorb some of the worry she was carrying inside.

Determining that she'd create a more honest, unbiased report if she took the night to distance herself from the situation, Heather put away the extensive notes she'd taken that afternoon, locked up her office and headed out to the Mustang convertible she'd purchased the previous fall. It was early. She wasn't due for dinner with Charles until seven. A drive down the coast with the top down, the salty air against her skin, the ocean right there beside her, would be good therapy.

Not that she needed therapy. She just had to clear her mind. To take a couple of deep, cleansing breaths. To talk to Raine.

In the back of her mind, she'd known that if the drive alone didn't do the trick, she could always stop in at YoYo, Raine's—who would have believed it?—incredibly successful yoga and yogurt studio on the beach between Santa Barbara and LA. A certified yoga and reiki instructor, Raine also had a handful of employees who were as calming and as nurturing as she was.

Raine might not be earning millions, but she was supporting herself comfortably enough to be happy. But then, it took a lot less to make Raine happy than some people.

"I had lunch with Cedar," she blurted out the second she and her college roommate were privately ensconced in Raine's apartment above the studio. Then she corrected herself. "Or rather, I walked out on a business lunch meeting, and he brought me my lunch and I ate it alone. At my office. Before my afternoon appointment."

There. She'd put it all out there, which would clear her mind. Like taking a pill for a headache.

And Raine was her "pill" when her thoughts were trying to trip her up.

"Why'd you walk out on him?" In bold, multicolored leggings and an orange tank top, Raine could've been any man's dream. But she hadn't met anyone who made her heart beat faster just by walking into the room.

That was a definition of love they'd come up with together during their freshman year of college. One that hadn't panned out in the long run for Heather, either—with Cedar, as the first case in point, her heart had definitely beat faster, but… and Charles as the second—he was going to be the love of her life and her heart remained steady every time he walked into a room.

Cedar still turns me on.

"Because I'm not going to let him suck me back in."

"And that was happening?"

She thought about the conversation she and Cedar had at the restaurant. Really thought about it, being completely honest with herself. "No," she said. "He asked me for a favor. He used his knowledge of me to get what he wanted, starting with the suit he chose, ordering my tea, even mentioning The Lemonade Stand. I knew it. I saw it, Raine. My walls were firmly in place. It's like I told you, I'm over him."

"And you left. Good." Raine's blue-eyed gaze seemed more concerned than celebratory. Although Heather had looked away from her friend, she caught the glance in the mirror they were both facing. It was oblong, decorative, almost a chair rail along one wall of the living room. There to make the room appear larger, Heather assumed. It had been there when Raine bought the place. She'd put her couch against the opposite wall, with her television mounted above the long mirror.

There they sat, two thirty-year-old women, both blonde and blue-eyed, looking not much different than they had when they'd met a decade before. Heather's hair was pulled neatly into a ponytail at her nape, while Raine's was tucked in a scrunchie on top of her head.

In college, they'd been called the Bobbsey Twins a time or two. Completely inaccurate, of course, as those twins from the books her mother used to read to her were two sets and a boy and a girl.

"Hey." Raine touched her arm, and Heather looked directly at her. It was why she'd come. To see herself reflected back at her with no judgment— and not just in the mirror. She wasn't afraid. Wasn't feeling weak. Didn't need reassurance or a kick in the pants. Lianna would've been closer to run to, but she didn't need strength. She needed understanding.

"I didn't tell Charles that I was meeting him," she said. She hadn't lied to her fiancé, but she'd been duplicitous all the same by deliberately keeping the information to herself, until after the meeting. It wasn't like her.

Unless Cedar and his manipulative ways had worn off on her without her being aware of it.

Raine's expression seemed to ease. As though she wasn't so worried anymore. Which eased Heather's level of tension, too.

Good. She'd been right to come. She'd been overreacting and…

"And when you did tell him, he got upset?" Raine asked.

"I haven't told him yet."

"Lunch was what…three hours ago?"

She shrugged. "About that."

"And you haven't called Charles in all that time?"

"It's been a busy afternoon."

"Yet you had the time to drive here."

If she'd been sitting with Lianna, the statement would have sounded more like an accusation. But the point being made was the same. Just more delicately put.

Was that why she'd come to Raine? To be

treated like a hothouse flower, rather than the strong, capable woman she expected herself to be?

She unloaded in a rush. "I have to do the favor Cedar asked," she said. "Charles is going to think it's because I'm not really over him, or that he has some kind of hold on me. But I swear to you, Raine, I had no problem telling him like it is." She told her about Dominic Miller's woman-friend. About Cedar giving her a chance to help right an egregious wrong. "I might be the only one who can get through to her in the little time we'll have. Residents can't stay at the Stand for longer than six weeks max. At least, not without special per-mission." The Stand didn't have to adhere to state mandates, and sometimes residents did stay on...

"You don't need to convince me, sweetie." Raine's brow was creased, but she was smiling, too. "This sounds like any number of other jobs you've done. It's precisely why people call you."

She had a good point.

"So...you think Charles will understand why I have to at least go talk to the woman?"

Raine's shrug was noncommittal. "I can't speak for Charles and don't know him well enough to make an educated guess."

Raine had given the problem right back to her. What was she missing that her friend could see? And expected her to get? Or was she slowly losing her mind, thinking everyone was seeing things she couldn't?

She shook her head. There was a shadow side to everything. Doubt and uncertainty… And when it came to her ability to put herself in others' shoes, to read them more accurately than most, that shadow side could interfere.

No…that problem hadn't surfaced until Cedar had used her. She hadn't questioned herself until then. Not like she had since.

"You think I'm overreacting as a side effect of having seen Cedar?"

Raine shrugged again. "Maybe."

"What else would it be?"

"I could see you needing some space to process the whole Cedar thing before being ready to defend it to someone else."

Yes. For the first time since Saturday night, when she'd agreed to the meeting with Cedar, her stomach settled.

"What I went through with him…the intense love and then the horrible betrayal… Of course I need time to process seeing him again." It all made sense now.

"Which is why I was worried about you and Charles getting engaged so soon."

Heather's stomach clenched again. "You think I'm not over Cedar?"

"I think you're over being in a relationship with

him. You're over some parts of having been in love with him. The rest... I don't know..."

"What rest? What else is there?"

"The residual effects. I don't know," she repeated. "I'm not a professional counselor." Heather had seen a counselor the year before, when she'd broken up with Cedar. Because of her job, she'd had to make sure her head was on straight. "It seems to me that the damage Cedar did... Well, you need to give yourself time to cope with that. And then to find out who you are when you come out the other side."

How was it possible that a heavy weight would lift at the same time that that one settled on her? That peace would come with dread attached.

"I'm ready to be with Charles. Just not ready to be engaged..." She said the words aloud, but she'd recognized the truth of them before she spoke. "I need to learn how to be in a relationship in a healthy way before I commit myself to anyone... I have to be fully recovered..."

She wasn't sure she'd ever fully get over the damage that Cedar had caused her psyche, her heart. She'd thought she had, until she'd seen him again.

Whenever she'd thought about him since seeing him at the party—and he'd been on her mind far too often because of the "secret" meeting she'd agreed to have with him—those thoughts had been accompanied by a horrible feeling inside her.

"I don't know about a full recovery," Raine said with a real, no-frown-attached grin. "But I'd say that you at least need to be able to talk to your fiancé about him."

Her *fiancé*.

Oh, God. "I have to give Charles his ring back."

"Or take it off for now. Postpone the engagement."

Charles was in such a hurry to get married. Remarried. The first time hadn't worked out, and his chances of being young enough to be the kind of involved father he wanted to be were diminishing.

He'd been completely honest with her, and she'd understood. But that didn't make the quick engagement right for her...

"He's the man for me," she said now, still certain of that. She enjoyed being with Charles. Looked forward to their visits. Was entertained by his company. And felt absolutely none of the debilitating emotional-rollercoaster ride Cedar had taken her on. Charles was steady and affectionate, even in the hard times. Understanding.

He was going to be devastated.

"I'm having dinner with him at his place tonight," she said, sitting forward. "At seven. He's grilling steaks, and we were going to share a bottle of wine on the upper deck and talk about the wedding." She'd been looking forward to the upper-deck dinner, the wine. The ocean view, the handsome man.

Raine was meeting her gaze, silent.

"Don't worry, I'm going to talk to him."

"I wasn't worried about that. I'm just... I'm here if you need to talk, okay?"

Raine was worried about her getting hurt. The same way Heather worried about Raine ever finding the man of her dreams.

"You want to go up to wine country this weekend?" she asked, liking the idea even as it occurred to her. "A girls' getaway, like we did in college?"

"I have class until noon on Saturday. I could go after that."

"If we fly up, we can take the early Monday flight back and be home in time for work." Just like they'd made it back for Monday-morning class more than once.

Raine stood, grinning. "I'll make the reservations," she said, reaching to give Heather a hug. "And why don't you ask Lianna? We talked some the other night, and it seems like we should all be friends, rather than pulling you back and forth between us..."

Feeling as if a part of her life was finally flying high, while the rest of it was about to crumble, Heather hugged her friend back and then, keys in hand, headed for the door. "I'll call her as soon as I get to my car," she promised. And hoped that Lianna would be free. Spending time with her two best friends sounded like heaven.

CHAPTER FIVE

PULLING OFF THE sweaty bandanna tied around his head, Cedar walked over to his pickup truck in the employee parking lot of The Lemonade Stand. He was one of a dozen men on the construction crew, building new bungalows on previously unused acreage on the other side of the swimming pool. But right now, he was alone as he unbuckled his tool belt in the deserted lot. Dropping it on the floor behind the driver's seat, he climbed inside, pushing the ignition button before closing his door. In the July heat, the Chevy was like a sauna without the steam.

A blast of warm air hit and he reached into the cooler on the floor below the passenger seat for his last bottle of water. Downed it. And glanced at the gray suit on the seat next to him. He'd donned it before lunch and quickly changed back into work clothes after delivering Heather's salad to her office.

Heather.

She'd be coming to The Lemonade Stand, but there was no reason she'd ever need to know that he was working there. It wasn't that she *couldn't* know, but he didn't want her to. He didn't want to be responsible for swaying her in his favor again. Didn't want anyone to convince her he was at the Stand as a way of proving that he'd changed. Or as an attempt to get her back.

His atonement was between him and…him.

The bungalows to which he'd been assigned were acres away from the main building, where Heather'd be meeting with Carin Landry, Dominic's girlfriend.

The parking lot she'd use was a small space intended for general visitors, on the opposite side of the now seven-acre complex. It was the only parking available without a pass card—giving access to a small, nondescript outer reception area, through which she'd be admitted to the main building after showing her identification.

He'd finalized the details that afternoon, during his break, and then worked an hour of overtime to make up for the extra minutes he'd been away from the job. And maybe to work off some extra tension, too.

Seeing Heather…

Damn, he missed her.

He needed a beer.

Throwing the truck in Reverse, he heard his phone ring. Whoever it was could leave a message.

Unless…what if it was Heather? Lila McDaniels Mantle, the Stand's managing director who had absolutely no idea—from him, anyway—that he and Heather knew each other other than professionally, had said she'd call Heather to arrange the appointment with Carin.

After putting the truck in Park, he grabbed his phone out of the heavy-duty case clipped to his jeans. And almost dropped it. The number on the screen was on his speed dial, but...

"Randy Cedar-Jones?" he said before the phone was even fully to his ear. His father was calling him!

Elation went to immediate alarm as he realized that something must be terribly wrong. Randy Cedar-Jones had never called him. Not once. Ever. They'd never met. He had the private number as part of a legal agreement designed by his mother. For all he knew, the line was only for him—set up when he was a kid. He called. Left messages. They were never returned. Never.

Most people didn't even know that the famous pop singer had a son. Cedar's mom, who'd been a groupie having a one-night stand, had chosen to keep it that way. She'd told the singer about him, and had signed a legal document that she'd helped him draw up, valid until Cedar's eighteenth birthday, agreeing never to approach Cedar-Jones or speak of Cedar's parentage—including no paternity testing—in exchange for child support. She didn't want her son raised in an unrealistic world, nor did she want him to be part of a two-family, two-home lifestyle. One with her and an entirely different one with Cedar-Jones. Her one demand had been that Cedar, the man's only child, always had his private phone number.

His mother, a kindergarten teacher, had never married or had other children. And she'd never made any secret of the fact that she was such a Cedar-Jones fan that she'd named her only son after the singer. Randy Cedar-Jones had sent flowers to her funeral when she'd been killed in a car accident shortly after Cedar graduated from college—but he still hadn't picked up the phone when his son had called to thank him.

Nor returned that or any subsequent calls.

"Cedar! Is this a good time?" To talk, he figured his father meant.

And with a mind that felt encased by sludge, he tried to sound as nonchalant as the old man did.

"Sure, what's up?" Something obviously was. But Cedar still couldn't contain the excitement churning inside. His father had called him.

Thirty-four years into his life, and it had finally happened.

His mother would be glad. He had to tell Heather...

Slowing his thoughts to adult level, Cedar listened as Randy said he had a favor to ask. And he felt another rush—of an emotion he'd waited for all his life.

Wow. A younger Cedar had lived for this day.

"I've got a…friend…who's gotten himself into a bit of trouble…"

Cedar listened, his mind racing ahead to possible fixes, thinking along the lines of cleanups and protection, even before he heard the gist of the problem.

"It's not unlike that case you had three or so years ago, the one where the guy skipped the country and you were able to get him to give you evidence to clear his partner, since they couldn't prosecute him if they couldn't find him…"

The time he and Heather had gone to Egypt. And come home to meet Charles at her parents' barbeque.

"And the case from last year where the guy was found with 1000 kilos, but you were able to show enough doubt as to the ownership and how it came to be where it was, that he walked…"

Dominic. Cedar had shown sufficient doubt, and then, just before he'd rested his case, the prosecutor had turned up with reports of 911 calls from neighbors, reporting suspicious activity at Dominic's home. There'd never been any charges for anything as a result of those calls. Until then, he'd never known about them. And though one would expect there to have been a police report, none could be found. Other than the incoming calls to 911 that had been too vague to draw from. Concerned neighbors calling in suspicious activity. Dominic had been certain they had the case won, that the calls wouldn't change that, so he wouldn't come clean about them. Dominic had been willing to risk his freedom on the certainty that those calls wouldn't matter, that no one would find a single report that would explain the calls, but Cedar hadn't been willing to risk his win.

He'd risked his relationship with Heather, instead.

Cedar-Jones listed a couple of other cases, and Cedar began to see the link. They'd all been seemingly definite convictions—mostly white-collar crime—and even with digital trails, he'd managed to pull a rabbit out of the hat every time, and his clients had walked free.

He saw something else, as well. All those years, when he'd called Cedar-Jones after every case... his father had been listening to his voice mails.

He sat there, half listening, knowing without a doubt that he'd give his father the affirmative he was after. And that whatever the old man had to say about the case wouldn't matter nearly as much as Cedar doing his own digging.

What mattered right now was that, when his famous father had finally acknowledged him, he could give him exactly what he needed.

For the first time in his life, he felt…good enough.
Complete.

Holy hell!

CHARLES HAD INVITED another couple to dinner. A
friend of his, Rebecca, from college, who'd been
in LA for a church conference and had an unexpected free evening. And her husband, Anthony,
who loved to play golf as much as Charles did.
They were a thoroughly enjoyable couple. Becky
was a dentist, too, and Anthony a chiropractor.
They had two teenage children and a lovely home
in Chicago and invited Heather and Charles to
visit them the following summer—promising to
take them out on their boat, which was docked at
their property on Lake Michigan. And they insisted on getting an invitation to the wedding, too.

The bottle of wine, and the next one, disappeared quickly, but they ate inside, in Charles's
formal dining room, not out on the deck. No view
of the ocean. And Heather helped with the cook-
ing, preparing the salad and side dishes, while
Charles entertained his friends and grilled the
steaks on the grill out on the deck. She was at
home in his kitchen, enjoyed her time there, which
was why she offered to take care of the dishes
while Charles and Becky and Tony continued to
chat. They were talking about a couple of bands
they all used to like, music she'd heard of, but to

which she'd never really related. Turned out that Tony and Charles, who hadn't known each other before that evening, had both been to more than a few of the same bands' concerts during their college years. Heather had barely been born.

She tried to follow the conversation as she rinsed dishes and loaded the dishwasher, cleaned the pans she knew Charles always did by hand and wiped down all the counters. It was a struggle, though. Her mind kept wandering, just as it had all night long, even when the conversation going on around her had been engaging.

Before she went home that night—and she definitely planned to go home, which would be another issue, since Charles was expecting her to stay—she had to tell the man she loved that she couldn't be engaged to him. Yet. He was going to think she was some kind of kook. Or worse, that she still had a thing for Cedar.

Which she didn't. She scrubbed hard at a spot on the frying pan—until she noticed that she was leaving slight scars on the bottom of the pan. The only true feelings Cedar raised in her were negative ones. Left over from the trauma he'd put her through.

The trauma she'd allowed herself to fall into.

But even if Charles didn't worry about Cedar, even if he took her conversation for what it was, it was going to be difficult for him. Including on the most surface level—they'd just announced their engagement in a big, celebratory way to everyone he considered a friend.

He wouldn't be wrong to feel upset with her for not realizing, a couple of days sooner, that she wasn't ready to marry anyone.

Yet.

That *yet* kept surfacing. Maybe if she led with that part, her news wouldn't be so horrible.

"Are you sure I can't help you with anything?" Becky was back from the restroom, where Heather had directed her minutes before. It was the third time Becky had offered assistance.

"Nope, all done here," Heather smiled, hung the cloth she'd just used to wipe out the sink and turned back toward the dining room.

The last thing she needed was girl talk. Unless it was with one of *her* girls, and she wasn't even up for that at the moment.

DEAN DISALVO, his father's friend, had a lot of money. He offered a sizable chunk to Cedar, who wasn't taking it. He'd promised himself he was done working as a lawyer, at least for a while. Maybe forever. He was done selling his soul. Done taking money for a job that had controlled him to the point that he'd sacrificed his conscience to succeed. He was helping his father. Period.

About five minutes into their conversation

Monday night, DiSalvo finally got that Cedar meant what he said—that he wasn't in it for the money.

His father never came up. Whether Cedar-Jones had mentioned anything to DiSalvo, other than the name of a lawyer, Cedar didn't know. If DiSalvo wondered about the name likeness he didn't say. DiSalvo could think what he liked about why a seemingly high-powered attorney would work for free. Cedar really wasn't interested in what the man thought.

The case interested him, though. Cedar-Jones was right. An intricate trail of money-making deals had veered off course, and DiSalvo was being framed. Or he said he was. They always said they were. Usually they weren't as innocent as they claimed, but there were ways to make them look as though they were. Cedar knew that firsthand. And knew, too, about the people whose palms could be greased, by a lawyer or the accused, to make things disappear. And people who'd roll over to keep themselves out of hotter water. It was exactly the kind of case that used to make Cedar salivate. After a quick shower and a ham-and-mustard sandwich, he sat out on his deck, with the ocean in the distance, a glass of milk in hand, his laptop on the table in front of him and his body alive in a way it hadn't been in too many months.

DiSalvo had sent a shitload of files. Cedar wasn't going to bed until he'd perused every single one of them.

And maybe not even then.

His father had called on him.

He had work to do.

And a job site to be at in the morning.

Good thing he was used to getting by on minimal sleep.

HEATHER STOOD AT Charles's side, a slight step behind him, as they waved goodbye to his friends. Could anyone tell her palms were wet?

Cedar would have known from the arm across her midsection that she was holding back. Holding in. That something was bothering her.

She dropped her arm. Kept waving. Concentrated on the smile on her face. And was caught unawares as Charles turned around and kissed her deeply, his tongue in her mouth.

"Thank you," he said, as soon as he lifted his head. "I know this wasn't the evening we planned, but it was perfect in a different kind of way."

Perfect wasn't even close to a word she'd have used, but then she'd known what was coming and was sure that had clouded what might otherwise have been a wonderful time.

All except for the conversation about bands, maybe.

"They're nice people," she said, stepping away from Charles—wanting another glass of wine, which would require opening a third bottle. Which they had.

Was it too late for him to go along with their original plan of wine on the deck?

"Becky's a sweetheart," Charles was saying, following her into the kitchen. "You really liked her?"

Hovering near the wine cooler, Heather smiled at him. "I did. Truly."

"So you'd be up for going to Chicago to see them?"

She imagined Charles and her together, but not engaged, and smiled again. "Of course."

It was awkward, just standing there in the kitchen. He might be ready to go to bed. She wasn't joining him.

She needed some time to figure out the total impact of the feelings assailing her because of her contact with Cedar. She should've realized there'd be an initial backlash. She hadn't seen it coming. And she had to deal with that first.

"Shall we have another glass of wine?" she asked, feeling like a kid asking for permission to stay out past curfew. Which was ridiculous. Charles was the late-night one. "We could sit out on the deck."

"Sure!" He shrugged, looked happy as he

pulled out a bottle of her favorite unoaked chardonnay, while she slid a couple of fresh glasses off the rack mounted above the cooler.

She loved him in this mood, so easy, so supportive. Would it hurt to put off the conversation until later?

Following Charles through the house toward the deck, she considered her options. Her appointment with Carin Landry wasn't until Wednesday, and she wouldn't be seeing or speaking with Cedar again until she'd had more than one appointment with the woman. She needed preliminary conversation with her before she could form a list of questions. She could have Charles over to her house for dinner on Tuesday night. After his golf game. Unless he had dinner with the others in his foursome, all doctors.

She'd been thinking about stopping by Lianna's after work the next day. Her friend hadn't said no to the weekend in wine country, but she hadn't said yes, either. She'd sounded decidedly unlike herself. Maybe it was time for Heather to be a friend, rather than just have one...

Charles pulled open the sliding glass door that led to the upper deck at the back of the house. She followed him out. She took a deep breath of air, convinced she could taste a hint of the ocean's salt in the breeze. Growing up in Santa Raquel had given her what seemed like a biological need for that very special air.

She handed a glass to Charles, exchanged the other empty for the one he'd filled, and stood by the rail waiting for their traditional toast.

"To us," he said, clinking his now-full glass to hers.

She nodded, mouthed the words and hoped he didn't notice that they didn't actually pass her lips. Hoped they'd still be an "us."

CHAPTER SIX

CHARLES SAT ON his usual side of the padded wicker love seat they normally shared. He lifted one leg and rested his ankle on the opposite knee. He seemed ready to sit for hours.

She wasn't sitting.

"Out with it…" His words were soft. Infused with the caring that had touched her from the moment he'd said hello the summer before.

"What?"

"I'm just wondering when you're going to tell me whatever it is that's bothering you."

Her genuine surprise bothered her. She really hadn't expected Charles to notice. Shouldn't she have? Considering that he was the man she intended to spend the rest of her life with?

Current necessary conversation aside, if Charles would wait for her, she'd marry him.

"I've been wondering the same thing," she admitted, turning to face him, but not joining him on the love seat.

He couldn't avoid seeing the difference. She always sat next to him.

"Seems like now's the time." He was holding his wine in one hand, letting it rest against the arm of the love seat.

She took a sip of hers, and then set it on the railing beside her. Her situation was clear to her—how to express it in a way that would hurt him least was not.

"I'm struggling," she started. And stopped.

"Obviously." He wasn't smiling anymore. Nor did he seem angry. "I'm here to help."

Oh, God. She wanted his help. So badly.

And yet...she didn't. Something about leaning on Charles just then seemed wrong.

"I want you to know that my feelings for you haven't changed."

His nod was reassuring. "Good," he said. "That's one hurdle passed."

"I still very much want to marry you."

He took a sip of wine. "I have to admit, I'm relieved to hear that."

"But I can't be engaged to you right now."

He looked out at the ocean, and then back at her. He studied her. She studied him, too, willing him to see inside her. To know how sincerely she wanted to marry him.

"I'm feeling all kinds of negative things, Charles. I'm doubting myself. Not my feelings for you, or my desire to marry you, but things that go...deeper than that."

"You still have feelings for Cedar." He sounded as though he'd been expecting as much.

"No!" Why did everyone keep accusing her of that? "At least, not in the way you mean. I shudder—with fear—at the very idea of being with him again." She took a deep breath, stilling those shudders. "But seeing him again, it was like an episode of what I'd call a very mild and temporary case of the past coming back to haunt me. I'm not myself."

He waited.

She had to finish.

Or begin.

"Saturday night, as I was telling Cedar goodbye, I agreed to see him."

Charles's chin dropped to his chest.

"Not like that!" she quickly reassured him, waiting until he looked back up. "I swear to you, it wasn't like that at all." She could look him straight in the eye on that one. "He said he had a business situation to discuss with me. He was certain I'd want to know about it…"

"Of course he did. He wants you back."

No. No, he didn't. And even if he did…just, no.

She shook her head. "I felt he was being completely straightforward." When he'd made the request. Not earlier, in the kitchen, when he'd been about to kiss her.

And she'd been about to let him.

A reflexive response, due in part to the shock of seeing him. Since she'd already labeled him a no-show and was no longer expecting that he'd be there.

"As it turns out, he was—being straightforward, that is."

Charles's gaze narrowed. "You met with him, then?"

She and Charles had been together most of the day on Sunday, roaming around at an art fair, stopping at a local wine-tasting. Having dinner...

She nodded. "Today. For lunch. Or rather, during my lunch break. I didn't actually eat lunch with him."

That detail seemed to matter to her a lot. She'd mentioned it to Raine, too.

Although she'd eaten the salad he'd brought. Like he'd said, it was her favorite. He'd paid good money for it. And she'd needed to eat.

Sitting forward, his elbows on his knees, Charles pursed his lips and glanced toward the ocean again. His hands weren't clasped, leaving his body language open. He wasn't completely writing her off yet.

"I should've told you Saturday night when he asked, or Sunday, even."

He looked back at her. Nodded.

She'd disappointed him. She hated that. He didn't deserve it.

"And that's part of the problem," she said, standing straighter. When she'd promised to marry him, she hadn't realized she couldn't. And she'd allowed a party to celebrate their engagement, with no idea that she wouldn't be able to go through with it. But she'd purposely withheld information from him…and that was inexcusable.

"I was afraid of your reaction, afraid you'd think what you seem to be thinking—that I'd still have feelings for Cedar. I wanted to find out what he wanted before I told you about it…"

"And now that you know, you're telling me." He sat back, lifted his ankle to his knee again and drank some wine, watching her.

"Yes." Sort of.

"I want to hear about it, of course, about whatever business he had that still interests you, but I have a more pertinent question first."

A feeling of dread ran through her. "What?"

"How could you possibly be afraid of my reaction? Have I ever…*ever*…given you cause to fear me? Or reacted in such a way that made you feel unsafe coming to me?" He seemed honestly perplexed.

"No, you haven't," she told him, feeling stronger in her purpose by the second. This was why Raine had been so concerned. She knew Heather wasn't acting in a healthy manner. Or reacting in one.

"It's me, Charles. I'm not emotionally healthy enough right now for a committed relationship. I overreacted totally. My fear of telling you about Cedar was irrational. And I was over-the-top with him, too. I was far ruder to him than I should've been, considering that I not only opened the door that he'd kept shut between us—out of respect— by inviting him to our party. And then by agreeing to meet with him."

"Maybe you need to consider why you did either of those things."

"I know why I did them." She didn't waver, although she was getting frustrated with having to continue trying to get anyone to understand her on this. "I did them because I *know* I'm over him. Because I also know that if he's still in town, we're bound to run into each other. Our fields tend to cross. It's kind of surprising that they haven't already over the past year."

"Maybe he purposely stayed out of your way."

"Maybe." But the past year didn't matter right now. "The point is, I was certain I'd be able to see him and that our encounter would be…empty… at best. I was hoping for a distant friendliness between acquaintances."

Or some such thing. She and Cedar had a ton of shared memories. He was bound to creep into her mind now and then through the years. She'd like to know he was okay.

As long as it was from a distance.

"You said you *were* hoping as though that's not what happened."

There he was again, implying she had feelings for Cedar. Anger shot up within her, and just as quickly died.

"Seeing him brought up all kinds of self-doubt," she told him. "Before Cedar's betrayal, I didn't question my own mind. I trusted my thoughts and feelings—and then, when I'd realized how easily he'd duped me, I didn't trust my own mind. I started to question what I really knew and what I only thought I saw. My mind was playing tricks on me. I doubted my ability to see things as they really were. Feared that I couldn't discern. It was horrible at first. I went through counseling, as you know, and haven't had a problem for months. Now, though, it's back. Maybe worse than ever because there's no grief to overtake everything else like there was then…"

"You had an important client this afternoon."

"Yes." She'd told him what she could the day before—that a child's life was involved. Nothing else.

"Did you struggle to do your job?"

"No. It's not affecting my work. Strangely enough, it never really did. Probably because I'm tuned outward when I'm working, and my struggle is inward. I'm acting weird around Raine and

Lianna, though, being defensive around them. And you... I need some time, Charles."

"I'd like to ask how much time, but clearly you wouldn't have any way of knowing that."

He was going to dump her. She could feel it coming.

And part of her was relieved. She wouldn't have to worry about hurting him any more than she already had.

But another part of her, the part that had been happy to have her future mapped out and rosy, the part that thought she was going to spend the rest of her life with him...

"I understand your time concerns," she told him. That had been the only true source of discord between them. The one time she'd stood up to him. She wouldn't marry him until they'd been engaged at least a year. "I really do understand them. They're real and important."

He seemed to be watching something on the horizon—as though he wasn't just staring off into the ocean, but was focused. She didn't turn around to see what might be out there. She was too concerned about him.

Looking for a way to make things better for him.

Charles turned back to her, his gaze so serious, her stomach felt like lead.

"They aren't as important as you are." His words were soft. And yet solid. Blessedly solid. Tears sprang to her eyes. She wanted to run to him. To hold him. To thank him.

But…she wanted to stand her ground, too. "I have to break our engagement."

He didn't speak.

"I need time to get myself back before I can promise myself to anyone else."

"Do you intend to date other people?"

Cedar, he meant.

"Absolutely not." But then…they were back where they'd started—her being pledged to him, without the formality, without the ring. "But… until I sort this out, I need to be free to feel, to not feel guilty for feeling, whatever I feel. I need to be able to know what's real for me without feeling obligated to consider how what I feel affects someone else. I need to be single, Charles. I can't be in a committed relationship right now."

"But you can date…say, me?"

"Of course!" She wanted that. "As long as you understand that I'm promising nothing for now, that it's only a date. And…" She hated this part, but knew it had to work both ways. "If you meet someone you want to, say, have dinner with, then you're free to do so. And not tell me about it unless you want to."

It couldn't possibly work. A couple couldn't go from being engaged to completely single, and then get married. Could they?

"When you determine you're ready to commit, do you see yourself being happy with me for the rest of your life?"

She couldn't lead him on. It wasn't fair. But she couldn't lie to him, either. "At this point, I do."

He nodded and held out an arm to her, and she couldn't resist. She needed to feel his warmth as much as he seemed to need hers. Snuggled beneath his arm, she sipped her wine, her stomach cramped with tension.

"I hate not being able to trust my own mind," she said. "I hate doing this to you."

"I'd rather it happened now than after we're married."

As though they were still getting married. And maybe they were. A dangled carrot, but one she was glad to see hanging out there.

"I'm so paranoid all of a sudden."

"It's only been a couple of days."

He was right, of course. Her melodrama was proof. Sitting up, she put her glass of wine on the table. Saw the ring on her finger, and her stomach took another nosedive. She reached to pull it off, but Charles's hand on hers stopped her.

"Might I suggest you keep that on? At least for a little while?"

She shook her head. There was no way... He didn't get it... She *couldn't* be engaged...

"For a couple of reasons," he said, when she met his eyes.

She listened.

"First, selfishly, I'd like a little more time to pass between our engagement party and any kind of official breakup," he said. "Just to spare me discomfort with my friends. Since, at my insistence, we made the engagement so public."

His request was fair. More than fair. She nodded.

"And secondly, maybe the ring will help you as you work through whatever business venture you have with Cedar. You and I know we aren't engaged—that you're single and free. But while you sort things out, while you figure out what parts of yourself are real, what you can trust, you'll have that small bit of protection."

A ring wouldn't stop the Cedar she knew from pursuing anything with her if he wanted to. The almost-kiss on Saturday night proved that. Unless she'd imagined he'd been about to kiss her...

Still, Charles had a point. "He might draw the wrong conclusion if he knows we broke up right after his return to my life." He might think he was the reason. That she still harbored feelings for him. He could hardly be blamed, considering that everyone who was close to her worried about the same thing. Which brought up another problem...

"My parents," she said. She hadn't even thought about them. About the conclusions they'd draw. They'd been so worried about her. So thrilled when she'd started seeing Charles.

"We don't have to tell anyone, Heather. At least, not yet. Let's find our own way on this, give it some time—and then decide about announcing a breakup."

He was offering her the best of both worlds. And that wasn't fair to him. Unless…

"As long as you know, in your heart, that I'm not yours. We *are* broken up, Charles. I can't worry about every move I make affecting you. I need you to think single. If you meet someone else, someone who wants to get married right away and start a family with you…"

His finger over her lips stopped the completion of her sentence, but the important words had already been said.

"I understand," he told her. "And, in truth, if I meet someone who interests me, I will most definitely ask her out. If nothing else, it'll show me that you're the one I want—even if it means being a father in my old age. Or…"

He could fall in love, and she'd lose him forever.

The idea, while hard, wasn't nearly as awful as the way she'd felt meeting with Cedar behind Charles's back.

She laid her head against his shoulder. She wanted some more wine, but knew she should leave what was left in her glass. She had to drive.

"I'd better be going," she told him—the first mention either of them had made about the fact that she wasn't going to be sleeping with him that night as he'd been expecting.

"It's getting late," he agreed, gathering both glasses and the bottle of wine as he stood. He followed her to the door, the glass stems between the fingers of one hand, the bottle in the other. He waited while she collected her purse and opened the door.

She didn't want to kiss him good-night. But didn't want to just walk out on him, either. Glancing over at him, she struggled for something to say. Besides the "I really do love you" that was entirely inappropriate.

"Drive carefully," he said, raising the two glasses to her.

"I will."

She left, tears streaming down her face as she closed his door behind her and climbed into her car.

She'd done the right thing.

And it hurt like hell.

CHAPTER SEVEN

DiSALVO, HIS FATHER'S FRIEND, was being investigated for tax fraud. Criminal charges were expected to be filed soon. He wasn't only looking at having all his assets frozen, but could be facing prison time, as well. Like most in his income bracket, DiSalvo had a myriad of interests, not all related. Businesses he'd purchased as a silent investor, some he hadn't purchased outright but invested in. And as Cedar had, the man had someone prepare his taxes every year.

Alvin Hines, tax specialist to the rich and famous, was the first person Cedar looked at once he had a more complete picture of the situation. Not because he was certain the man was guilty of fraud—he wasn't sure of that at all. He'd found some numbers in the files that had been provided to the preparer by DiSalvo's people, numbers that didn't add up. Deductions taken without evidence to prove they were legitimate. Purchases made with no proof of goods having existed. Services paid for, with no accounting of those services having been received. Like the landscaping that was done for a property DiSalvo had bought and sold. The property was wooded, with forty-year-old trees. It didn't need landscaping.

Didn't mean Hines had done anything wrong. He reported what his clients gave him.

In any case, the fraud of which DiSalvo was being accused was on a grander scale. Companies in which he'd invested once, a relatively small amount of money each time, were included in the list of everything that was being investigated and named in the criminal charge. And the money that had been invested had come from another source he'd never really owned. All of which gave wiggle room for getting him off. And gave doubt to his innocence, too.

Cedar spent all of Monday night following paper trails—and coming up with dead ends. Investments were tied to other investments, and yet DiSalvo wasn't tied to most of them. Or an investment that was named was tied to one that wasn't.

After almost ten hours of work, he'd come up with two key points. First, the timeline—threads had started to connect three years before, during the summer. Ties between investors started there. Like a massive family tree filled with branches, and that was when the trunk came into sight. Almost as though the people had met in person. Concocted a plan.

Or an event had happened that triggered the

events that followed. Or fostered the financial relationships that grew out of it.

Second point—an entity, HHC, had shown up in some emails, and he'd found no reference to what the acronym stood for.

A tangled mess, in other words. His list of questions was long. He wouldn't stop until every single one of them, and any others that arose, were answered. He'd been waiting his entire life to be his father's son, and if this was his opportunity, then so be it. He'd help, and then move on.

One thing he was pleased and relieved to see was that his father wasn't part of any of it. Whatever Cedar-Jones did with the millions he raked in, he didn't do it with his friend DiSalvo. Or the tax preparer, Alvin Hines.

After a brief nap about an hour before sunrise, he showered, pulled on the jeans that still didn't feel like work clothes, tied up his leather boots and, grabbing another ham-and-mustard sandwich, headed out the door, his filled cooler in hand. Helping his father didn't diminish the moral debts he had to pay.

Thinking of those moral debts brought Heather Michaels to mind. Sitting with her at the restaurant the day before—*their* restaurant—he…well, if not for his father's phone call precipitating a night trying to sort out that incredible turn of events, he'd have spent the previous hours with a six-pack, maybe more, trying to forget everything he'd lost.

And everything he'd taken from her. A woman who'd once approached the world with gusto now seemed closed off. Not just to him. She'd been different with her friends, too. Less effervescent. And with that fiancé of hers... They'd seemed more like affectionate friends. Like she wasn't letting the guy far enough into her life to touch her at her core.

Cedar knew. He'd been that far in. That far in was where he'd hurt her most.

How the hell could he heal the damage he'd done to her?

On his way to work, pushing the button on his steering wheel, he gave the command to call her. It was just past seven, but she'd always been up with the sun—as though she couldn't bear to miss out on anything.

"Hello." Although she answered on the first ring, her tone didn't sound welcoming. Of course she'd know it was him calling.

She'd answered anyway. He took that as a good sign.

"I just have two quick things," he started, wishing he'd had the forethought to make an actual list. She'd get that; she was used to his lists. Particularly the one where the top item was "Be financially set for a luxurious life by thirty-five."

He had a year to go. He would've been able to cross that one off the list if he hadn't quit his job. And didn't worry about it either way. He'd thrown away the list.

"What?"

He'd give the fortune he'd amassed to know what she was thinking.

She didn't trust him, but she'd answered. And was still on the line. Giving him a chance?

"First, I heard from Lila Mantle regarding Carin. She said you have an appointment with Carin in the morning and—"

"I do. And you are to stay away, Cedar. I'm only talking to her, in case I really can help her. To make sure things are as you say they are. If you've got something else up your sleeve, something else you hope to gain by this, I will not—I repeat not—allow you to manipulate this situation to your own benefit."

Part of him felt a smile coming on. His tigress still had her claws when it came to those she sought to protect. The rest of him felt a sadness so deep, he knew he'd never completely recover from it.

"I just want to help," he told her, pretty sure her mind was closed to the possibility. "I have some information that will help you form questions that could lead her to tell you the truth. Particularly when she's hooked up to the polygraph. She'll be more apt to be truthful if she suspects the machine could point out deception."

He slowed at a light and slammed his hand against the steering wheel. He sounded like an ass. An immoral, trying-to-convince-someone-of-something ass. Because he'd used those same words on her before, when he'd been exactly that. A manipulative ass.

Heather of all people knew the power of her work. And how to find the truth.

"As I said, Cedar, you will not have the opportunity to influence things for your own gain."

The light changed and he sped up, signaling his next turn. He'd be at the Stand in a matter of minutes, pulling into a parking lot that would be filling with pickups and good guys heading to a day of hard, hot work. He wasn't part of their morning hello call-outs, jokes or commiserations, but usually listened to them.

"I know. I expected no less. I have no goal other than to see that this woman's life is saved, if at all possible. To that end, I'm offering to help." He understood what went into the preparations she made—and believed he could contribute.

His new way was not to exploit, but to let those around him make their own choices, without controlling them.

At the same time, if you knew something, and

knew it could genuinely help, it would be equally wrong to withhold that information.

"I won't be compiling questions until after tomorrow morning's session," she told him.

He was aware of that. He passed his turn into the Stand's employee parking. Signaled to go around the block.

Would she be calling on him when she did get around to creating her list of questions? Or had he just received a polite Heather brush-off?

He'd never had one of those before, although he knew of many people in her professional world who had. No, when he'd pissed her off, there'd been nothing polite or restrained about the way she'd told him what she thought of him.

And what he could do with certain body parts.

"You said there were two things." She spoke into the silence that had fallen.

The second was trying to help heal the damage he'd done to her...but he felt powerless. He was certainly familiar with the theories and the rhetoric. Apology was a powerful force...yada, yada, yada.

"I just want you to know that I'm conscious of what I did—telling you I wanted the truth when, in fact, I was only using you to get what I needed to free Dominic—was deplorable. I wanted the truth, but only so I could protect Dominic from it, if it turned out that's what I needed to do. I told you I'd do the right thing, and I had no intention of doing that unless it turned out to be what would win me the case. It wasn't. Instead, you exposed another offense, a horrendous one, and I ignored it. I was wrong, Heather. Absolutely, completely wrong. I take full responsibility for that. And I'm sorry. So sorry. You're an incredible woman, and... I hate what I did to you."

He was on his second trip around the block. Her silence carried on for so long, he would've thought she'd hung up if not for the *call in progress* notation showing on his phone.

"So you did do it knowingly. Purposely."

As opposed to?

Had she actually still been giving him the benefit of the doubt? Thinking that maybe he'd manipulated her without meaning to?

For a second, he considered accepting the small bone she'd apparently thrown him. For a very brief second.

Shaking his head, he turned one last corner, and the employee parking lot came into view on his left. His soul was already in the red. He couldn't afford another mistake.

"I did."

Cedar wasn't at all surprised when she hung up on him.

CHAPTER EIGHT

HEATHER HAD THREE appointments that day. Two were from LA—one a defendant on a court-approved attorney request and the other at the request of law enforcement—and the third was with a local defendant who had consent from both the prosecuting and defense attorneys. Only one, the local one, was a domestic violence issue. The law-enforcement case was emotionally draining, though, as it dealt with a missing person. An adult missing person. A sister who lived with the young man who'd gone missing said she didn't know anything about his disappearance, but detectives were convinced that she did.

Heather had met with the woman and knew she'd have to give the case a very high priority. She'd be traveling to LA on Wednesday, having a second appointment in the woman's apartment before drawing up her first set of questions and administering a polygraph exam.

At their first meeting, she didn't think the woman was lying about not knowing where her brother was. Heather didn't suspect her of foul play. She had no idea whether the police considered her a suspect or not. She got information on a need-to-know basis only. Her purpose was to get to the truth, not to prove suspicions correct.

She did, however, agree with police in their assessment that the woman knew more than she was saying.

The day filled her mind, took all of her focus, and it wasn't until she'd changed into a tank-style, tie-dyed casual cotton dress and was heading over to Lianna's apartment that she felt the weight of her personal circumstances returning. She hadn't spoken to Charles all day. Couldn't help wondering how he was doing. How his day had gone.

She hoped he was playing golf that evening, as he normally did on Tuesday nights. And that he played well. Good golf scores were important to him.

She'd spoken to Cedar and could hardly bear thinking about the end of that particular conversation. She was thankful she didn't have to tell Charles about it.

Not just what Cedar had said, but the fact that the conversation had happened at all.

That alone told her she'd made the right choice where Charles was concerned. She'd had to answer Cedar's call.

They had a critical common business interest. And a history that needed to be better understood so she could get over the mental and emotional hurdles facing her.

But with Charles in the picture, she would've felt guilty.

"Hey, girlfriend, I've got sushi and wine on the patio," Lianna said as she opened the door of her second-floor apartment. The fact that her smile was a flyby and that she turned immediately to lead the way in concerned Heather even more than their call the day before. Something was definitely not right in her friend's life.

Lianna had changed out of the colorful scrubs she always wore to work. She had on shorts and a full-flowing top that accentuated her breasts and long legs without drawing attention to shoulders that were broad enough, she'd always said, to handle it if she chose to be a linebacker.

As a nuclear-med technician at the new Santa Raquel children's hospital in town, Lianna carried a lot of weight on those shoulders.

Maybe they'd lost a patient she'd known well. No way could anyone get through that without some hard moments.

Usually, she called Heather at times like that.

The wine, an unoaked chardonnay Heather had turned Lianna on to after Raine had introduced it to her, was chilled and waiting. Lianna asked how her day had gone as she poured them both glasses and then took a seat, facing the beach and the ocean below.

The view was spectacular. Even better than Charles's and her parents'. It was the reason Lianna still lived in a rented apartment.

Her feet bare, she rested them on the white wooden railing as she held her wineglass in both hands and sipped, staring out.

"What's going on?" Heather didn't want to talk about her day. Didn't want to think about her life.

Lianna shrugged, still staring outward. That was so not like her that Heather faltered for a moment. Lianna had had it rough growing up. An abusive father early on, and things hadn't improved much later. She'd learned to be tough when life came at her.

"You're not sick, are you?" she asked, fearful.

"No." Still no tough-girl grin. Lianna's stunning red hair was up as usual, but the curls had lost a bit of their normal flair.

"You're scaring me. Look, if I pissed you off by asking you to go with me and Raine, for not planning our own time, I'm sorry. I just thought… You know I'll always give you whatever time you need. It's just that, after last weekend, the way you two seemed to be getting along… But it doesn't matter. If you want us to take our own trip up north, then that's fine."

"It has nothing to do with that." Lianna frowned

and pulled her head back as she turned to Heather. "Why would you think I'd get pissed at something like that? We're thirty, not ten."

After slipping off her flip-flops, Heather put her feet up on the rail, too. She had no idea why she'd jumped to that childish conclusion. Or maybe she did.

The same reason she'd broken up with Charles. Because she was struggling to understand herself at the moment. Overreacting due to post emotional overload.

But this wasn't about her.

"I'm not letting you derail the conversation, Li. Tell me what's wrong." She hadn't had to play the strong girl in their relationship often, but she knew how to. And knew when it was needed.

"I'm thinking about breaking up with Dex."

What? They'd been together almost a decade! She'd been expecting them to set up house together soon, even if they weren't going to get married. To start a family. Lianna loved kids, had always wanted at least two. And Dexter had just turned forty.

Sharing a house would mean having to leave the apartment, but she and Dexter both had good jobs and could afford a place close to the beach, if not directly on it.

"Why?" The question was there, demanding to be asked.

Lianna's shrug surprised Heather. Her friend was usually so sure. About everything. Or was damned good at faking that she was, although Heather was one of the few who could usually see through her faked responses. But that night, she wasn't even trying.

"He wants to get married. Buy a house together. Have a family."

All the things Lianna had always said she wanted.

"And?"

"After your party on Saturday night, he proposed. Gave me a ring."

Lianna's ring finger was glaringly without a stone.

"And?"

"I don't want it."

She didn't like the ring? Heather shook her head. Lianna couldn't care less about stuff like that. And if it was truly hideous, she'd probably just exchange it. Or go buy a cheap one she could live with.

Heather didn't like that her friend still wasn't looking at her. Lianna was big on catching your gaze and grilling you, with just a look.

"Why?" Heather asked the only question that presented itself. She was holding her glass of wine, but hadn't taken a sip since she sat down. Hadn't studied the view she loved so completely, either. Lianna was all that mattered at this moment.

Her repeated shrug was frustrating at best. "I was fine with a wedding in the future," she said, sounding despondent. Almost as though she had no fight in her. Not like herself at all. "But seeing you with Charles felt…wrong. Horribly, completely wrong. And then Raine was all uptight about it, too, so I knew it wasn't just me. I don't know. I…"

Oh, God. "You and Dex aren't Charles and me!" Surely her friend hadn't broken off a ten-year relationship because of her! "Anyway, I broke up with him last night, not that anyone's supposed to know yet, so please don't say anything."

Lianna's feet dropped. Sitting forward, she stared at Heather, a look that would scare a kid in a principal's office on her face. "Please tell me you are *not* getting back with Cedar Wilson."

"Of course I'm not." And would everyone please, for the last time, get *off* that?

"But you're not going to marry Charles?"

She hoped she was. "We'll talk about that later. Right now, tell me what's going on. You love Dex. He loves you. He's offering you everything you always said you wanted. I don't get it."

Lianna's recurring shrug wasn't a satisfactory answer. "I wish I could tell you," Lianna said. "I saw you with Charles… I'm so, so, soooo relieved that you broke up with him, by the way..." Lianna, feet back up on the rail, looked at Heather, grinned and took a sip of wine, before returning her focus to the ocean.

"There was no spark between you. No fire... not like there was when we left you alone in the kitchen with Cedar." She shook her head full of glorious red hair and it was like mini-flames sending out the energy she usually directed at everything she tackled. "I knew we shouldn't have left you alone with him." Her glance at Heather was more pointed this time. More like the Lianna she knew. "You swear to me you aren't getting back together with him?"

"I swear." She didn't look away. Didn't even blink. She had no desire, whatsoever, to be back in the relationship she'd so narrowly escaped. What if she'd married Cedar and then found out that his heart was too damaged, his soul too empty? That he wasn't capable of doing the right thing? Even when it came to her...

Had he done it on purpose, callously used her, she'd asked him that morning. A question that had haunted her since the day she'd found out what he'd done.

I did.

The words had been like daggers to her heart. Remembering them caused a similar stabbing pain.

Lianna's stare was long and hard. She didn't let

up easily. And then it was over. Obviously satisfied, she took another sip of wine and turned back toward the ocean.

"Dex is comfortable. The way Charles was to you. Sex with him is nice. Fine. I like it. But I like taking hot baths, too. I already have a lifetime of being able to take hot baths ahead of me. I don't want to sign on to a lifetime with only hot-bath-feeling sex, you know?" Her voice was soft, a tone she rarely used, Lianna looked over at her again. A sheen of moisture covered those bold green eyes, and Heather almost wept.

"I know," she whispered.

She knew about the fire. Had been held captive by it. Addicted to it.

When she'd been in Cedar's arms, when the universe had faded until it was just the two of them...there'd been nothing like it. She'd known moments of pure ecstasy.

But she also knew she'd spend the rest of her life with someone like Charles, soaking in a warm bath, rather than getting burned by those flames a second time.

CHAPTER NINE

CEDAR WASN'T IN the best of moods Tuesday evening, when he drove up the coast to meet Dean DiSalvo for a late dinner. He'd used the SUV's Bluetooth capabilities to stream his father's music from his phone, something he used to do a lot when he was younger, but then tuned it out with thoughts that wouldn't be silenced. Mostly revolving around Heather. Then and now.

DiSalvo had picked their meeting place, an Italian eatery off the beaten path, yet packed to the brim. Vehicles spilled out of the parking lot, onto side streets in an old neighborhood, part of a small town he'd never even heard of, which forced him to park a block away.

Because he'd stopped at home to change into what to him were normal business clothes, one of the couple of suits he'd saved, he was sweating beneath his collar and tie before he'd reached the door. He was shown to a private alcove off the dining room, out of hearing range but with a perfect view of the place. An older guy, probably in his fifties, also in a jacket and tie, stood as he approached and held out his hand. He was the only person there.

Not that Cedar had expected anything else.

Hoped maybe. Foolishly. He wasn't a kid anymore with visions of rock-star moments stalking his dreams.

"Thanks for making the drive up," DiSalvo said after introducing himself.

Cedar could have told him that he preferred doing business away from home. The only office he kept now was little more than a shell for meetings he might need to have as he worked toward helping those who'd been hurt or damaged as a direct result of his blind drive to win. It also served as a storage place for the ten years of case files he had on record—files he was slowly going through, one by one, on a journey to find and rescue his self-respect, on the way to making peace with his conscience. The desk was opulent because he was using the one he had rather than buying new. But he'd donated the rich leather conversation ensemble, the bar, even the art. All that was left was carpet, file cabinets, his desk and chair, and the two chairs in front of it. Not the type of place in which he'd want to host a friend of his father's.

DiSalvo was already well into a glass of amber liquid on the rocks. Whiskey of some kind. Cedar wanted a cold glass of milk, but ordered a beer.

Though he never apologized for his penchant for cold milk while he was working or explained himself to anyone, he'd received enough raised eyebrows at various dinners not to order it. If Cedar-Jones heard about this meeting, he wanted the man to be impressed, not amused.

They ordered. He got the salmon at DiSalvo's suggestion, but passed on the wine, and they drank and got to know each other a little bit. Neither played golf. DiSalvo was a professional provider of big outdoor adventures—hang gliding over the Alps, big-game hunting, shark fishing— and he pandered to the rich and famous. His excursions weren't cheap.

That was how he'd come to meet Randy Cedar-Jones—and he told Cedar that he knew his mother was a big fan, to the point of naming him, her son, after the famous singer. He also knew Cedar had actually never met the man. DiSalvo was under the belief that Cedar-Jones had put out feelers for the best defense attorney going and Cedar's name had come up.

He clearly did not know that Cedar was Randy's son.

His father didn't seem to have any qualms about Cedar keeping that secret. And why would he? Other than Heather, he'd never told anyone who his father was, even after he'd turned eighteen and the agreement was null and void.

His mother had told no one, either—including her family—and he respected her wishes, even when her family came to her funeral. It wasn't as if they were close. She'd had a sister who lived back East, whom Cedar had seen a handful of times in his life. Her parents had been alive when he was little, also back East, and he'd seen them, but didn't remember much about them. They hadn't approved of her having a baby outside of marriage and then raising him on her own.

They'd been gone by the time his mother died.

The salmon was good. He liked DiSalvo and was kind of interested in a shark-fishing expedition. They'd be dropped off on a small, uninhabited island, have tents, minimal medical supplies, food and drink, and spend three days fishing off the beach. No boats. No way to get off the island. Sketchy cell service.

And, because of the laws, nothing to show for it when the trip was done, except for photos. It was all catch and release.

The irony of that final detail landed on him. That was what his life had been about. The cops would catch the bad guys, and then Cedar would get them released.

He'd helped a few innocent men go free, too, of course. Early on in his career. But the real money had been in getting the rich guilty guy off. The guilty were willing to pay exorbitant amounts to protect their freedom.

DiSalvo had offered to pay him a shitload.

"Your signature is on your tax returns. Did you check them over before signing?" Cedar asked. He wasn't there to make a new friend.

"Do I look like a guy who signs his own tax forms? Of course I didn't check them over. I didn't even sign them. It was done electronically. And I have a signature on file."

"Who has access to that file?"

DiSalvo shrugged. "My wife. My executive assistant, Leon Anderson. That's it."

He'd have to speak with both of them.

As a starting point, he could deflect tax fraud to the preparer, Alvin Hines, if he could prove that DiSalvo hadn't been responsible for those forms.

"Who gave Hines the information he used on those forms?"

"Leon."

"At your direction?"

DiSalvo looked him in the eye. "Between you and me?"

"Of course." That went without saying. He still had his license to practice law. And at the moment, it meant something to him.

"I am fully aware of what was sent to Hines."

"Then you're also fully aware of what was on those forms. Even if you didn't examine them."

"Yes."

Cedar nodded, satisfied. As long as DiSalvo was honest with him, he could get the job done. One way or another. Everyone made mistakes, including those on the right side of the law. It was up to him to find one—a legitimate one—that could become DiSalvo's loophole. But first, he had to know the truth. Every last little dirty drop of it. He had to know what DiSalvo was into. And how deep.

"You ever have anything to do with Santiago Holdings?" One of the questions on his list. "Their Cayman Islands Account is a problem." One of DiSalvo's "interests" had sent money to it.

"I saw that," DiSalvo said. "I swear to you, I'd never heard of Santiago until a month ago. I haven't been able to find out who they are. Who's behind it. And I sure as hell never sent money to a Cayman bank account owned by them."

Cedar noticed the qualification. *Owned by them.* Going down his list, he continued to grill DiSalvo as the waitress took away their empty plates. A little later, he was ready to conclude the meeting, and, other than that brief mention at the beginning, Cedar-Jones hadn't come up once.

Why he'd thought he might hear something of a personal nature about his father, he didn't know.

"What's HHC?" He was almost through here. Ready to head back home and get to work, looking forward to another long night ahead. He'd napped for an hour before dinner. And he'd catch another few hours before work in the morning, but was thankful to have his mind so satisfyingly occupied. Heather would be meeting with Carin in the morning.

She was going to see that he'd been completely up-front this time. Dominic Miller wasn't eluding arrest, facing any charges, wasn't even his client. Would Heather be relieved? Glad? Would she call him? Or...

"HHC? I have no idea," DiSalvo said. Cedar almost missed the reply completely in his uncharacteristic mental wanderings down an inappropriate lane. HHC. DiSalvo was unfamiliar with the initialism.

"Why do you ask?" the older man sipped his whiskey, his third since they'd been together that evening. "Another Cayman bank account?"

"Not that I know of. So far, I'm not sure what it stands for. There've been a couple of mentions in emails that Hines gave to the IRS that mainly regarded other issues. 'Don't forget HHC.' And 'HHC is a win.' That's it."

"Sounds like a horse to me."

He'd already looked that up. No winning horse by any name with those initials had run in the past three years. He couldn't come up with any whose name included HHC or even HC, either.

It would be almost too easy to find a tax preparer advising an IRS agent of illegal gambling on horses. It was so commonplace in certain circles, if you knew where to look. He knew where. And had looked. No HHC.

DiSalvo picked up the bill. Told their waitress, whom he'd been calling by name all night, to put it on his tab.

"If you're serious about the shark fishing, we've got another adventure coming up next month," he said as they walked out to the parking lot. "I've got a couple of guys already booked, two doctors who graduated from med school together. You'd be perfect as their third. And who better than a doctor to have with you on a deserted island?"

Cedar was tempted. But knew he couldn't guarantee he'd be able to get away. Not if Carin went back to Dominic. Not with the target open date of the new bungalows at the Stand being September 15. Not with all the old cases in his office still waiting for him.

Not with Heather getting ready to marry a man who didn't seem to bring the sparkle to her gaze, that lift in the tone of her voice, that Cedar had grown to take for granted...

"I first met Randy on a fishing expedition," DiSalvo said. "Though I haven't personally run one of the expeditions in twenty years, I go along sometimes, to keep my own adrenaline hopping."

They were at Cedar's SUV, but he didn't pull out his keys. DiSalvo had his complete attention. Other than the little bits he'd gotten from his mother, the only time Cedar learned anything about his father was from the news. Just like the rest of his millions of fans.

"That trip was a two-day one, on this mammoth boat off the New England coast. We were after bluefin tuna. The record noncommercial catch is over a thousand pounds. Those fish can reach eight feet in length and swim like rockets. Get up to twenty-five miles an hour, some of them. We were hoping to hook at least one, but ended up taking in nearly twenty. Nowhere near that big, of course, but we had one that weighed in at nearly six-hundred pounds!" Grinning, DiSalvo held his hand above his head. "Higher than this when we brought him up..."

Cedar grinned back. Sounded like a trip he'd have loved to be on. So maybe he'd look into that. Or the shark fishing.

For now, he had to get back to work. The evening had gone well. He was pretty much where he'd expected to be. DiSalvo was in deep enough to go to jail. But not nearly as deep as the charges were claiming. He was, Cedar suspected, a gameboard piece, one among many. Cedar's job was to find the game's creator.

If worse came to worst, he could get immunity for DiSalvo in exchange for testimony.

He didn't like that option and knew DiSalvo wouldn't either, which was one reason he didn't mention it.

Still, it was important to have an escape hatch. Even if just to use as a bargaining tool somewhere down the road.

"THEY SAID YOU talked to Dominic. That you helped get him off on those drug charges last year," Carin Landry said.

Who was "they"?

In brown pants and a beige silky top, Heather flipped a lock of her hair over her shoulder, crossed her legs and stared for a moment at the brown wedge dress shoe she had on. She'd come here, to the Stand, to help.

Had to take herself out of the picture to do so.

But she couldn't help without the truth, and the path to that had many diversions.

"You want to go for a walk?" she asked Carin Landry, knowing that she was going to blow this if she didn't get herself together. The other woman, in jean shorts and a tank top, nodded. The bruising along her jaw had begun to yellow. The swelling around her right eye had gone down, but the discoloration in her beautiful honey-colored skin was going to be there for a while.

"We can go out to the Garden of Renewal, at the back of the property. Pick some wildflowers. If we get roots and all, we can put them in water and keep them alive. They have pots here for replanting them. You can take one to your bungalow, and I'd love one for my office."

Flower "transplanting" was a new program they'd started at the Stand that summer. Lila had told Heather about it the day before, when Heather had asked how everything was going. Though she and her parents supported the Stand financially and had attended fund-raisers a few times, Heather didn't get to visit the place all that often. She'd thought the transplanting program sounded cool.

At the moment, she just needed something to do, to distract her from her jitters, and suspected that Carin did, too. Since they'd entered the private room they'd been shown to for their meeting, Carin had been looking around, in corners, along baseboards, almost as though she thought the place might be bugged.

"I'll leave my bag and cell phone here," she offered, holding up her hands. "Just you and me, flowers and talk. No notes. No record of anything."

The petite woman's eyes narrowed. "You some kind of shrink? They said you were a polygraphist. That I'd take a polygraph test, answer your questions, and then everyone quits asking me how I got these bruises."

She hadn't known they'd made a deal with Carin. But she hadn't asked, either. She was there to learn the truth about Carin's injuries, to help the woman stay safe. The rest was none of her concern.

"I have a degree in psychology and a counseling certification, but no, I'm not a shrink. I also have law-enforcement training, but I'm not a cop, and I can't arrest anyone. I'm a criminologist with polygraphic training." If she wanted the truth, she had to tell the truth.

"You work for the cops, though." Carin's gaze darted around the room again, and Heather stood. She had to get the woman out of that setting or they'd be wasting their time. And because Carin was in a safe house—resort-like though it might be—there were only so many places they could go.

"Walk with me," she told Carin, who was waiting by the door. Despite everything, Heather still wasn't sure she was there for the reason she thought she was.

If Carin so badly feared the cops, then did that mean Dominic was in custody, after all? Or, more likely, about to be, and Cedar needed to know what Carin would say about him? To form a defense that would get Dominic off in the event that he was arrested?

This probably wasn't about domestic violence at all. Cedar wanted to know if Carin was going to squeal. And what she'd say if she did. *That* was what it was about.

At least, Heather now feared it was.

Based on how Cedar had played her in the past, the idea made perfect sense. And made her sick, too.

Carin wasn't moving.

"I work at the behest of law enforcement sometimes," she said, answering the question. "But not this time. I'm doing this as a favor."

Carin's head tilted at the word *favor*. Her brown eyes wide now, she looked straight at Heather. "A favor for who?"

Heather had to be honest. And she had to choose her words carefully, too, if she wasn't going to blow things. Cedar's intent aside, if she could help this beaten woman, it was something she had to do.

"A favor to the people here who are trying to help you, for starters," she said. And then, "Listen, fighting the mental manipulation that's part of domestic violence is why I got into this business to begin with. My aunt was abused. Her husband loved her, but he had anger issues. He had her convinced that if she left him, others would get hurt, including their children. He also had her convinced that he needed her. That only with her help could he get better. That he was already a lot better than he would have been because of her. Everyone knew he was hitting her. My mom and dad went and got her and her kids one time when he was away on a hunting trip. Brought them here to Santa Raquel. But she still wouldn't testify against him or admit that her injuries were anything but accidents caused by her being clumsy. He got back from his hunting trip, called my mom, looking for her. My aunt overheard and, in the end, went back to him. He had such control of her mind, through fear, love, whatever, she couldn't even reach out for help when she was away from him."

She'd often told the story before. But this time, she felt tears close to the surface as she held Carin's gaze. The woman retained her defensive posture, the stubborn set of her chin. And yet, in her eyes, Heather saw something more. A softening. Vulnerability. Fear, maybe.

Without relenting or showing any indication of cooperating with an intent to put her abuser away, Carin stood and followed Heather out the door.

CHAPTER TEN

"IT'S NOT THAT I have anyone to testify against," Carin said as Heather walked along the garden path with her. They'd yet to pick any flowers, but Heather had eyed a few. She'd like a bouquet for her office, and wanted even more for Carin to have one in her room at the Stand. A thing of fragile beauty that could grow and thrive in more than one place, that could be uprooted and find new soil in which to flourish. A fragile, beautiful life that managed to exist in spite of the ugliness in the world. The way trust did. And true love. The way a bruised and battered life could.

Heather could use the reminder. And was certain Carin could, too.

"But I'm willing to cooperate with you in terms of the test. Just so everyone will let this go. I already told them how I got hurt. Dominic's friend was drunk. He thought I was someone else. That he was after a threat. He meant to be protecting his own..."

Questions sprang from all corners of Heather's mind. She tried to corral them, file them for later, without missing a step in the here and now. Cedar had said that Carin was claiming someone else had hurt her, someone who'd been drinking, that it had been an accident. Exactly what Carin was saying now...

"Then you should do just fine with the test, when we get to it," she said. "I'm here for a preliminary conversation today. I'd like to meet with you one more time before the test, and then we'll do it, if that's okay with you."

Carin shrugged. "Whatever. Is that how it's always done?"

"That's how I usually work. But no, that's not how a polygraph is usually administered. Most times, it's just one preliminary interview, and then the test."

Carin stopped, gently worked a yellow flower up by its roots and continued walking slowly beside her. "But what you're doing with me, it's no different than what you normally do."

Trying to figure out what prompted the question, Heather came up blank. "Every case I have takes on a quality of its own," she said.

Carin took another flower. Purple this time. Heather bent and took one, too. They were everywhere, the wildflowers that had been planted and grown for just this purpose.

"How successful are you?" Carin asked as they walked along.

Heather had questions to ask, but sensed that listening to Carin's questions was the better course right now.

"Depends on how you measure success."

The other woman glanced at her and then back at the flowers around them. She took a red one, adding it to her bouquet. There were other people in the acreage that composed the garden. A couple of women sitting on a bench by a beautiful fountain. One or two strolling among the trees. There was a feeling of freedom out there. Of peace.

And yet there were also security cameras everywhere. And electric fences surrounding them, keeping evil out. At least the evil that hadn't yet had a chance to strike.

Most of the residents at the Stand—and some of the staff, too—had some kind of evil attacking them from the inside out, through the memories that lurked in their minds, sometimes attacking them in dreams and in hearts that had lost the ability to trust. Hearts that were often barricaded against any future storms.

"How do you measure success?" Carin's question made Heather look at the woman in a new way. Carin was a woman of intelligence, of mental ability, not just an emotional and physical victim, and she'd been remiss to treat her as though she was. She knew better.

Was Cedar's effect on her now impinging on her ability to assess people accurately?

The thought came. And went. She had a job to do.

"Am I out to please those who hired me, you mean?" she asked.

Scuffing her flip-flop along the cement, Carin tossed her head to one side. "Maybe."

"I'm out to find the truth," she said. After stopping to pick a yellow flower of her own and another purple one, as well, she stood and looked Carin right in the eye. "Only the truth will set you free."

The woman nodded. Walked on. Picked a couple more flowers. Said something about having enough to share with her bungalow mates. She seemed to have run out of questions.

"Are you aware of any imminent or pending charges against Dominic?" she asked.

Carin's head shot up. "You said you aren't working for the cops."

"I'm not."

"Dominic trusted Cedar Wilson. When my counselor here said that Cedar wanted me to talk to you, I thought you were on our side."

Heather's heart started to thud. Her mind seemed to stop. As if a white blanket was wrapped around it. And then it cleared.

"I'm here as a favor to Cedar first, and the

Stand people second," she said. "Cedar's the one who approached me about speaking to you. His request was seconded when I spoke with Lila." She assumed Lila and Cedar had met over Carin, though she hadn't asked.

Carin studied her, hard. Heather bore the scrutiny easily.

Carin nodded and continued on the trail that would eventually take them back to where they'd started. They were in the thick of the woods now, with only natural vegetation surrounding them. Heather held her flowers in one hand, at her side. Carin carried hers as a bouquet, in two hands in front of her, as if she was in a wedding.

"How long have you and Dominic been together?"

"Since high school. He was the first boy I ever kissed." Not the only? Had the woman ever had a relationship with someone who wasn't a criminal? Sensing a struggle inside Carin, she hoped so.

"You and he ever talk about getting married?"

"Sure we do. He wants to."

"But you don't?"

That shrug came again. "I'm already his woman. Everyone knows it. What's a piece of paper going to change?"

"Do you love him?"

"More than anyone." The answer came quickly. With confidence.

She loved him, but something was keeping her from marrying him. If she was telling the truth about his wanting to marry her. Heather knew one question that would be on the test for sure.

They were rounding a corner, and would soon be passing another resident, a woman about Carin's age, also in shorts and a T-shirt. Her arm was in a cast up to the shoulder. Carin avoided looking at her. Heather smiled, but the woman didn't glance their way.

"So…are you aware of any imminent or pending charges against Dominic?"

Carin's hands seemed to tighten around the flowers. "You trying to tell me something?" she asked.

"No! I absolutely am not!" she said, stopping again to look Carin straight in the eye. "I have no knowledge of Dominic beyond the case Cedar Wilson had with him last year. I interviewed Dominic then, which Cedar said you knew."

Carin nodded.

"I hadn't heard of him since, until Cedar met with me on Monday and asked me to speak with you."

"Is he afraid Dom did this to me?"

"I am not here to discuss what he knows, and truly don't care what he thinks or what he wants. I'm interested in what *you* know. What *you* think. What *you* need. And I might or might not ask you some of these same questions when I administer the polygraph test. That's how this works."

And she wanted to learn if she was being set up. Carin had clearly been beaten. She was at The Lemonade Stand willingly. And was refusing to press charges or name Dominic's "friend" who'd hurt her. But maybe this was all so that Cedar could find out what Carin would say, how close she was to rolling on his client...

Cedar had said Dominic wasn't a current client.

Or had implied as much, anyway. She couldn't remember the exact words he'd used.

Carin dropped her arms to her sides, still clutching the flowers in one hand. "If there are any current investigations involving Dominic— other than that the feds always seem to be watching him—or if any charges are pending, I don't know about them. Which means, unless it happened in the few days I've been here, then no. There's nothing."

Did that mean Cedar was telling the truth? Carin was frowning, her arms still at her sides.

Or had something come up as a result of Carin's beating? Were the threats to Dominic's freedom that new?

Didn't really matter, did it? Carin needed help. So Heather had to do what she could.

They'd reached their starting place. "We done

here?" Carin asked. "I'd like to get a bit of green-ery to go with these before I head back up."

She *could* be done. They'd have another, more formal interview, one where she'd take notes, be-fore she scheduled a test.

"I just have one more question, and I'd like an honest answer," she said. Polygraph tests might not be a hundred percent accurate. There might be ways to trick them. But for most people, even the thought of being asked a question during the exam brought on enough tension to ensure some version of the truth.

"What?"

Carin must've been aware that if Heather wasn't fully convinced she'd heard the truth, the question would end up on the test.

"Why don't you want to marry Dominic?"

Whether or not he wanted to marry her was an-other issue. One she'd definitely take to the test. Carin needed to see Dominic for who he was. But right now, this question seemed far more critical to helping Carin. So Carin could see herself.

"Because, as soon as we get married, he'll want to start having kids."

And clearly, judging by the stricken look on her face, Carin didn't want to do that.

That expression, the words, hooked Heather completely. Carin might not be willing to protect herself, but she was already protecting any unborn children.

Carin didn't want Dominic's children. Heather had to make certain that before they were done, the woman understood why that was. And hoped she'd also be able to see another truth.

That she, Carin, deserved the same protection.

It was a truth Heather could help her see...

If she did her job right.

THE APPOINTMENT HAD been at nine thirty. Cedar knew that Heather wouldn't be anywhere close to where he was working, but every time he took a break for a sip of water or to refill his nail pouch, he glanced in the direction of the main building. He couldn't actually see it. The pool house and a stretch of bungalows along the winding walk blocked his view, but he looked anyway.

If nothing else, the meeting would show her that he hadn't lied to her. That he wasn't using her.

At least he hoped it did.

Where he went from there with his newly formed quest to help her heal from the hurt he'd caused her, he had no idea. He'd always been good at coming up with things on the fly if a prosecutor threw a wrench in his original plan.

Mostly because he knew every aspect of his cases, inside and out.

He'd once known Heather that well.

So maybe he just had to trust his instincts where she was concerned.

Lunch came and went. She'd have left the Stand by now. But he took a walk anyway while he ate his sandwich. He didn't have clearance to be past the construction site, and, in fact, there was a fence preventing him from going any farther.

As a new donor to the Stand in the past year, he'd been inside. Had toured the place. And planned to visit, with a temporary clearance, only to the main building, to meet with Carin at some point. Technically he wasn't her attorney, but she'd named him on the forms she'd filled out when she was admitted. There'd been a place to write down your attorney's name and a box to check if you wanted him or her to be called.

She'd checked the box.

He'd already known she was there. He'd had Dominic on his radar for months.

With the assistance of the private detective he'd hired as part of his overall "make amends" plan.

He had yet to meet with her, though. He'd sent a message, through Lila, that he'd set up a time later in the week. He'd wanted her to have some counseling first.

And to talk with Heather.

Then he'd have to figure out how he was going to handle his professional end of things. He'd recuse himself, of course. He'd been her boyfriend's attorney. She'd been abused. It was obvious to him that there could be a conflict of interest.

But he didn't want to just cut her off, either.

Not if she was reaching out for help.

Hence, the meeting later in the week. After he'd spoken with Heather.

He'd hoped Heather would call as soon as she was done. He hadn't really expected her to, but he'd hoped.

By the time he was climbing into his SUV that night, dirty, tired, but completely geared up, he was fairly certain she wasn't going to call. Business hours were over for the day, and she'd made it very clear that her association with him was business only.

Did she care at all that he'd been straight with her? Did she find it odd that he was willing to risk his career, as she saw it, to help his client's girlfriend?

Was that why he was doing this? Because he wanted her to know? To care? He'd denied that possibility a few days ago; it might, however, be true.

Had he become a better man in the year since she'd left him? Since her leaving had shown him the truth about himself?

He wanted to think so.

He had no legitimate reason to call her. Not by her standards, anyway. He'd already offered his services, offered to help her formulate questions that might persuade Carin to disclose the truth. She'd acknowledged the offer.

And all the while his mind kept concocting scenarios that would allow him to make that call, he shut himself down. Over and over. As he drove home. As he showered.

Yeah, he could probably manipulate a situation that would let him speak with her.

But he wasn't going to do it. Heather's life was out of his control.

Always had been. Her love had been a gift. He'd been lucky that she'd chosen to share her life with him. But the choice had always been there.

He just hadn't been smart enough to see that.

CHAPTER ELEVEN

HEATHER'S NEXT APPOINTMENT with Carin was mid-morning on Friday. She'd have one more interview and then on Monday, after her return from wine country, she would administer the polygraph test. Arrangements had been made through The Lemonade Stand; they'd allocated an appropriate space. She'd be doing the test on-site, obviously, as Carin was under the shelter's protection. She had no idea whether Dominic Miller knew his girlfriend was there. Had no idea what Cedar might have told him.

She couldn't worry about those things.

But she woke up on Thursday morning thinking about them. The Cedar she'd thought she'd known, the man she'd thought she'd been living with all those years, wouldn't be in contact with Dominic. But the man he became, the man she now knew him to be? Who could tell?

After throwing off the covers with a little more force than necessary, she went into the bathroom and turned on the shower. Cedar's motives, his actions…his heart…were of no concern to her. She had to stop thinking about him.

And yet, as she showered, had her coffee and fiber bar and headed into the office, he was still on her mind.

He'd probably been telling the truth about Carin. He'd given Heather the chance to help him undo the wrong he'd done. Unless Dominic was in some new trouble. Was Cedar manipulating her again? And if so, to what end?

She thought of the kiss they'd nearly shared in her mother's kitchen the previous Saturday night. At her engagement party.

Charles. He was a truly good guy. Great-looking. Kind. Life with him would be like the potted flowers she'd brought to her office from The Lemonade Stand, the day before. Wonderful to look at. Sweet-smelling. Peaceful. She'd called him the night before, just to see how he was doing. He'd been out with friends, having dinner. Had told her he'd call her back.

She'd forgotten to wait for his call. She'd been getting ready for bed, after an evening of specifically not thinking about Cedar, before she realized Charles hadn't called her back.

Not that she blamed him.

Once she was in her office, behind her desk, fully professional in a black skirt and white-and-black polka dot blouse, pumps instead of sandals, and hair in a twist on the back of her head, she dialed Cedar's office number. Something else she hadn't forgotten.

And felt let down when she got his voice mail. She'd been mentally and emotionally prepared for the call…and now she'd have to do it all over again. That was all.

She wanted this done. Now she'd have to wait.

After leaving a message, asking him to call as soon as he got in, she hung up and went about her day. Listening for her phone. Checking for messages the second she returned if she stepped out. She was administering a test at the county jail that afternoon and forwarded her office phone to her cell.

He didn't call. Charles did, though. He asked if she'd like to come to his place for dinner Saturday night. She would've accepted if she hadn't already made plans with Raine, and told him so. Lianna called, too. She and Dex were taking a break from each other. And she wanted to know the flight Heather and Raine were taking up north. She wanted to join them.

A weekend away with both of her best friends at once. Heather almost started to cry.

Life was so unpredictable. Doors closed and others opened. She wondered about doors that didn't close all the way.

The last one to vacate her floor of office suites

Thursday evening, Heather left just before six and let the door closing behind her signify the end of her workday. She wouldn't think about Cedar again until the next morning. At which time she'd try once more to reach him. Her appointment with Carin was mid-morning, although she wasn't testing her then. His input would be better before the morning's interview, but not completely critical.

He'd know that. Lila had told her she was keeping Cedar apprised of Carin's situation. Which told Heather that he was professionally involved.

To what end, she didn't... No! She wasn't going to spend her evening spinning in circles. She knew why *she* was involved with Carin. Nothing else mattered.

She'd asked Lianna if she wanted to get dinner, but her friend had some kind of meeting that evening. Stopping by to see her parents was out of the question; her mother would monopolize the conversation with wedding talk and rehashing how well the party had gone the previous weekend. Heather would have to hear what each of her mother's friends had to say about the event. About how she and Charles made such a great couple. No way could she sit through that.

Nor did she feel particularly good about lying to her parents, if only by omission. This was a situation she'd have to handle soon. But not until she'd talked to Charles. Keeping their possibly temporary breakup a secret had been his request, and she owed it to him to honor that.

As she pulled into her garage, she thought about driving down to see Raine, who had evening classes on Thursday, but she didn't feel like doing yoga. Which meant she probably should go and do yoga. So she did. She stayed and had a cup of chamomile tea with her friend afterward, too. Talking about the weekend. Where they'd stay. The wineries they wanted to visit. How excited she was that Lianna was coming. She thanked Raine for making the suggestion.

She didn't talk about Cedar. Didn't even bring him up. He was business. If she mentioned him, her friends worried about her, and there was no longer any reason for them to worry.

On the drive back to Santa Raquel in the dark, she thought about him without meaning to. One of the diners she passed had a sign that lit up the night and it reminded her of the time she and Cedar had been driving home from LA, late one evening, and had stopped there for a cup of coffee. He'd seen a headline in a rag mag about Cedar-Jones's worth and quoting him as saying that he had no heirs.

Cedar-Jones had never said whether he believed that Cedar was his son. He'd only placated a one-night groupie who'd said he was. There was no obvious resemblance between them. They had the same color hair. That was it.

Cedar had acted as though the article didn't matter. Said it was no different than any other time his father hadn't acknowledged him as his son.

She'd suggested that maybe he should petition for a DNA test to prove paternity once and for all.

He'd declined. Said it didn't matter one way or the other. His mother had maintained all her life that Cedar-Jones was the only possible candidate, and Cedar believed her. A DNA test, no matter how discreet, was bound to leak to the press. He didn't want the cacophony that would follow.

Heather had always suspected he didn't want to piss off the man he still hoped to meet someday.

He didn't want the man's money. Or any part of his lifestyle.

He'd just wanted to matter.

Cedar had always been self-sufficient. Capable. Strong.

And yet, he had that one vulnerability—this need to be important to his father, the man whose genes made up half of him. To be good enough to get the man's attention.

To be someone Cedar-Jones would want to acknowledge, maybe even get to know.

And there, in the quiet darkness of her car, driving along the coast road that was mostly peaceful that time of night, Heather's heart gave a small tug in the Cedar direction.

Until she pulled onto the lighted streets of Santa Raquel and remembered what he'd done. Not just to her, but to so many others, by creating legal loopholes to free criminals who would continue to hurt the people with whom they came in contact.

And yet… She drove past the street that would take her by the office he'd kept in town—one she assumed he still kept—and went right on driving. But she thought about the justice system. About the people who'd been wrongfully accused and, without Cedar's help, would most likely have gone to prison. Those who'd been charged with greater crimes than they'd committed, people Cedar had successfully championed. That had been in the early days. Before his ego had gotten in the way. Or winning had gotten hold of him.

When had he stopped taking the cases of those who were wrongfully accused? Or people he'd believed had been? At what point had the challenge of winning pushed him to prove guilty people innocent in the eyes of the law?

It was when he'd started taking on clients he knew were guilty, just so he could succeed at more difficult wins. When he'd started to care more about the money they paid him and the notches on his lawyerly bedpost—that was when things had changed.

So had he always been like that, deep down? Was there a moral compass in there that had malfunctioned along the way?

Did it matter anymore?

He'd deliberately and knowingly manipulated her, used her to set free a man who'd been violent with his girlfriend. Those weren't the charges Dominic had been up on. There'd been no domestic violence charges, no proof that Dominic had hurt Carin. But there'd been several 911 calls about his address—all made by neighbors—concerning suspicious behavior. The calls had become a potential stopping point for Cedar's win, because of other evidence that had also been presented. That evidence suggested Dominic, who made frequent trips to Mexico, was dealing out of his home. A home that had cost him several million dollars, but, like most real estate in LA, was situated close to neighboring homes with disgruntled occupants.

Dominic kept insisting to Cedar that the calls were because of loud music and absolutely wouldn't budge from that story. Police records didn't stipulate. There were records of the calls from the neighbors reporting suspicious behavior—"something not right is going on over there." And then nothing. No charges, no further details. Cedar had been fairly certain that Dominic had paid someone on the police force to make sure there was nothing.

And Dominic told Cedar he was paying him enough for Cedar to take the truth and win.

Going by the jury's reaction during the prosecution's presenting of evidence, Cedar knew those calls, the suspicion without a strong explanation, posed a serious threat to his win. He'd asked Heather to help him find out what those calls had really been about.

Already concerned about some of the names on Cedar's client list, she hadn't wanted anything to do with Dominic. She was an independent operator, so she could choose her cases, give her time and energy to the ones she believed in.

He'd led her to assume that if she found incriminating evidence, he'd still use it. Her report would tell the jury the truth, one way or the other. He'd said if worse came to worst, he'd argue some kind of plea deal for Dominic. Convince the man to take it. He'd do his best for his client, but he needed the truth.

The fact was, Cedar had needed an explanation for those calls—an explanation that had nothing to do with drug dealing. He'd suggested questions for Heather to ask based, he'd told her, on things he knew. In reality, the questions had been loaded with innuendo that would lead Dominic to the answers Cedar wanted. He'd been manipulating both Heather and Dominic to get a result that would stand up in court and give him his win. He'd expected her report to exonerate Dominic.

The interview hadn't gone as Cedar had planned, but Cedar had gotten exactly what he was after. A way to explain the calls that had absolutely nothing to do with drug trafficking. The neighbors hadn't known more than to report unusual activity and sounds of violence. Someone after drugs and drug money the prosecutor claimed. Heather gave him the truth—the calls had been domestic violence–related—trusting him to do the right thing by having her findings admitted as evidence as he'd promised her he'd do. He'd be able to show that the calls weren't drug-related. And he'd be exposing Dominic's additional crime. Something that couldn't be prosecuted without Carin's help.

Instead, he'd used the information to get Dominic to testify about a disagreement between partners, with no injuries to report, no medical treatment sought, to repudiate any drug-related connotation. Cedar had used Heather's information to set the man free. And then ignored the underlying domestic violence issue in spite of the fact that he'd known more.

Thinking back about the "more" he'd known, Heather treated herself to an instant replay of that interview. Dominic had lied to Heather several times, and she'd called him out every time, based on his polygraph-test readings. Eventually Dominic had admitted to Heather that the 911 calls hadn't had anything to do with drug dealers coming and going from his home. They'd been about fights between him and his girlfriend. He'd admitted he'd had a little too much to drink and been loud, she'd asked about the violence, and he'd admitted that there'd been some. When she'd asked if Carin had been the victim, he'd said yes.

He'd also, later in the interview, admitted to having drugs in his home, and to sometimes traveling from Mexico with them.

Instead of taking the truth as he'd promised he'd do, Cedar had refused to have the test admitted as evidence, as was his legal right as Dominic's attorney, and without his consent, her findings didn't make it into court.

What he did, though, was call Dominic to the stand and ask him to tell the jury why there'd been prior 911 calls to his home. And Dominic's reply, coached by Cedar, had made it sound as if Carin was the one who'd gotten out of hand. When the prosecution, in recross, called her to the stand, she'd corroborated his story.

And then, even knowing that Heather's entire reason for going into her line of work was because of the women who were silent victims of domestic violence, he'd hung Carin out to dry. He'd won his case and he walked away.

Once she'd told him what she'd found, Heather had trusted him to recuse himself from the case, if nothing else. To care about more than his win.

To protect Carin.

Or at least try.

Of course, she hadn't known back then that he'd purposely misled her from the beginning. He'd convinced her that if Dominic was guilty, Cedar would work out a plea agreement that benefited his client. Something that would provide for another chance at a better life for Dominic in the future. But that he'd let the truth stand. He'd let justice win.

He'd done exactly the opposite.

And he'd done it all with forethought. With planning.

Now he had questions he wanted her to ask again. Good luck with that. She had questions she wanted to ask *him*. It wouldn't work both ways.

Not this time, or ever again.

No matter what the topic.

She didn't trust him.

CHAPTER TWELVE

CEDAR WAS HALFWAY through his third glass of milk, sitting at his side of the partners desk he and Heather had chosen a couple of years before. It had a space for a person on each side and was in a room she'd never seen. Dressed in the sweats he'd pulled on after his shower, he'd run his hands through his hair half a dozen times. It had dried. His T-shirt had seen better days, but he'd put it on because…he wanted to. It was a memento of the first cruise he and Heather had taken—six months or so after they met. The shirts had been in their tiny cubicle of a stateroom, a free promo for a new rum being served on the ship.

No telling what had happened to hers. If she still had it when she left him, she'd probably burned it. Or, more likely, considering that it was Heather he was thinking about, she'd donated it someplace where someone would get good use out of it.

He'd loved that about her—the way she always thought about other people. Her awareness that the world was full of people in need, and that she could help fill that need.

That same awareness had given him a sour taste, too. Because he hadn't had it. His mind just didn't naturally go there. If he actually saw someone in need, it did. He wasn't a complete jerk. He'd stopped more than once to help change a tire. Held doors for people on a regular basis.

She'd start conversations while standing in line, just to make someone feel noticed. He used his standing-in-line time to go over details on a case. Or think about other lists in his life. To make lists, mostly.

He'd made a little more headway on DiSalvo's case. Found out that one of the companies in which he'd invested was attached to a company that dealt in the buying and selling of rare items. Collectibles for those with a lot of money. Didn't mean DiSalvo himself was attached to that company. Only that he'd invested in another company that had been.

That particular find was a good one. Illegality— money laundering in particular—was often paired with rare collectibles. He could show doubt that DiSalvo had had anything to do with a money laundering charge that might arise from that segment of the investigation, which would clear him of any tax fraud resulting from it.

It was after eight. Why hadn't Heather called? Her meeting was in the morning.

He knew why, of course.

Because he'd wanted her to call. Really, really wanted it.

The other night, she hadn't seemed…okay. Sure, she didn't trust him. Wasn't eager to get involved in any business dealings with him.

Wait.

Business.

Staring at the computer screen in front of him, the spreadsheets that could blind a man if he couldn't figure out how to find what he was looking for, he had a thought.

Grabbed his cell phone.

Heather was treating their current association as all business. And knowing her like he did— knowing the walls she'd rightfully built against him—if she had to reach him, she'd call his business phone. Not the cell he'd used when he'd called her.

He still had the landline in his office, hooked up to a voice mail service. For all intents and purposes, he was out of business, but had wanted a number to give out if necessary, as he dealt with the moral debts he had to pay. And although he'd sent all current clients letters telling them he was taking a sabbatical, at the very least, and referring them to a peer he respected, he'd wanted them to have a number where they could reach him if something arose connected to work he'd done for them in the past.

It was the decent thing to do…

He'd already punched in the code to his voice mail and was listening to the messages that had accrued in the past few days. One from a cleaning company trying to sell him a monthly service. Another offering him insurance. And then…

"Cedar? If you get a chance, I'd appreciate a call back sometime before morning. I've got a couple of questions to ask you."

There she was.

Right where she'd been since eight o'clock that morning.

Disconnecting the call, he pushed her number on speed dial. Maybe he should have deleted that option. He'd thought about it, but hadn't gotten around to it yet.

She answered on the first ring, and from the hollow sound, he guessed she was in her car.

"Sorry for calling so late, I just heard your message," he said to quickly kill any idea she might've had that he hadn't considered her call important. Or had forgotten to return it.

Both sins from his past that would continue to haunt him.

"Seriously," he added when she didn't immediately respond. "I was out all day…on a…job, and then came straight home to work here. I thought you'd call my cell…"

"It's fine, Cedar. As I'm told you know, the actual test isn't until Monday."

"Your message said you wanted to speak with me before morning." That was his excuse for calling so late.

Or else, he was just using her for his own… comfort. Because he'd needed to talk to her.

"I… Actually, it would help if I could ask you a few questions. Can you give me a few minutes to get home? My notes are there."

"Take whatever time you need. I'm always up late, you know that."

No. Scratch that last line. He didn't want to reel her in with reminders of a closeness that was no longer there. Didn't want to reel her in at all.

Whatever Heather did, didn't do or would never do was her choice. He couldn't influence her. He'd promised himself.

He probably hadn't needed to worry in this particular case. She'd already hung up. He wasn't even sure she'd heard his last line.

Or the one before that.

HER HAND WAS shaking as she picked up her phone. She'd taken a moment to change out of her yoga clothes. She'd felt too…exposed in the tight leggings and sports-bra top. The shorts she'd worn to Lianna's on Tuesday night were in the laundry hamper so she'd pulled them on and the blouse, too, covering the sports top.

There was no room in her bungalow for an office, so—as she frequently did—she went outside, to work on the deck. Across the street, and through another yard, she could see hints of the ocean in the distance.

Porch light on, electric screens raised to keep out the bugs, she sat at the redwood table and opened her file on Carin. After a couple of focused hours studying her notes from the day before, adding her own thoughts and impressions, she felt she had a pretty good start.

Cedar picked up immediately. She'd imagined him sitting at his desk, waiting for her call. Wondered which desk he'd be at. The one from the apartment in LA, or the one they'd had in Santa Raquel. If he'd kept either one of them.

She hadn't wanted any of the furniture they'd bought together. Maybe he hadn't, either. Could have sold the house furnished. Or given it all away. Bought new.

It was nothing to her.

Picturing the desk from LA because she knew what it looked like—and it wasn't the partners desk they'd shared in town—she got right to the point.

"I have a couple of questions that arose from

yesterday's interview," she began and then continued before he could comment. "First, how are you connected to this case?"

She was going to ask her questions regardless. She needed the answers, and he'd offered to give her anything he had. But she needed a baseline in terms of Carin. Was she under the protection of Cedar—Dominic's lawyer? And therefore less apt to speak up if she thought Heather was in contact with him or a professional associate of his?

"Just as an interested party." His seeming evasiveness pissed her off.

"I need more than that." She could ask some pointed questions, but wasn't going to push him into lying to her. Let him give her the truth he wanted her to know.

Probably should've done the meeting face-to-face, so he'd be easier to read.

She found herself shivering at the thought of being alone with him at either of their homes this late. She knew he'd never hurt her physically.

But there was no way they needed to put themselves in any kind of intimate situation. If that almost-kiss in her parents' kitchen was any indication—and only to herself would she admit that she feared it could be—she had to keep herself away from temptation where he was concerned.

Apparently the body didn't always listen to the

mind when it came to matters of attraction. Or maybe the message just took longer to arrive.

"Dominic isn't a client of mine anymore. I don't know if Carin is aware of that or not. She put me down as her attorney and asked that I be contacted when she was brought from the hospital to The Lemonade Stand. Lila Mantle called me and you know the rest. I have strongly advised Carin that she tell the truth about who hurt her, and promised her that I'll do everything in my power, from a legal standpoint, to see that she gets full representation if she presses charges. Obviously, based on my former relationship with her boyfriend, it wouldn't be in her best interests to have me as her attorney if this matter goes to court. Between you and me, if she comes forward, if she wants help, wants out, I'll pay for her protection myself until she's safe from him. And if her testimony implicates her in any wrongdoing, I intend to represent her. My plan, at that point, would be to seek immunity for her in exchange for her testimony."

Wow. Where was the Cedar who kept all his cards close to his chest?

Unless he was playing her?

The air was warm, the street quiet, and she took comfort from the familiarity of being in her hometown.

"Does she know all this?"

"I don't know if she knows that I'm no longer

representing Dominic. He's certainly aware, but he has no criminal charge threat pending, so he's had no reason to need me."

He was serious then?

"Why are you no longer willing to represent him?"

It wasn't a business question. And she shouldn't have asked it.

"Forget that," she said as quickly as she could. "The question was inappropriate, and I apologize."

"Apology accepted."

He wasn't going to answer. She'd given him the out.

So now what? She was supposed to draw her own conclusions? Had Dominic fired him? Was that what this was about? Getting back at the drug dealer?

She couldn't imagine it. Not even from Cedar. He wouldn't stoop that low.

Would he?

But then, she'd never have thought he could use *her* the way he had.

What did she really know about him?

And…if Carin's life was saved in the process, what did she care?

"Carin mentioned a friend of Dominic's. Some guy named Renaldo. Sounded like a close friend.

Do you have any idea who this guy might be? What their relationship is?"

"Dominic definitely has a crew. I can think of three who stand out. Renaldo is one of them."

"Would she have access to their homes when they aren't there?" Carin had said she'd surprised him. That he'd thought she was someone else.

Wouldn't "he" have known if she'd been coming over?

"Definitely not."

So maybe he'd hit her outside his home? Thinking she was someone else coming to the front door. That made sense.

"And if, for some reason, she'd been inside the house, Dominic would know about it," he continued. "He has guys watching the homes of his top people, for obvious reasons."

So *someone* would've seen whoever beat up Carin? Or known if anyone else had hurt her. Assuming it had happened in one of their homes.

This was good. To her growing list of test questions, she added a couple regarding the location of the attack.

If Dominic wasn't the abuser, but knew his girlfriend was being abused and was doing nothing about it...

"Where does Dominic think Carin is now?"

"I have no idea."

"Do you know how she came to be at the hospital?" She was going to ask Carin the next morning, but...

Was she testing him now?

Or testing Carin?

She needed to find out if there were any differences between their versions of the truth. Had to have a set of questions she was confident Carin would answer honestly, so she could set the standard for the test. While generally those questions were neutral and easily provable—like birth date, address, that kind of thing—she usually added some emotional questions. That way, she'd have a comparison for reactions that were emotional. She'd be able to tell if her test subject was telling the truth.

"She told me the attack happened the night before Dominic...left the country for a few days."

Meaning he was making a drug run to Mexico?

"She gave him enough time to cross the border, and then took a couple of different buses out of LA to a smaller area north of the city," Cedar explained. "After that, she hired one of those bike-carriage drivers to take her a block from the hospital. She walked the rest of the way."

She was smart. And didn't want to be easily traced. If what Cedar was saying was true.

Heather couldn't come up with any reason he'd lie about such a thing. But then...

She shook her head.

She was going in for a glass of wine, as soon as this call was over.

Carin had ridden two buses and a carriage while she had a broken eye socket. Hadn't anyone thought to offer her assistance?

Or maybe they had and she'd refused. Clearly this wasn't the first time she'd been hurt.

"Are you aware of any other medical records for her? Any indication of repeated injuries?" Lila had told her there weren't any.

Why was she asking Cedar? She wasn't here to test him.

"There are none."

She nodded. Glanced across toward the ocean. Saw very little, but thought of it out there. Guiding her back to her true self.

The woman who was strong and capable. Confident and secure. She needed that woman. Badly.

"What would Dominic's friend be protecting?" She didn't give him any context. She wanted a general idea.

"Could be drugs, of course. But it might also be his reputation, depending on the situation. Could be one of his crew. A family member. These guys don't rely on the law to protect them. They take care of things themselves."

Her assumption had been correct on that one.

CHAPTER THIRTEEN

CEDAR ATTEMPTED TO get back to work after Heather's call. He presented himself to the spreadsheets on his screen, the files he'd printed that were labeled and neatly lined up in front of him, and the list he was working off for the case.

And heard Heather's voice in his head. Not words so much. Just the voice. The tone. Her mistrust of him ran so deep, it was like she didn't even know him. Like she was a stranger.

It had taken everything he had not to remind her how well they knew each other. Not to refer to something intensely private, just to break through the wall she'd built around herself.

Thank God she'd ended the call before he'd made such a colossal mistake. She needed those walls. He needed her to have them.

Going for a fourth glass of milk, he turned back when his cell rang. It was almost nine. Too late for anyone in his current life to be calling him.

He wasn't seeing anyone. And he didn't know any woman who could hold his interest like Heather had.

Didn't have any family to speak of, unless... Cedar-Jones?

He grabbed the phone and sank into his chair.

"Heather?" he answered. He'd told her to feel free to contact him if she thought of anything else...

"Did you coach Carin to corroborate Dominic's story last year? When the prosecutor called her to the stand, after the defense called Dominic to the stand and he testified about those phone calls... When they re-crossed because she'd been added as a witness, did you coach her? Did you tell her to admit she was the one who'd gotten violent in their arguments?"

He'd wondered if that was going to come up. "I did not." He'd drawn the line there.

"Did you know she'd do that?"

"I suspected."

"And you didn't try to stop her."

He no longer wanted milk. Or to look for ways to make any upcoming charges go away. He wanted a beer.

And Heather in his bed. Not even for sex. He'd settle for holding her. Or...he didn't actually have to touch her. Just to hear her breathing next to him. To have her soft, flowery scent on his sheets.

"She refused to meet me without Dominic present." He'd asked for a meeting, so if that constituted trying... "I had the impression that if I pushed things, she would suffer. Dominic made that quite clear."

So he'd let it go. Just as the police apparently had when there'd been calls to the home. For some reason he didn't fully comprehend, Carin was unable to get herself away from the situation. From the man.

"Did he say that?"

"No." It was there, though, in the looks he gave her. The possessiveness he revealed around her. The jealousy when a court deputy offered bottles of water…

But that was only Cedar's impression.

"Do you have any idea why she stays with him? Anything you can tell me without betraying client confidentiality?"

He'd do it in a heartbeat if he thought he could help. But he didn't figure opening that door with Heather again was a smart move. It could make him appear untrustworthy—a lawyer willing to ignore a client's right to confidentiality.

"Nope. I've done some reading on the topic of victimization in relation to domestic violence, but other than the fact that many women stay for various reasons, I have nothing."

"If I need to reach you tomorrow, after the interview, when would be a good time for you?"

She'd be picturing him at his office—meeting with clients, handling cases, maybe in court. As much as he wanted to tell her he wasn't doing that anymore, he didn't. Because he might go back to it. He might be that man again, sometime in the future—or a better man at that job. Protecting the innocent against erroneous claims. Or getting the best plea deals for the guilty.

If he could trust himself not to let the win take control.

"I'll be out most of the day," he told her. "It's best to call my cell. If I can't answer, I'll call back as soon as I'm able to have a private conversation."

He didn't want her to know what he'd be doing while he was out. No one at the Stand, other than Lila who was rarely at the actual work site, knew that he'd been a high-powered defense attorney. He'd learned construction in high school and college; it had been a way to earn good money during the summers.

This sabbatical, his current journey, was a very private one. He was on it for intensely personal reasons.

If he told Heather, she might soften toward him. Which was why he so desperately *wanted* to tell her. He wanted her to be able to see, to believe, that he was trying to be the man she'd fallen in love with. Trying to be the man he'd expected himself to be.

And knowing that telling her could gain him

what he wanted and needed meant he couldn't do it. If she found out for herself...so be it.

But if he told her, it could look as though he was manipulating her.

She might then think that he was only doing the work to impress her, which might make him doubt himself on that score.

And that was his bottom line.

His current way of life was too fragile to expose it to disbelievers. Too critical to risk receiving praise.

HEATHER COULDN'T CALM DOWN. She was on her couch, curled up with a pillow on her lap and one of her favorite mindless shows on TV. She was watching it. Listening. Trying to quiet her mind, stop the zooming in her veins.

She'd been off the phone for almost an hour. Inside the house for half that time. She was on her second glass of wine. And couldn't relax.

A character she particularly liked made a witty comment, and she smiled. Heather was paying attention to the screen and anytime her mind tried to stray, she brought it back to the show.

But her breathing was off. Her feet wouldn't keep still.

When the show ended, she grabbed the phone she'd carried in with her. Looked for recent calls and tapped his number.

He answered immediately. Almost as though he'd been sitting there, waiting. Knowing she'd call.

In the old days, she would've been certain that was what had happened. Not that she'd mention it to Cedar. He wasn't the woo-woo type. But she'd been certain their souls were connected on a level that was pure and true. That they communicated on that level.

Then she'd discovered she'd been wrong.

"Why?" The question was forbidden.

"Why what?" he asked.

She wasn't entirely sure. Hadn't thought it through. She'd been watching TV, and now…this.

Why did he help Dominic beat the charges instead of getting him a good plea deal? Why didn't he recuse himself? Why did he use her? Why did he choose to betray her?

Why had he asked her to assist now?

"Why are you helping Carin?"

Because the Stand had called him? Did he know someone there he was trying to impress? The Lemonade Stand had some incredibly rich donors.

"Because she called and asked for help."

Her system calmed. The answer was so Cedar. Exactly what she'd expect from the man she'd known. The Cedar who would've risked his relationship with a former client to help a woman in need.

"Is she paying you?"

The answer was none of her business.

"No."

"But if she's in criminal trouble, she will be."

"I can't speak to that." He was right to shut her down. She'd crossed a line. And couldn't seem to stop herself. No way should she have called him back after two glasses of wine.

Even as she had that thought, she knew the wine wasn't really to blame. It had loosened her inhibitions, but she'd needed to make the call to clear her mind so she could focus totally on Carin and ask exactly the right questions, in the right way, to bring out the truth. Whatever that might be.

In some respects, her job mirrored Cedar's in that she was resolute in her attempt to guide people to tell her things. But the difference was, she had no preconceived notion about what those "things" might be. While Cedar wanted to lead them to a place that would serve his purposes, her only purpose was to lead them to the truth.

Not a version of it. Not someone's perception of it. But as close to the pure truth as they could get.

"Still, you know she has the ability to pay you well…"

It was more statement than question. An assumption that didn't put him in a good light, so, basically, she'd just insulted the hell out of him.

"I'm under the impression that Carin has no income of her own, other than what she spent to get to the hospital and a few hundred she's managed to stash away one or two dollars at a time. And before you ask, that information came from her, and she knows you and I are discussing her case, and she was fine if I filled you in on it."

"She said that you, or 'they'—so maybe that meant the people at The Lemonade Stand, too—agreed to leave her alone about what happened if my report shows that she's telling the truth."

"That's correct."

"But you don't believe her."

"In terms of Dominic not hurting her? No, I don't."

He'd said he had things he could tell her...

Shaking her head, she took another sip of wine. If she hadn't had to be sharp the next morning, she might've just gone ahead and emptied the bottle.

She didn't want to know what he had to tell her. She couldn't trust that he wouldn't be leading her in a direction that served a purpose other than the truth.

He'd agreed to let the whole thing drop if her report showed that Carin was being truthful. But he *knew* she wasn't. He knew things Heather didn't. And he was trusting her to get Carin to admit them.

Tears sprang to her eyes, and she blinked them away. Blaming *them* on the wine.

"You have that much faith in me?" Her vulnerability was showing. She'd have been better served to keep quiet. Told herself to hang up.

She *had* to hang up.

"I do."

She disconnected the call.

WORK HAD ALWAYS been a driving force in his life. An adrenaline rush. Even in high school. The more he worked, the more he made, the more he was worth. Not merely in financial value, but in the value of his existence. His importance.

That changed when Heather walked out of his life.

On Friday, after work, having waited all day for a phone call that never came, having spent hours wondering how her second interview with Carin had gone, work became his remedy. His relief.

Or should have. Shortly after getting home, he sat down at his desk and spent a couple of minutes staring at the empty partners desk across from him. He couldn't help thinking about the times he'd looked up from his case files and seen Heather sitting there, smiling at him. He opened the DiSalvo folder. DiSalvo had said he met Cedar-Jones during a tuna-fishing expedition. Without consciously deciding to take a break from the time-consuming task of finding missing pieces, hidden facts, in the DiSalvo money trail, he turned to the adventure company records. With the excursion file open, he searched for when DiSalvo had said he'd met Cedar-Jones. He found two different excursions that summer, three years before. Neither of the registration logs bore his father's name.

So maybe DiSalvo was mistaken about the date. Cedar searched for his father's name over the entire company database. And came up empty. He tried a couple of other searches, other ways in, and found...nothing.

There was a reasonable explanation, he was sure. But he was disappointed. He'd needed to spend a moment with his father, even if it was only vicariously.

The thought of Cedar-Jones was about the only thing that seemed to ease the ache that losing Heather continued to bring. It was a momentary fix. But it was something.

Feeling stupid—but at least he was alone, so *stupid* didn't stop him—he went back to the two tuna-fishing trips that had taken place that summer, three years before. He read the trips' manifests one more time. Looking more carefully at details.

There were names he recognized, a couple, anyway, that had come up during his perusal of files. He'd go back and put the names together with his notes later, to have the references in case they became important in the future. But for now, he was…eavesdropping. Or the equivalent of eavesdropping—hoping to find an "in" to his father's private life. Just for a momentary…connection.

Cedar-Jones wasn't anywhere that he could see. Not under his own name or in any way that Cedar could tie to him. But he did learn something useful. In the accounting of food onboard during the two-day cruise, he saw HHC listed. The acronym that had shown up in a couple of emails the accountant, Hines, had sent. *HHC is a win. Don't forget HHC.*

He'd searched online for HHC, and all he'd been able to find that even came close was an investment group. He'd thought he had a possibility, until further digging showed no connection at all. He'd found a hospital network. Had checked that out, too.

HHC wasn't a horse. It wasn't a reference to another set of investments or an investor. Or anything else nefarious.

HHC was food. A catering company of sorts.

CEDAR WENT BACK to work. Sipped milk and concentrated. Potential game plans were forming on a flowchart, like little guys on a field, readying for battle. If one possibility turns out to be correct, then we go this way. If another one did, then...

He was out of milk. Went to pour another glass and noticed he'd gone through almost a gallon in the past three days. Didn't much care other than that he had to get more.

He thought about going to the store. Made himself a sandwich instead. Ham and mustard again. Because it was easy. Comfortable.

Because he liked it. To hell with the fact that it probably wasn't good that he'd had it a lot that week. He'd had steak and salad and baked potato one night, too. Vegetable soup for lunch the day he'd gone to a diner. Takeout Chinese another night.

He checked his phone, just to make sure he hadn't missed a call. Checked his voice mail at the office for the second time, too. Since it was almost six now, she would've left her office.

As a last resort, he opened his email program. Now that he was a construction worker, he didn't use the account very much, as his inbox was generally consumed only with some form of newsletter ad or other. Apparently everyone had a great deal that he certainly wouldn't want to miss.

It used to be that his email inbox had been filled with business for him to attend to. Clients, prosecutors, judges, other defense attorneys...they'd all had things to say to him. Important things.

He'd been practically addicted to his email. Because work, the rush he got from it, had been that important…

Heather Michaels. He had an email from Heather.

One click and it was open. She'd emailed instead of phoning.

That brought him back to the way she'd hung up on their last conversation, the night before, without even a goodbye. So not like Heather to be impolite.

And now she didn't trust herself to call him?

Cedar,
Just a couple of questions from today.

Do you know Renaldo's last name? Do you know who lives on Becker Lane?
Thank you.

The next few lines were her official email signature. She'd been sitting across from him when she'd first set up that signature. A couple of lines were different. The LA office and its phone number were gone. Everything else was exactly the same. As far as her professional life was concerned, the only thing that had changed in the past year was that she'd ceased renting an LA office.

He should have married her while he had the chance. Then at least maybe his name would still be part of her life. If she'd taken it.

Shaking his head at the ridiculousness of that thought—if they'd divorced she'd have taken back her own name—he clicked Reply.

He told her the Renaldo he'd referenced was Bentley and that Renaldo Bentley lived on Becker Lane.

He added a line about being available if she needed anything more. Deleted that. Changed it to *Call if you need anything.* Deleted that, too.

Hope you had a good day disappeared to be replaced by *Hope everything went well,* which also got erased.

They all sounded as though he was opening a door. Even if just a crack. That was exactly what he wished he could do. Wanted to do. Needed to do.

But wouldn't.

So he hit Send.

She'd asked; he'd answered. He wasn't helping Carin, or involving Heather in the process, as an attempt to get Heather back.

CHAPTER FOURTEEN

CEDAR MADE A milk run. Literally. He put on tennis shoes and jogged to the convenience store closest to him, and then walked back.

He fed the stray cat that came by once or twice a week and meowed on his back patio.

He took a walk down the beach.

All with his cell phone in the pocket of his basketball shorts, resting against him so he'd feel any incoming calls or messages vibrate against his skin, even if he didn't hear the ring.

When he finally headed back to his desk, he took a beer with him.

He'd get through the rest of his flowchart that night. DiSalvo was expecting tax-fraud charges to be filed early the next week.

But first…

He opened his browser and clicked on the Facebook tab. He had a profile, but only as a way to access the information hub. Heather had helped him set it up years before, when social media had begun to sway criminal and civil-court case decisions. There was nothing to show on any of his profile tabs. No pictures. No About section at all. And not a single post.

He had one friend—Heather Michaels—and was surprised she still hadn't unfriended him. Or blocked him. He'd noticed that each time he'd signed in over the past year, looking for one piece of information or another.

He'd never so much as clicked on her name. What she did or didn't post on Facebook was none of his business.

In the search box, he typed the name of DiSalvo's adventure company. He wanted to see what, if anything, was posted there about the company. He also wondered if there'd be any photos that included Cedar-Jones.

He'd taken the case at his father's request, but didn't seem to be getting any closer to him. Cedar-Jones had a page, too, of course, with over a million likes, but someone in Randy's employ obviously did the posts. Cedar wouldn't be surprised to hear that his father had never even visited the page. He didn't either that night.

Sorry… Just looked up Renaldo's page. A girl on there, Chloe White, is asking about Carin. There's no mention of Carin on Chloe's page, and nothing personal about her, either. She hasn't posted in over a year, and her moniker is a kangaroo. Do you have any idea who she is?

The private message popped up into the corner of his screen, accompanied by a small sound notification.

Cedar read it again. She could have called. Or texted. Or sent another email. Her Facebook would have showed her he was online.

What did it mean that she'd private-messaged him? A step removed from phone, but less impersonal than email.

It meant that she'd seen he was online and was using the quickest means possible to get a question answered. She was working.

He typed a response. Hang on.

He wasn't sure, but he thought he recognized the name. He pulled the Dominic Miller file from the corner of his desk. Sifted through to a time of year, a weekday, trying to find a particular conversation he remembered. One that had taken place shortly after the man had signed with him. Cedar had asked for an accounting of family members—something he always did when taking on a new case. Family coming out of the woodwork could blow a case to hell.

Yes. There it was. He responded to Heather.

Carin's little sister. She was put in a foster home when their mother was killed. As far as I knew, Carin had no contact with her. There was no reason for me to question her.

Maybe she still didn't have any contact. Heather had found a mention of the girl on Renaldo's Facebook. If Carin had said anything about her during their interviews, Heather would have known who she was.

If they have no contact, how would she know Renaldo, to ask for Carin?

The question came back in seconds.

It was a good one and should probably be on Carin's test. But he'd die before he said so. He was not going to affect Heather's process in any way.

He went to Renaldo's page and saw immediately what she was talking about. Each day, for the past few days, the girl had been on there… asking about Carin. There'd been no response. And no other posts, either. Not for quite a while.

He could hypothesize. But instead, he clicked back to the DiSalvo adventure company page.

Sorry to bother you on a Friday night.

He stared at her newest message. Because he hadn't answered the previous one? Did she think he was ignoring her? She could see that he was still online, thanks to Facebook's posting of those details.

No bother. I told you to contact me anytime, and I meant it.

He could see by the little waving dots in the box that she was typing. Took a sip of beer, all the while watching those dots.

You at work?

No, why?

She was engaged, he reminded himself. To that dentist.

And he couldn't allow anything to start up with her, even if she wasn't engaged. Even if hell froze over and she wanted him back. He had to do good for the sake of doing good, not for his own good. He couldn't benefit personally from the penance he was doing, or it wouldn't be penance.

The little dots were waving again. He sat up, beer in hand, and watched them. Eager, in spite of himself, to see what would appear next.

I'm not quite sure about asking but...

That was it. The sentence hung there. Unfinished.

Dots waved. He waited.

Based on something Carin said today, I need to
see the interview I did with Dominic. I need to see
my report. I'm assuming you have a copy.

She knew he had one. She'd sent it to him.
What kind of game was she playing here? Set-
ting down his bottle, he sat forward. Typed. Yes.
Dots. Then more words in the box.

I'd like to borrow it.

He'd said he'd help in any way he could. And
the information she was requesting was her own
work. He couldn't figure out what she was doing,
though. Where was her copy of the report? Or did
she have a different kind of motivation altogether?
Trying to reinstate the past in the present?
Reminding him of the greatest mistake of his life?
Of the fact that he was the one who'd screwed up?
As if he'd ever forget.
He'd give her the damned report. Had it right
there in Dominic's file. But…
She was typing again.
And he waited again.

I destroyed my copy.

Holy hell! Heather had destroyed an official report she'd written? He hadn't seen that one coming.

Hol-l-ly-y hell. He'd hurt her that badly.

He wanted to run it right over to her. To tell her, face-to-face, how sorry he was. How he'd do anything to take back the past, to undo what he'd done.

Which was precisely why he typed…

I can leave it in your office drop box in the morning.

She wasn't testing Carin until Monday. That should give her plenty of time to prepare.

Heading out of town for a weekend of relaxation. Our flight leaves at 7. Not back until Monday morning.

Our flight. Lucky Charles.

Damned lucky Charles.

Cedar finished off his beer in gulps. Karma flashed him a memory of walking into Heather's parents' barbecue after their Egyptian idyll and meeting Charles for the first time. Coupled with a more recent memory of reminding Charles of that very event, just six days before. Karma was a bitch.

Heather was waiting for an answer.

Nice. Where you going?

Not his business. Not his business.

Not a leading question, either. On the contrary, he was twisting the knife inside him, handing down his own punishment.

Wine country.

He went for another bottle of beer, gulped some of it down, but it didn't numb the pain. He'd been the first one to take her up north, to ride the tour trolley and sip wine until they were both tipsy and turned on. He remembered private, stolen, intimate touches in a cellar. And the way they'd fallen straight down on the mattress the second they'd stumbled into their room, stripping off their clothes…

Back at his desk, he half expected to see that she'd signed off from Facebook. A good four or five minutes had passed.

She knew he had the file. Could call him. Or text.

He'd said he'd do whatever he could to help. And this wasn't about him.

That reminder had him sitting up straighter. No one said redemption would be easy. He'd never expected it to be.

I have the file here at home. I can scan it if you'd like. Email it. Or, if you want the exact copy, to make absolutely sure I don't alter it, I can drop it by your place, you can come here, or we can meet. Whatever works best for you.

He didn't know where she lived. He could've found out easily enough. She would've bought a place and tax records were public.

I can come there. I'll need the address.

He almost dropped his bottle. She was coming to his home? When he'd offered to meet her anywhere she'd like? The fact that she didn't trust him to scan and email the file didn't surprise him. He also didn't dwell on that fact.

He typed the address so quickly, he had to backspace twice to correct mistakes. Heather had opted to come to him, rather than meet somewhere impersonal.

She'd invited him to her engagement party.

There was something personal in that.

This wasn't a big deal. It meant only that she was taking responsibility for her actions in destroying an important piece of her work.

Which she'd done for a very personal reason.

And had just admitted to him that she'd done it when she could have made up an excuse as to why she didn't have the file. It could be in storage someplace or...

He wasn't going to have hope. Could not allow

hope. He wasn't trying to win her back. He was making things right for others, making amends, trying to help those he'd hurt.

He'd do best to keep that firmly in mind.

IN THE TIGHT-FITTING, ankle-length navy dress pants and short navy-and-cream top she'd worn to work that day, Heather signed off the internet and went straight out to her car. To get the chore done and over with.

She'd been driving herself crazy most of the afternoon, going back and forth about whether she was going to ask Cedar for that damned report. She'd held out some hope that she'd stored a copy on her home computer—after trying to find one on her hard drive at work. She'd even had a computer tech come to defrag and do whatever he could to recreate lost or deleted files. Hoping.

There'd been nothing.

And if she was going to have the best shot at getting the truth out of Carin, she had to have that report. There were definite discrepancies in what she remembered Dominic saying and what Carin had told her that day.

She needed facts, not memories.

Those facts were in that report. And it was the only work-related report she'd ever written that she didn't have. The only work file she'd ever shredded.

All during the time it had taken her to cook and eat a frozen dinner, she'd toyed with ways to ask Cedar for that report. Had come up with scenarios for why she didn't have her own. In the end, as it always did, the truth had won out.

Her unprofessional temper tantrum could not get in the way of her doing her job right. She wouldn't let her pride cause further damage to an abused woman. So she told him the truth and asked for the file she needed.

What did it matter what he thought of her?

She didn't really believe he'd alter the report when he scanned it. But she didn't have the time or energy to fight any doubts that might plague her. And going to his house was the appropriate thing to do. She'd created the issue. She was the one who should be put out by it.

Once she heard his address, she knew basically where his house was. Knew the cul-de-sac of homes that backed up to a private stretch of beach.

Being curious about the place was only natural. She'd lived with Cedar for five years. Had thought his home and hers would be the same for the rest of her life. He'd given her the gate code for his new place, and she hated that her fingers were shaking as she stopped at the keypad and typed it in.

She was relieved when the big wrought iron

gate swung open. She'd had visions of having to type and retype, push and then push again, until he'd have to come out to rescue her.

As she pulled into the five-home area, glanced around and wondered if any of Charles's friends lived there, she felt a huge stab of guilt. Would they recognize her car?

She had every right to be there.

Cedar was a person in her life. They had history. And were working on a case.

Charles hadn't answered her call that afternoon. For all she knew, he was out on a date. As she figured out which house was Cedar's, and pulled into the drive, she kind of hoped Charles *was* on a date. He was a good man and didn't deserve what she was doing to him.

That happened in life. Good people hurt good people without meaning to.

Not to be confused with what Cedar had done to her. No, his deliberate betrayal was on a much different scale...

The house was beautiful. Exactly what she would've picked if they'd purchased it together. Not too imposing, it didn't scream money, and the two stories—the white-painted second story with dark green shutters, the brick along the bottom, the windows and circled fountain out front—all spoke of quiet elegance.

They'd looked at homes together. Had talked about what they liked.

She was glad he'd found it.

She climbed out of her car, hurried toward the front door, but then slowed. What was she doing?

How could she be eager to get to that door? To catch a glimpse of the inside of Cedar's house?

To see him for a moment?

Just because it appeared that he was honestly helping Carin in order to do something good didn't negate the harm he'd already done.

He'd always done good things. *Some* good things.

But he'd become a man who felt no compunction about crossing lines when it served his purpose.

He wasn't evil. He was untrustworthy.

With her heart rate slowing, she got to the porch. Lifted a finger to ring the bell. And her gaze caught the manila envelope sitting on the little wrought-iron-and-glass table in an alcove with two matching chairs, to the left.

Her name was scrawled across the top of the envelope.

She recognized Cedar's handwriting.

He wasn't coming to the door.

He'd already been.

CHAPTER FIFTEEN

THAT CLOSED DOOR bothered Heather all the way home. It told her there was something unresolved between her and Cedar. They had to be able to meet casually, to have nothing between them other than a respect for a shared past, perhaps a bit of sadness for the pain of their breakup and then a healing that sent them both on to a happy future.

It was the whole reason she'd invited him to her engagement party. To prove that she was healing, that it was sending her to a happy future.

Instead, she'd just broken up with her fiancé.

And was running over to Cedar's house, disappointed because she hadn't seen inside.

She was acting like a schoolgirl, not a healthy, successful grown woman.

Looking at the envelope on the car seat beside her, after she'd pulled into the garage, she thought about reading through the report. Getting her mind back on solid ground.

Told herself that her reaction at Cedar's was perfectly normal, considering that it was the first time she'd been to his home since they'd broken up. Since he'd moved.

She wondered if she'd find something in the report that would give her a valid reason to call him.

And picked up her phone.

"I think we need to talk," she said as soon as he answered. She wasn't going to second-guess herself. Or chicken out.

She was in control of her life. It was time she acted like it.

"Fine," he said. And nothing else. Which was how it had been since she'd agreed to help Carin. As though whatever happened or didn't happen, whether they talked or didn't talk, was solely up to her.

It wasn't natural, and she didn't like it.

He was the one who'd come to her for help and... Oh!

He was forcing her to make all the rules. She got it now.

"I'd suggest a place to meet, but this is a small town and I'd rather no one saw us together. For the same reason, your car at my house is out, and I don't feel comfortable talking in yours."

"How about two cars parked down at the beach? We could walk."

Almost as though he'd been reading her mind.

The idea shouldn't surprise her as much as it did. She used to take such things for granted. Just because Cedar had betrayed her didn't mean he didn't also understand her, know what she'd like, or think in ways that were often similar to hers.

The things that had drawn them together still existed. It was something she'd missed in all her efforts toward complete understanding, letting go, healing.

"That's fine," she said, and then suggested the public beach halfway between their homes. And when he asked that she wait in her car until he got there, if she beat him to the parking lot, she agreed.

They'd been in town, still together, the previous year when a Hollywood actress, a daytime soap opera star who'd been living incognito among them, had been attacked on that very beach. The would-be rapists, teenagers, had been apprehended and prosecuted.

Kacey Hamilton still starred on *The Rich and The Loyal*, but she now lived most of her life in Santa Raquel with her husband, Michael Valentine, a computer genius who ran a repair business and training sessions at the Stand during his free time. And when Kacey was in the apartment she owned in Beverly Hills, Michael, an introvert with scars inside and out, was right there with her.

Heather had never met either of them, but would love to do so.

SHE'D CHANGED OUT of the work clothes she'd worn to his house. It was the first thing Cedar noticed as Heather got out of her car. Not that he'd ever want her to know, but he'd watched her car pull into his drive. Watched her walk to his front door and take the report she'd requested. He'd given her the option not to have to see him. She'd taken it.

So would most people who'd seen what they'd come to collect sitting outside, waiting for them.

If he'd hoped she'd knock on the door anyway, thank him or something, then he was more of a fool than he'd realized.

He didn't recognize the running shorts or tennis shoes she had on. Probably hadn't seen that exact tank top before. And it wouldn't have mattered if he had. He'd still be hard. Salivating. Her long legs, those ankles...he knew the size of her toes, even though they were hidden in the shoes, and the exact shape of her breasts beneath that bra.

He had no business thinking about any of it.

Thankful for the loose-fitting basketball shorts he'd changed into after work, Cedar tugged at the hem of his T-shirt and turned immediately toward the beach as they met up at the end of her car. When he'd been about to take her hand as they reached the paved path at the edge of the sand, which he'd always done, she took a step away.

"What's up?" he asked as they headed down the path, staying on the pavement. Something else they'd always done. It would lead to a sidewalk that ran along the road, keeping the ocean in sight, without having to deal with the shifting sand.

"I've been walking on the sand this year," she said. "It's nice. The ocean is right there, part of the walk."

She wanted him to know she'd changed?

"You want to walk on the sand now?"

"Kind of."

"You wore tennis shoes," he pointed out.

"Because I knew I was meeting you, and you like the sidewalk."

He didn't like shifting sand as much as solid ground. True. But… "I like the sand. Not for exercise, though. I've got a private beach behind my house, and I've been spending some time out there."

TMI. Why would she care?

Back at their cars, they divested themselves of shoes. Walked barefoot to the sand. That was new for them—walking together in the sand, just to walk. Not to find a place to lay a blanket and park themselves.

They walked in silence for a long enough period that he wasn't sure what she expected him to do next. Was there something he was supposed to say?

"I'm sorry, Heather. I know it's not enough. I know it changes nothing. And that I've said it all before, but I'm truly, deeply sorry. Using you like I did was the single biggest mistake of my life."

"It's in the past," she said, as though—just like that—he could dismiss the wrongs he'd committed.

And he had nothing else to give. Apology. And help any recovery effort, or fix any damage, he could.

Silence descended again. He wasn't altogether sorry. Walking with Heather, even in total silence, was a gift.

An hour ago, he'd been at his desk alone, figuring himself for a lifetime of being alone, and now here he was, walking on a moonlit beach with the love of his life.

Not *with* her. But being in her presence at all was more than he'd expected.

And the extent of what he could have. No matter what she offered. Because making this about him would forever leave doubts as to his true intentions.

The only way to find true redemption was to give up oneself for others.

"I'm struggling, Cedar."

Here it comes. Whatever their conversation was supposed to accomplish. Almost relieved at that point to know he'd have something to do, a reason for being there, Cedar walked in silence, waiting.

"I ended things between us so abruptly... I had to. You'd left me no choice. But I'm finding that

I left a lot of things just hanging, unanswered somehow."

She wanted answers? Fine. He'd give them to her, no matter how painful the process might be. If he had them. He wouldn't make them up. Or make do. He'd give her the truth. Or nothing. A lesson he'd learned—too late—from her.

"I need to understand, Cedar. What we were, what we had. Because what I thought it was turning out to be was wrong, and now I'm second-guessing myself on everything. Except my work, thank goodness. I still have my confidence there…"

So sweetly Heather to just put it out there.

And so Heather to hand him a challenge he wasn't sure he could meet. It had always been like that with him. Her so full of love and giving, so always knowing the right thing to do and the right time to do it, while he'd pretty much screwed up every step of the way.

Except with his courtroom win record.

He hadn't called when he should have, hadn't shown up on time, or at all. He'd thought she'd understand that he'd just been doing his job. What she'd understood, and he hadn't, was that he'd been increasingly consumed more by the win than by anything else. Including her.

He didn't believe for a second that she'd ever have left him over those infractions. But he realized now that they'd eroded their bond.

He'd loved her more than anything.

But he'd taken for granted that she'd always be there. The courtroom triumph wasn't going to be—unless he fought for it. Worked for it. Put it first. Every second of every day.

Just as Cedar-Jones had done with his career. Something Cedar had never consciously realized until right then. That there was any correlation between his father's choices and his own fall from grace. If Cedar-Jones hadn't been out there on tour and constantly making new music, fighting for his share of the audience among an ever-expanding group of artists, he might have faded into the woodwork. Randy's single-minded focus on his career meant they had essentially no relationship. Cedar had never even met him, and yet he was still there for him. Because this was his father...

His mother had always adored the man, too. Been happy with the crumbs he'd given her. Raised his son alone so Randy could have the life he wanted.

Life wasn't always mom, dad and the kids. Sometimes it turned out differently, but that wasn't wrong. Or even bad. It just was.

Cedar's thoughts traveled off into the night as he walked. He looked back at their footsteps in the sand. One after the other.

"I'm...still affected. Not feeling or acting like

myself. You were such an integral part of my life. I can't just wipe you away as though you never were."

He felt a rush of hope, immediately quelled by the part of him that knew better. He was a man who was on a quest to redeem himself. If he screwed this up, there'd be no other chance, no way he could ever convince himself he wasn't the bastard he'd become.

"I'm over the hurt," she said. "Past the loneliness. The missing you."

Then she was one hell of a lot further along than he was. Relief swept through him, even as the well of sadness grew a little deeper.

"I don't want to try again or anything. I need to be completely frank and up-front about that…"

Honest, almost to the point of brutality. That was new.

Or maybe it just felt brutal to him. Not that he was open to trying again, either.

After the initial stab of pain had subsided, he knew that Heather was being kind, not brutal.

Taking a deep breath of ocean air, he felt the sand sliding through his toes and wondered why he and Heather hadn't taken walks like this when they were together. He could have held her hand. Lain with her on the sand, in the moonlight.

There were people scattered about on this beautiful summer night—another couple, some kids, a guy walking his dog—but if they were on his private beach, they could have made love under the stars. Accompanied by the sound of the ocean, the waves riding the tide of passion right there with them.

Why, in five years' time, had he never thought of that?

"I think I need you in my life, Cedar..."

What the hell? He tuned in, completely focused on the present now. They weren't getting back together, that had been firmly established.

"I think that's why I invited you to my engagement party. Because, as much as I wanted to marry Charles, I didn't feel right about doing it without your support."

Wow. He hadn't seen that coming.

And...*wanted? Didn't?* Past tense?

"Do you still want to marry him?"

"Yes, of course. I just need to work all of this out."

So, speaking in the past tense... That was because she was explaining how she'd felt when she decided to invite him to the party. No reason to make any more of it than that.

Unless... Could this be a cry for help? He'd witnessed none of the spark between Heather and Charles that had been there when they'd been together.

He'd told himself he'd do what he could to save her from a passionless marriage. That he owed her for crushing the heart that had been so open with him.

Two women passed, deep in conversation, and Heather watched them. Was she missing Raine? Or Lianna?

He'd always been a little jealous of her closeness with them. Because he couldn't seem to get that close to her.

And yet, here they were, on the beach, deep in meaningful conversation.

"I…sometimes… If I need to call you, or answer the phone when you call, it's because it feels like the right thing to do. We share memories, but we were also connected, you know, in our thoughts…"

He felt a tremble begin inside him—something powerful. And dangerous. Possibly familiar, and yet, not really. He had to suppress it. Couldn't let his own feelings take over here.

"I guess what I'm saying is…it feels like we're meant to be friends. To be able to call each other if there are times we know the other will understand a particular circumstance or situation or case."

He kept his gaze down on the sand in front of them…with an eye out for anything the ocean might have swept in, live or otherwise. "Okaaayyy," he said with a certain amount of trepidation. His love for her was so intense. Could he give her what she needed—friendship—without that love getting in the way?

Did he have any choice?

the was

CHAPTER SIXTEEN

THIS WAS IT THEN. The source of her distress. She
hadn't been looking at the whole truth. While
she'd been right to leave Cedar, and knew she
couldn't trust him, she also couldn't just walk
away. The bond they'd shared, at least in her heart,
was not one from which you could walk away.
She'd known he was a forever person in her life
as soon as she'd met him.

She'd tried to pretend it wasn't so after he'd
betrayed her.

But it was.

Other than "okay," Cedar hadn't said a word.
And the okay had been drawn out…more of an
acknowledgment of what she'd said. Not an agreement.

"I want to see your house, to picture you where
you're living. I want you to see mine." And if she
married Charles, she'd want Cedar to visit his
house, too, although that scenario wasn't ringing
as strongly as the rest.

Because Charles wasn't really in her life at the

moment. When he was again, his role would score on her internal truth-o-meter.

Still no reaction from Cedar. Was her idea ludicrous to him? Or was he considering it?

"I can't feel guilty for thinking about you. Wondering how you are." She kept talking, because she didn't know what else to do.

"Are you feeling guilty right now?"

"Not at all." The truth was so clear. She was where she needed to be.

He wasn't saying much. Although she didn't know what to make of that, she was prepared to carry this out to the end. To either reach a mutual understanding, or not.

She couldn't go on the way she was.

And she knew how to get to the truth. She just had to ask the right questions.

"I need to understand what *you* thought we were, Cedar. How you saw our relationship."

When she caught herself holding her breath, she let it go. Took in a deep gulp of the ocean air on which she thrived.

Finally, she felt she was moving forward. Preparing to thrive, rather than just figuring out how to live.

"I thought we were going to be together forever." He spoke slowly; she could tell that he was considering his words. His hands were down at his sides and as he glanced over at her, she detected no sign of subterfuge.

"Why?" she asked.

"Why what?"

"Why did you think that?" Did he feel what she'd felt? Something that drew them to each other? Or was it simply that they were incredibly good in bed and they'd *said* they were going to spend their lives together?

"I...you've got me at a bit of a disadvantage here..." His words dwindled away. "Don't get me wrong. I'm open to the conversation. Just give me a second to catch up."

To figure out what she was looking for and offer it to her? If he lied, where would that leave her?

Knowing she'd have to wait and see, Heather focused on the sounds of the waves, the moon over the ocean. There were still a few people around. They were far enough away that no conversations could be heard. It was dark enough that no facial distinctions could be made. Everyone was part of the landscape, which gave her a sense of joined humanity, and privacy, too.

"I would say the most obvious answer to your question is that we spoke about spending the rest of our lives together." Nothing in Cedar's posture or tone of voice had changed. "I believed we meant what we said."

So had she.

And yet…she was the one who'd ended things.

Because his actions hadn't been those of some-one who'd be there for life. She had to know why.

But first, she had finish the question she'd already begun.

"Why do you say 'the most obvious answer'?"

They walked a few steps in silence.

"Because there's more than just that."

"Like what more?" She'd pushed in the past. He'd always bailed on her. Made a joke. Or distracted her with the physical proof of their connection. Taking her to bed and showing her how much he loved her.

"I'm trying to figure that out."

"Trying right this moment, or in the process of trying at this point in your life?"

His chuckle caught her unawares. "I pity your test subjects," he said. "They've got no hope of avoiding truth against you."

She started to grin, but immediately sobered. "I know I've said it many times, but I really believe the truth sets you free." Her subjects benefited from her attention, or so she hoped. In the long run, if nothing else. "And you didn't answer my question."

"I'm trying to put it into words that express what I feel," he said.

"Take your time." She sidestepped what could have been a sand crab, probably a dead one, as far from the water as they were. Could also have been a partially buried bottle top, although the Santa Raquel public beaches were raked every night. Still, nothing was fail-proof.

"When I met you, my life changed," Cedar said. "I can't really explain beyond that. You didn't always agree with what I said, and I didn't always agree with what you said. And yet…there was this agreement between us. I could always understand where you were coming from. And I always felt you understood me, too. On a level that went deeper than the words we spoke."

As if they were soul mates.

"It's like I recognized you even though we'd never met before."

She could've been washed out to sea in that instant and not have noticed. She felt heady, in an intense other world she'd never really entered before.

And then it dawned on her that he could just be saying what she'd needed to hear. To get what he wanted from her.

"What do you want from me?" she asked. Aside from her help with Carin, which was a given at that point. Was he hoping to manipulate her into having an affair with him? Playing along with her to make her malleable?

Barely beginning to open her eyes in that other

world, that new world, she found that her thoughts offended her.

And yet, in the real world, they seemed a necessary reminder of all that had happened, all that was.

Cedar stopped. The warmth of his hands was gentle on her forearms as he looked straight at her, his eyes glistening in the moonlight.

"I want you happy, Heather. Whatever it takes, I want you happy."

She knew he was speaking the truth.

"And what you said before?" she asked. "Was that because you *thought* it would make me happy?"

"No." He paused. "I failed you," he said after a few seconds. "I failed us. It's too late to undo what I did. Betrayal isn't something the human heart is likely to forget. I know all of that. I also know that the one thing I can do for you is give you the one thing on which you put supreme value. The truth."

His words were almost too perfect to believe.

"Why did you do it?" she asked.

He didn't turn away. Didn't even look away. His breathing unsteady, he held her softly, watched her, but said nothing for a bit. And then, "Because as much as I loved you, I had to value myself as well, and I took my sense of self-worth from the win. The bigger, the better. I put my own value above how I felt about you. I mattered more."

There was no doubting the truth of his words. Or the tremendous pain they caused her.

And yet, they were freeing, too. Allowing her to see a way out. And still be true to herself.

She couldn't be a life partner to Cedar. Couldn't trust him, in any ultimate sense. Which meant there was no danger of falling for him again, as her friends had feared.

At the same time, she could move forward into a friendship with him. Something real. Honoring the connection between them. And yet…distant, too.

But there was another question that had to be asked, one that bore seeds of doubt that could grow and flourish.

"What about now?" Her words came over dry lips and a parched throat.

He shook his head.

"Considering what you just said," Heather began, "do you think, given the same circumstances, you'd do it again?"

For the first time in a while, he looked away from her. Upward and then out toward the ocean.

"I'd like to be the man you need, Heather," he finally said. "I'd like more than anything to be him. But do I believe I am? No, I do not."

"What I meant was, under the same circumstances, would you choose yourself over me again?" She couldn't afford to let doubts linger.

They'd disallow any friendship between them, because they could create a need for more than that. More than friendship…

"I think it's possible."

Truth.

Sometimes it hurt.

And still…it set you free.

NOT UNDERSTANDING THE myriad of emotions attacking him, Cedar pushed them deep inside as he walked beside Heather, back toward their cars. He focused on what he could control—his outer world.

Heather had just offered him the opportunity to be her friend. She'd be in his life. He was welcome, needed even, in hers.

More than he could've hoped for.

He'd also lost any hope of being her life partner.

While the finality of that seemed almost debilitating, he also knew that he was to blame.

If he couldn't trust himself, how could he ask her to trust him again? Or hope she'd be capable of it?

Forever seemed too far away to let hope go. He couldn't face life without it.

And he knew he had to find a way.

He wasn't happy about that. Was actually pretty damned pissed. At himself. At a world that had watched, without warning, while he screwed himself for now and evermore.

"All this talk about friendship," he said, "are you sure you can follow through on that if you're so afraid of someone seeing us that we had to meet here, in the dark? You don't do anything without talking to Raine or Lianna first. And yet no one even knows we're together tonight." He wasn't proud of his tone. Or the fact that he was turning some of his anger on her.

Hell of a friend he was being already.

But he had his limits and she'd asked something of him, something different. Wanted him to be there for her if she called, to stay in touch with her. He'd already sort of agreed with his "okay." But not really. Yet. And as badly as he wanted to, wanted that tiny bite of cake without icing, he wouldn't accept unless he honestly thought he could be the friend she was seeking.

"Everyone thinks I'm still in love with you." Her words made it almost impossible to keep the hatches battened down on emotions too dangerous to free. "They think I invited you to the engagement party because of that, and they're afraid I'm going to get back with you."

Other emotions, same intensity. He couldn't speak.

"I was all out of whack, being duplicitous with Charles, paranoid with Raine and Lianna, and not trusting myself. So I can't blame them for making the assumption they did. I knew they were wrong. I kept telling them, but they didn't believe me, and the harder it was to convince them, the more frustrated and paranoid I was getting. I knew I had to take care of me, to take a step back and figure out what was going on, and now I have. But I didn't feel it was appropriate to tell anyone else until I'd spoken with you. This isn't just about me, Cedar. It's about us. About whatever it is that pulls us together. First, I needed to know it wasn't just something I'd conjured up inside me. I needed to know I wasn't the only one feeling it. That it was real and worked both ways."

It is. It does. He tried to get the words out. His throat was too dry. He swallowed. And swallowed again.

There was still a lump in his throat.

"Once we decide how we're going to handle 'us' from here on out, I'll tell everyone else. And there'll be no hiding after that."

He could just imagine how Charles would take that. Or, rather, he couldn't, since he still didn't get a guy being okay with his fiancée inviting her ex to their engagement party. If it were him, there was no way he'd be all right with a "Cedar" in her life.

Maybe Charles could approve because he didn't fully understand.

Maybe only Cedar and Heather would ever get that.

The idea was a huge comfort. And posed danger, as well, in its implied intimacy.

And yet, didn't that same intimacy demand his presence in the relationship in some form?

Or was he justifying himself in order to manipulate the situation to his own end?

He hadn't suggested friendship. Or anything between them. She had.

But was he in it for her, or for him? Was he making amends, or doing what he had to in order to get what he wanted?

Because, more than anything on earth, he wanted Heather.

Losing the truth in his life had shown him the truth about himself.

They were halfway back to their cars when she stopped.

"So…where do we go from here?" she asked. And when he didn't answer, added, "Can we be friends?"

The polygraphist had landed on a question that required the million-dollar truth—one that was filled with nuances almost too hard to comprehend.

"More accurately, *can* you be my friend?"

He had to be, didn't he? But that wasn't what she'd asked.

They were getting closer to the cars and this

portion of beach was better lit. A party had started on the beach, with the beginnings of a bonfire.

He walked on. Searching himself, the world, what he knew, and wondering what he was missing.

Heather had grown silent, and he sensed that she wasn't going to ask again. That this night, like so many, would fade into their memories.

That seemed…wrong.

"I can try." His words sounded too loud, which made him shudder. As though he might just have nailed his own coffin shut.

She stopped him this time, her hands on his arms, so soft. Warm. So…Heather. Her touch brought life to his body, warmth to his being. Why had he never realized that before?

"I don't want you giving me anything because you feel you have to, Cedar. Like you owe me or anything. That's not what this is about. The past is past. We both lost a lot. Now we're here. And what I need to know is…do…you…want…to… be…my…friend?" Her speech slowed more with each word.

Finally, she'd asked a question he could answer without pause. "Unequivocally."

CHAPTER SEVENTEEN

HEATHER WASN'T READY to leave. They were at their cars. It was getting late, and she had an early flight in the morning.

Knowing Cedar, he probably had a full day of work booked the next day.

Still, she didn't want the conversation to end yet. The decision to be friends wasn't enough. She wanted to talk a little more. Actually *become* friends.

He might want to get back to whatever he'd been doing. Might need a break from her intensity.

His new way with her appeared to be a matter of letting her call the shots. She didn't like it.

Having him more aware was one thing; docility…uh-uh.

A few cars lined the parking lot. The beach was open all night now, with patrols and stipulations, but the town was small enough, tourist trade minimal enough, that it was still quiet. Peaceful.

At the other end of the lot, a car had parked, and two couples were milling around the trunk. A girl pulled out a blanket and…

"I have a blanket in the trunk. You want to go back out and sit for a little while?" she asked Cedar. Going to her house, or his, didn't seem like a good idea. Especially when it was dark, and the late hour could give them the feeling of being in their own little world.

When trust didn't carry as much weight as getting naked and feeling his skin against hers again. His hands on her body...

"Okay." There was no inflection in his voice, no indication of whether he wanted to sit with her. She decided not to make an issue of it. He'd said he *unequivocally* wanted to be her friend. She felt as strongly about it. Establishing a new *them* was critical.

She got the blanket. Walked with him toward the bonfire. Far enough away that they weren't impinging on the other group's privacy, but close enough to see the flames.

It wasn't a cold night, but California evenings were generally not all that warm. Sixties was plenty cool, in her opinion, for a fire. And yet... she wasn't freezing without one.

They laid the blanket together. Sat down. There was a coolness to the sand, in spite of the sun's heat that had been warming it all day.

"Are you sure you want to do this?" she asked after a few minutes of silence. "Be friends, I mean? You aren't just here because you think *I* want it?"

His glance, warm and far too familiar, answered her question.

"It's going to be weird at first, I guess," she said aloud. Going from lovers to friends…nothing she'd ever given a lot of thought. Perhaps she should've given it more thought. "But like any relationship, if we both want it, work at it…"

He nodded, looking out toward the ocean, leaving her with doubts that he believed it could work.

But then, she doubted him, period. Which was why they could only be friends.

Still, something deep inside told her she couldn't give up on this.

"Tell me what you're thinking."

He glanced her way again, as though assessing…her? What he should say?

"I'm wondering what Charles would think if he knew you were sitting here with me. Or, if he already knows, how he feels about it."

She nodded.

"You're leaving in the morning for wine country," he continued. "Seems to me the two of you should be home, packing. Getting ready for your trip."

It was what they'd always done. The night before a trip had always been the beginning of their vacation, generally celebrated with a glass of wine, slow sex and then packing.

The memory brought to mind the kiss they'd almost shared six nights before, in her mother's kitchen. She'd wanted that kiss.

Wanted it even more right then.

A cross she'd have to bear, was willing to bear, to have him in her life. Unrequited sexual need for Cedar. Probably going to be a lifelong thing if the current situation was anything to judge by.

He'd asked about Charles—who'd asked her to keep their breakup a secret. To save face with his friends. To protect her from Cedar.

Cedar didn't know Charles's friends, or hang with them, even if he did happen to have some kind of business association. He'd grown up in Santa Barbara, not Santa Raquel.

And she didn't need protection from him. She needed to move forward with him. To a healthy place—one they could both inhabit and still have full and complete lives of their own.

She couldn't lie to him.

"I broke up with Charles."

He seemed to freeze beside her. No movement. Not even a blink.

"Not for good," she hastened to add. "We're just...as I told you, I'm struggling, not myself. I need time to find me again before I can be an honest and true partner to him." The words sounded…weak, at best. And kind of selfish, too. But it wasn't fair to Charles to keep things from him, or to be his partner when she clearly wasn't ready.

He glanced down at her hand on the blanket. "You're still wearing your ring."

"We just announced our engagement. He asked for a little time before announcing a breakup." What he'd asked was reasonable. "I'd appreciate if you kept this to yourself."

He shrugged. "Who would I tell?"

"Exactly."

"Maybe it would've been better to tell him about your…confusion before having the party."

The flames in the distance danced taller. Heather could see their reflection in Cedar's eyes as she studied him. "My confusion arose after the party," she said, admitting what she suspected he already knew. "After seeing you again."

There was no discernible change in his expression. But then, he had a good courtroom face.

She'd always thought she could see through it, but maybe that was just what he'd chosen to let her see.

"When I saw you at the party, you asked to meet with me," she said, testing her hypothesis that she'd seen what he wanted her to see, but more, just stating what she knew. "I needed to see what you wanted. You said it was a business issue, so I didn't feel guilty about it. But I did feel guilty about the Charles aspect. Should I tell him or not? I knew that no matter what he said, I was at least going to find out the reason for your request. That started it. It felt as though by being loyal to myself, doing what I believed was right, I was being disloyal to him."

She took a deep breath and continued. "Like I told you, I started getting paranoid about what he'd think, worrying that he'd assume more than there was. I was getting paranoid with the girls, too…" Things were becoming clearer, sitting there with him. Talking it out. "The thing is, I thought I was completely over you. I know we can't be a couple, that I can't be half of *your* couple, but I didn't factor in the rest of it. The…connection we have. You're going to be part of my life. I had to get that sorted out. And then move on."

"Back to Charles?"

She followed the direction of his gaze, out to the horizon, marked by glints of moonlight.

"Maybe," she said. He could always find someone else, could already be seeing her. "As long as he's okay with you on our friend list."

Yes. That felt…better. Much better.

"I just need some time," she reiterated. "I thought I was ready. I found out I wasn't."

"But you love Charles."

"He's a good man. A really good man. We have

a lot in common, Cedar. I enjoy the time we spend together."

"And you love him."

Of course she did. Why was it so hard to admit that to Cedar?

"I wouldn't have agreed to marry him if I didn't love him," she pointed out.

"Are you *in* love with him?"

What was with all the questions? She'd wanted him to engage with her, not put her on the witness stand and cross-examine her.

"I don't understand the question," she said.

They'd made a very clear agreement about their relationship and what it would and would not be. She was *not* going to get paranoid on him, too.

And yet…

The whole reason she wasn't with him was because she could no longer trust him. But the friendship thing…it was right. It had to work.

Which meant she had to maneuver through the doubts.

"You used to tell me you didn't just love me, you were 'in love' with me." His words fell softly into the silence. He was facing the ocean, not her, and yet she felt as though he'd touched her.

"I don't believe in the idea of being 'in love' anymore," she told him. "I used to have impossible expectations. I grew up." There was no bitterness in her words. She was actually thankful to have passed through that particular learning experience, to be on the other side of it. Life was much more peaceful now.

Less painful.

"I'm sorry."

She glanced his way. "What? Why? My expectations weren't your fault."

"Letting them down was."

Partially, yes. But… "No one could have lived up to them, Cedar." She hadn't spent the year just condemning him, blaming him for all her heartache. She'd looked at her own culpability, too. "You'd have had to be superhuman perfect not to fail, which has always been an issue for you. I sometimes wonder if my constantly pressuring you to be more…present than you knew how to be prompted you not to want to be there at all."

It was true.

"That doesn't even come close to excusing or forgiving what I did."

"No. But it's good to talk about this, regardless." She'd needed to tell him she knew she'd been unfair, put impossible demands on him. Feeling disappointed every single time he couldn't get away to call her. And every time he'd called, saying he had to work late due to circumstances outside his control. That only made it more difficult for him to make those calls when he could. She was always hurt when she felt he didn't place as much significance on emotional events as she did.

"If you and Charles split, who are you going to wine country with?"

Cedar had pulled up his knees, was resting his arms on them. Looking casual, relaxed and so, so, so hot.

"Lianna and Raine." She smiled at him.

"Both of them?"

"Yep! I'm really looking forward to the weekend." It was as if all the separate parts of herself were coming together.

Maybe she really was becoming the healthy, adult, confident woman she'd been assuming she was.

GOD, SHE WAS BEAUTIFUL. Those long legs… The sun-golden skin her shorts were revealing. The halo of hair around her face and cascading down her shoulders. Those breasts…

He'd always loved Heather's breasts. They weren't huge, but they called out to him. Their shape, their size, the way they fit his hand. Her nipples were gloriously responsive, too. To him, getting hard just from him looking at them sometimes. He used to make her wild just fingering them…

But it wasn't just her breasts that were calling out to him as he sat with Heather in the sand, with the sound of the ocean cocooning them in privacy, while the public beach kept them from any actual intimacy. Her intrinsic search for the truth, the way she was so honest with herself, were what compelled him the most.

He, a professional truth-smudger, was addicted to her truth-telling.

The irony wasn't lost on him.

Nor was the fact that he'd been a bit too pleased to hear about her and Charles. Maybe his satisfaction was premature, considering that she said she loved the guy and that they'd left the door open to get back together. Still, with his fear that his betrayal had been responsible for destroying her spirit, he felt as though a reprieve had been granted. She wasn't rushing into what had appeared to him to be placid happiness, as opposed to the passionate, intense happiness they'd shared at times during their years together.

Not everyone was capable of that kind of intensity, but because Heather was, and because he feared he'd been instrumental in its demise, he hoped to see it in her again.

She wasn't going to wine country with her lover. He got hard just thinking about that.

The fact that she'd be with Lianna and Raine, each of them a force in her life—he could only imagine how powerful they'd be, influencing her together—didn't thrill him as much, considering how much they both hated him now.

Justifiably so.

And yet...he was glad she'd be with them. Her best friends had her back. And her trust. If Raine and Lianna were displeased with this new friendship proposal Heather had offered, if they convinced her it was a bad idea, if she came back from the weekend having changed her mind... he'd respect that choice.

"Something else is bothering me." She broke into his thoughts.

"What's that?"

"This whole way you're with me now—like I call all the shots."

"I lost my rights where you're concerned."

"You lost my life partnership, Cedar. But if we're going to be friends, have any kind of relationship..."

Her words dropped off, and he wondered if she was already reconsidering...

"A relationship, by definition, is at least two parties relating. It's back and forth. Not one-sided. I want—I think I probably need—your friendship. But only if you're really in the relationship. I don't want or need a patsy. Because it's not the real you. And I can't trust what isn't real."

Trust. Everything came back to that. He'd betrayed her trust. Lost her trust. And she was a woman who based everything on trust.

Was this whole friendship doomed from the start?

He had to admit he was skeptical. And yet... he'd been completely honest with her when he'd said that he wanted it unequivocally.

He'd even begun to see how she'd been absolutely right to suggest it. How a friendship between them could be a great thing, could give him a means to always be there for her. Instead of spending a life with her as his partner, he'd have a lifetime to make amends.

Maybe the way he could help her heal was to help her trust again.

He took a deep breath. Living in total honesty was a tough order for someone who'd spent his entire life trying to explain the world around him. Justifying why his father couldn't at least pick up the phone. Ask to meet him.

Why his mother never got angry with Cedar-Jones.

Justifying why good people sometimes do bad things.

And then justifying the bad things bad people did...

He was getting a headache. And starting to crave a beer.

He wanted sex. With Heather.

He had to find a way to let himself be fully engaged in a friendship, with no expectations beyond that.

He wasn't sure it was possible.

But he knew he had to try.

"I can't refuse you." That was the truth. If it made him a patsy, it did.

"Of course you can." Her blue-eyed gaze had a bit of the old sparkle in it when she glanced over at him in the moonlight.

He shook his head. "No, Heather, I can't. You wanted the truth? There it is."

When her mouth dropped open, he instinctively leaned in. His lips were going for hers, going home.

And then…by some force he neither recognized nor understood, he stopped. Reached for her hand instead, and stood up.

"It's getting late. We should probably be getting back," he said. Aching with need.

And yet…feeling better than he had in a long time.

Maybe there was hope for him yet.

CHAPTER EIGHTEEN

HEATHER HAD EXPECTED to be the go-between that weekend. To have a friend on either side and tend to each of them. Sharing Raine memories with Lianna and describing Lianna times to Raine. She'd expected to show them both how very much they meant to her, and prayed that they'd get along even half as well as she hoped they would.

She'd assumed there'd be some possessiveness on each of their parts, as well, jealousy-tinged moments, and was prepared to handle those. And to drink a lot of wine.

Raine had made all the arrangements, had found a little one-room cottage, with a pull-out sofa and a roll-away bed, in a popular camp ground in between two wineries, and had booked them on the facility's trolley for the afternoon.

They'd tasted quite a bit of wine. Laughed a lot. Finally found a merlot that all three of them wanted to purchase for the cabin that night. Just as Heather had hoped, they shared memories, she and Lianna filling in Raine, and vice versa.

But other than that, nothing was as she'd expected. Lianna and Raine hit it off so perfectly, she didn't know why she'd worried about awkward moments. She'd suggested outings for the three of them many times over the years, and one or the other of them had always declined. But now...

The two of them—one with a bottle of wine, the other with a tray of cheeses, crackers and veggies—approached her as she sat on the couch in the cabin, just feeling good. Raine poured the wine as Lianna sat on the corner of the couch, opposite Heather.

Handing them each a glass, Raine offered a toast to the three of them. Heather sipped her wine—and noticed the glance that passed between her friends.

"What?" she asked. She'd been waiting all day for the right time to tell them about Cedar and felt that it was rapidly approaching, whether she was ready or not.

"We've got something to tell you," Lianna said as Raine sat in the chair closest to her. Both of them looked nervous, which made her nervous, too.

She smiled at them, though. "What?"

"We didn't just start talking last weekend at your party," she said.

"We've been talking for months," Raine added, a concerned frown on her face. "I was so worried about you after your breakup with Cedar, and Lianna was there in town where you were, so I called her."

Wow. She grinned. "So you two are already friends," she said. She'd been worrying about nothing. She felt relieved. And…a little bothered, too.

"Why didn't either of you tell me?" she asked, looking from one to the other. She felt left out, and far too needy. As if she was helpless and they were her caregivers.

"At first we were afraid you'd think we were ganging up on you."

Looking back to the first months post-Cedar, thinking of Raine's support and Lianna's, about how they'd always had the same message for her. Love. Support. Concern. Each inviting her to do things. Not accepting *no* more than once in a row.

She couldn't imagine having made it through that time without them. But knowing that they'd been conversing behind her back…that came with a little sting.

"And later?" she asked. She wasn't really angry with them. And even if she had been, it wouldn't last. They were her girls. And she was theirs.

She'd seen them both through some tough times, just as they'd been there for her when she'd left Cedar. Raine's inability to find a man who "fit," as she put it. Her mother's many relationships and then marriage to a man their age. She was okay with it now, but at first, she'd been completely lost. And Lianna…they'd had years and years of painful moments. Lianna's childhood had been unfair and horrible, with alcoholism, abuse, foster homes…

"Later we didn't…" Raine's voice fell off.

"We didn't tell you because we didn't know what was going on." Lianna's voice was strong. Sure and confident.

And Heather was totally confused.

"Going on with me, you mean? You guys have known everything all along." And then it dawned on her. "Is this about Charles? Is that what you mean? Because you didn't think I should be with him?" Still no reason for her friends not to tell her they were friends, now, too. As often as she'd tried to get them all together, they should know she'd be happy about it.

They were both watching her, looking almost sick.

"Well, you guys were right," she blurted, wanting to help them feel better, but…still lost. She turned to Raine. "I told you I'd talk to him, and I did." They both knew she'd broken up with Charles. At least temporarily. "And I won't be getting back with him again unless I know for sure that I'm ready to get married. Until I don't need a yearlong engagement to make it okay."

They didn't know about Cedar yet.

Unless one or the other of them had driven by the beach the night before and seen them standing by their cars. But that was a long stretch.

She helped herself to a cracker, picked up a slice of Havarti and carefully arranged it on the cracker. Took a bite. And another. Followed it with a sip of wine.

Her friends watched her. They weren't looking at each other.

This wasn't about Cedar.

"Tell me what's going on," she said, holding her wineglass in both hands. They were scaring her.

"We weren't sure ourselves," Raine said, her gaze filled with compassion. She was still frowning. "Not until this week."

"There's something I never told you," Lianna began with a quick, almost covert, glance at Raine. She turned on the couch then, facing Heather. "When you were in college, rooming with Raine…I was incredibly depressed there for a bit."

"You were in college, too, off in San Francisco, where you'd chosen to go, with new friends of your own," Heather said. But she nodded, too. She'd known that Lianna had been hurt by the onset of Raine and Heather's friendship. Heather had never meant to leave her childhood friend out. She'd tried to tell Lianna that she hadn't moved on, she'd just added on.

"My roommate was gay," Lianna said.

Heather shrugged. "So?" It wasn't as if they cared, any of them, about things like that. Choice was choice and respect was respect. Period.

"I had a relationship with her."

Her mouth dropped open. "But…you…we…" She shook her head. "You had a huge crush on Jamie Felder. All through high school. And…you went to the same college he did. You guys hung out. I thought…you said…"

"We did it. Jamie and me. Yeah, we did. It wasn't what I'd cracked it up to be." Lianna's smile was wry.

"And with Amy…it was?" She'd only met Lianna's roommate a time or two, but she'd liked her well enough.

"Nope. But it was better than it was with Jamie." She took a sip of wine. Heather did, too.

When she looked at Raine, she saw her friend's glass was empty.

So…this was girlfriend confession time? She could handle that—and she had something to contribute, too. But this moment wasn't hers. It was Lianna's.

And maybe Raine's? They both had things to tell her, apparently. Things they'd told each other over the past months, but never told her?

"I wish you'd told me. Not because I have a

problem with it. But because I'd like to have been there for you…"

She'd never had the desire to experiment with a girlfriend, but she knew several who had. Mostly in college. After painful breakups and a lot of drinking.

Since then, she'd known a few lesbian couples. A doctor in her current office building was half of a lesbian couple. She liked her, and felt completely comfortable around her. Lianna had met her, too, when she'd come to the office to meet Heather for drinks over the past year.

"I was in love with you." Raine's words came out of nowhere. Heather might have dropped her glass if Lianna hadn't taken it from her. "Or I thought I was."

Oh, God. How could…how had she not… She remembered Raine's inability to find a man who turned her on…

But she stared at her beautiful friend and felt… friendly love. Deep, abiding friendly love.

"Don't worry," Raine said. "It passed."

Okay, then. Good. She nodded, still looking at her. Not at all sure what to do.

"It was more a crush than anything," she continued.

"When?" As though it mattered. But it kind of did. All these years, she'd seen Raine in a certain way, as a good friend, a close friend…and Raine had seen her differently. She'd never known.

But Raine had told Lianna. Who'd understood.

"Senior year. That last semester. I knew we were going to be moving on with our lives, not living together anymore. I didn't want it to end."

"I didn't, either," she admitted. "That doesn't mean there was anything sexual in it."

"For me, there was." Raine's tone was as soft as always.

"So, all these years, you've been…"

Raine shook her head. "Nope. I've been loving you like a sister, loving Cedar for a while, too, like a brother. I was happy that you were so happy, and looking for my own happiness. Looking for the man of my dreams."

So it had just been a moment then. "You're sure?" Not that it changed her feelings for her friend, in any way. But a girl kind of needed to know if someone wanted her—or had wanted her—in that way.

If nothing else, she could have been more sensitive to Raine's struggle.

"Completely." Raine nodded. "I love you dearly. Like a sister."

Phew. Heather picked up her wine. Love was a sticky thing. You didn't always get to choose who you fell for. "You'll find the guy of your dreams, you know," she said, looking at Raine. And then Lianna. "You, too. I'm sorry about Dex, but..."

Her friends were looking at each other. Back at her. And then at each other again. Then they did the craziest thing. They linked hands. Like they had a pact or something.

The *or something* started to dawn on her when Raine moved over to sit between Heather and Lianna, much closer to Lianna.

Oh.

Oh!

Ohhhh.

Hands trembling, she didn't know whether to smile. Or cry.

Lianna took the glass from her hand. Set it, along with hers and Raine's, on the table, and pulled the three of them into a hug.

A long, loving, accepting hug.

Because that was just the way love worked. No matter who fell for whom.

WHETHER BECAUSE HE knew Heather was out of town, or because he was trying to avoid making too much of their time on the beach Friday night, Cedar spent all day Saturday completely enmeshed in DiSalvo's life. Using sources from Facebook and other social media accounts, to bank records, tax records and IRS reports, from company holdings and year-end reports, to employees and then back to social media, he built a picture. He had to know everything there was to know about his client—everything a prosecutor would be able to find.

As a defense attorney, that was his job.

And he was good at it. Actually enjoyed the challenge, the ability to find everything, to be able to figure out where to look, to see things around the next bend and then know how to get them.

One thing he'd prided himself on was that there'd never been anything he *couldn't* find. And find first.

Which was why it had infuriated him when Dominic wouldn't tell him the truth about those damned phone calls. He'd checked for police records. Had followed up on all previously dropped charges, talked to the earlier arresting officers about their impressions. He'd played the game like the pro he was.

He'd never thought to check 911 records. It had never occurred to him to ask about the address.

The fact that the prosecutor had known to do so had always bothered him. Until he'd realized that someone had to have tipped them off. Could've been any of a number of people who'd been after Dominic for years. Anyone in the police department, for instance.

Knowing who'd squealed hadn't mattered. Dealing with the calls had.

In walked Carin Landry. He'd known there was something going on in that home, hers and Dominic's, but…

In her own way, she'd been crying out for help back then, and he hadn't cared enough to find out why. It had nothing to do with his case, so he'd let her take the blame for the calls on the stand.

Lost Heather.

And now he had her in his life again. Friends instead of lovers.

Sipping from a tall glass of milk, he sat at his desk Saturday evening, right where he'd been all day, and tuned back in to DiSalvo.

There'd been a loose end that had bothered him for hours. A shell company—one that had no obvious business or assets—attached to another shell company attached to another—and he couldn't figure out where the common denominator lay. One attached to one but not another. Another attached to a fourth but not attached to the other two. Not by names involved, bank accounts or even type of business. Invoices and paid receipts for services in one place, for supplies in another and employee wages in a third. It made no sense. You didn't have a company that only invoiced or only paid employees.

Reading through the paperwork, actual photocopies of bills of lading, service receipts, locations, dates, amounts, he tried to find something that would connect all the different shell companies emptying into each other randomly for different purposes.

The only thing that seemed at all logical to him was that invoices were drawn up, receipts given, for whatever the writer decided to label them at the time. Fake invoices and fake receipts, in other words. And different writers.

Kind of ingenious in a way. Made tracking anything that much more difficult.

None of it had direct ties to DiSalvo. But he was tied to a couple of companies that had been tied to one or another of them.

And then he saw it again. HHC.

On an invoice.

Food being sold?

Food that was a "win" according to an earlier email.

Online, he started searching public records again for all the companies. Anything he could find. Anywhere.

And came up with HHC again. On a high-dollar purchase order for a rare, rudimentary musical instrument, a bronze flute that dated back more than a thousand years.

HHC was the purchaser.

And he found something else, too. A company DiSalvo had told him was a shell, wasn't. Again, DiSalvo didn't have direct dealings with the company, so he might not have been aware…but the company was real. Based in Japan, it bought and sold bluefin tuna. At exorbitant prices.

And a separately owned shell company attached to a company DiSalvo owned had been shipping goods to the Japanese company for more than a year.

It very much looked like someone from DiSalvo's adventure gig was bringing in a lot more tuna than was legal and, rather than registering every catch, as the law required, was selling it in Japan instead.

Not as bad as murder. Or drug dealing.

But not legal, either.

Question was, how much of this did DiSalvo know?

Had the man been lying to him all along?

If he was, and continued to lie, would Cedar be able to protect him from the law like Cedar-Jones had asked?

There was one way he could find out the truth.

He could, as a friend, ask Heather to test DiSalvo.

But even as the thought occurred to him, he threw it out.

CHAPTER NINETEEN

HEATHER SAT IN the window seat on the flight home early Monday morning, leaving the aisle for Lianna, who was larger, and the middle for Raine to sit next to her.

It was taking a lot of getting used to, her friends as more than friends. But she was fine with it. She'd still see Raine at her studio. She and Lianna would still have times alone.

But the three of them would be doing a whole lot more together, and she was honestly glad about that. It wasn't what she'd expected, and yet…it felt…good.

Odd. But good.

Raine and Lianna…in love. Each was such an integral part of her life…and they fit together. It hadn't been easy, she now knew, after listening to an account of their struggles the night before. Neither had been ready to see herself as a same-sex partner. But the more they'd tried to fight it, the more they'd been drawn to each other.

She was truly happy for them.

"So what's Cedar up to these days?" Lianna

asked, leaning forward to look at Heather as the pilot turned off the seat belt light.

She'd told them both about her talk with Cedar. About the new world they were entering together—friends instead of lovers—and about how she felt so much better, so much more honest, so much more her true self since he was back in her life. Ending their relationship had been the right thing to do. Cutting him out of her life had not.

They'd both supported her decision.

And they'd been worried about her, too. They hadn't said so; they hadn't needed to. They might be emerging into something new and beautiful together, but to her, they were still the best friends she'd known and loved for years.

And she read, loud and clear, that they didn't like Cedar being anywhere near her.

"I assume work," she said, answering Lianna's question. She saw Raine watching her, too. They were ganging up on her without wanting her to feel ganged up on. She could tell.

"I didn't ask him anything about work," she admitted to them. "I wasn't ready to jump back into the Cedar-defense-attorney arena."

"How can you be his friend without at least being aware of it?"

The question was fair. One she'd already asked herself.

"I'm willing to hear about it. I just can't be involved. And until this thing with Carin is done, it's best for us not to go there. I can't let anything I feel about what he does interfere with what we're trying to do for her."

They nodded. Didn't exchange any meaningful looks.

She took that as a positive.

All in all, it had been a good weekend.

And she was looking forward to getting back home. She could call Cedar if she wanted to. He might call her. They were friends.

It was okay.

CEDAR WAS ON the phone early Monday morning, talking to DiSalvo who was on the East Coast, getting ready to go out on another fishing expedition. As a fisherman.

"I need the truth," he told the older man. Not disrespectfully, but confidently. "I can't help you if I don't have the truth."

"I haven't lied to you," DiSalvo said. He was in his car, having left the restaurant where he'd been having breakfast so he could speak privately.

"You told me you aren't familiar with HHC."

"I'm not."

Cedar didn't find that unconvincing, but he

wasn't completed convinced, either. Nothing about HHC in the manifests, paperwork or spreadsheets had connected directly to DiSalvo, other than as a mention of food on one of his expeditions.

"You also haven't been totally up-front with me. Tell me about the fish you're selling to Japan."

"By damn, he was right."

Whatever Cedar had expected, it hadn't been a note of approval in the other man's voice. DiSalvo did know he could go to jail for some of this stuff, didn't he?

"Who was right about what?" He wasn't playing around here. Cedar-Jones was counting on him.

"Randy. Cedar-Jones. He said you'd find out about the fish. Told me to tell you about them in the first place. You're as good as he said you were." He'd been tested. And passed.

Felt some pride in that.

But his client had to be honest with him. There was no other choice. He'd walk before he'd lose due to a client's lying.

He told DiSalvo so, quite clearly. Listened as the man assured him he'd been hiding nothing else.

And hung up.

Half an hour later, DiSalvo was charged with a laundry list of counts.

All of which Cedar knew he could fight.

He wasn't going to let his father down.

THE TEST STARTED out like many others. Carin had clearly been tense as Heather hooked her up to the portable polygraph. Blood pressure cuff on her arm, galvanometers on her fingers and pneumographs around her torso.

They'd discussed all the questions she'd be asking, as was normal. No new issues would be introduced during the test. Other than base questions, name, address, that kind of thing, there was only one topic. There'd be a number of questions, but all dealing with that one topic—who was abusing her.

The base questions weren't just meant to give Heather a starting point on her reading, but also to calm her subject—Carin. Easy questions, right answers. No big deal.

All she had to do was tell the truth, and the rest of the exam would be just as easy.

"Remember, you have the right to discontinue the test at any time," she said before they began.

"Can I ask you a question before we go any further?"

"Of course."

"What happened to your aunt?"

Heather blinked. She'd been expecting a procedural question.

"My aunt?"

"You said that even after your mother brought her home, she still went back. What happened to her?"

"He continued to beat her. Then he'd repent and hit her again."

"Are they still married?"

She shook her head. "He's in jail, serving a life sentence for killing her."

Carin nodded, and Heather hoped to hell the woman would choose truth over possible death. Because, like Cedar, she didn't think her injuries had come from Dominic's friend.

Every question, no matter how Heather worded it, led to the same answer. Dominic's friend had hit her. She'd started the test establishing that they were talking about Carin's current injuries only. Test results would be skewed if they dealt with more than one thing at a time, since that would also mean more than one answer. A response that might be true for one incident, but not for the other. With no way of knowing what it really indicated.

"What's the name of Dominic's friend who inflicted this injury on you?" She was on the fourth question of twenty and so far, the test results showed that Carin was telling the complete truth.

"Renaldo Bentley."

"Where did the injury take place?"

"Becker Lane, I don't know the address."

"Was it at a house?"

"Yes."

"Whose house?"

"Renaldo's."

"Do you have a broken eye socket?"

"Yes."

"Do you have multiple lacerations on your chin and cheek that required stitches?"

"Yes."

"Do you have other bruising that did not require stitches?"

"Yes."

Because she was emotionally involved in the case, Heather wanted to ask if the woman was afraid of Dominic. If he was threatening her in any way. Ethically she couldn't.

She'd been brought in to find out one thing. If Carin was telling the truth about who'd caused her current injuries.

The questions were in front of her.

All she could do now was read them.

"Did anyone else hit you?" She moved down her list, thinking. Trying desperately to come up with something. She'd been so certain the results would show that Carin was lying.

"No."

Carin had answered truthfully, and yet, her gaze,

as it met Heather's across the table, had an almost desperate quality. And then Heather understood.

The next question read, "Was Renaldo the only one who hit you?" but came out, "Was Renaldo the only one who caused your current injuries?"

When Carin didn't answer as immediately as she had with the other questions, Heather's heart started to pound.

But, with years of training her voice to remain calm, she asked again, "Was Renaldo the only one who caused your current injuries?"

Carin frowned and then said, "Yes."

Heather noticed the spike immediately. All across the board. Dominic's girlfriend had just lied to her.

They had a chance to save her.

THE LIE WAS not an admission of who'd hurt her. Heather knew they weren't home free. But the agreement between Carin and the staff at The Lemonade Stand and Cedar, too, apparently, had been that they'd leave her alone about it—if she passed the test.

Wishing she could have Stand staff and Cedar with her as Carin finished the test and she printed out the results, Heather took a deep breath. Sara Havens Edwin, the Stand's chief counselor, and Managing Director, Lila Mantle, would have time with their resident, but by law, Carin was allowed to know her results if she wanted them.

And, of course, she did.

Sliding the printed sheet across the table, she looked at Carin. "According to this, you didn't tell me the truth."

Heather sat through the tense silence. She wanted to hear from Carin before she continued.

"You can't tell them I failed." Carin's tone was almost hard as she sat there, staring at the sheet. "I want the test results destroyed. I withdraw my permission to have anyone see them."

"What good will that do?" she asked. "You agreed to the test so they'd leave you alone about who hit you. If you withdraw the test, or if you fail it, the results are the same—they're going to try to find out what happened to you. The people here, they just want to help you, Carin. And I assume, since you're here, there's a part of you that wants help."

When the woman didn't immediately respond, Heather focused on that swollen and misshapen eye socket, which would probably require surgery to keep it from dropping lower than the other, and made a decision.

"We can do more testing, if you like," she offered. It was done sometimes, when results were inconclusive. "Ask different questions. Come at the issue differently."

Carin slowly raised her head, her eyes assessing Heather. "Renaldo hit me. I just… I needed a little time to get my confidence back," she said. "That's why I'm here. Just to…take a time-out."

"I believe Renaldo hit you. But these results—see how high that spike is? Across the board. It's clear that you're lying about Renaldo being the only one responsible for your injuries. Maybe someone else put him up to it. Maybe someone else was there…"

She shook her head. "No. Look, I do this sometimes. I take a time-out, like I said. Dominic knows I'll be back, and things are good."

"This isn't your first time at a shelter?"

Carin's gaze dropped. She pulled the test closer, appeared to be studying it. "Yeah, it is."

"Where do you usually go?"

She shrugged. "Just away. To a hotel someplace. I just, you know, hang out, watch TV, rest."

An idea occurred to Heather. "You stay away until the bruises heal. So people won't know you've been hurt."

Glancing up again, Carin seemed to be weighing her response. "Yeah," she said, as though daring Heather to do something about it. Make something of it.

Or find a way to help?

More was going on than Carin was saying. That was obvious. How much more, and what? She'd pretty well admitted that she'd been abused in the past. As everyone had suspected.

Heather wasn't a domestic-violence counselor.

But Carin was on the verge of some kind of admission…and seemed to trust her…

She also seemed to think that being hit was better than speaking up. Had Dominic threatened her?

"You know I tested Dominic," Heather said, going with her instincts.

"Yeah."

"During our interview, I found him to be overly confident and not particularly…kind."

"He's a powerful man. He does what he has to do, but he's loyal. And a great protector. He'd die for me. I'm certain of that. And when we just hang out…he relaxes then. He's fun. Funny. He treats me like a queen. His queen."

Would he also kill her if she turned on him? Or even, eventually, if she stayed?

"Did Dominic hit you?" Heather asked calmly.

"Renaldo did."

"I know. Did Dominic do it, too?"

Heather held her breath as she waited for the answer. There'd be no formal test result, but if she could get an admission…

"No. Dominic has never hit me."

Carin looked her straight in the eye as she answered.

Heather almost gave up. Gave in to the fact that Carin was telling enough of the truth. That Renaldo was the one who'd hit her.

That maybe, this last time, it had been an accident, just as she'd said, and Dominic's friend had mistaken her for someone else.

But she noticed that Carin's finger was running back and forth along the paper, almost as though the movement was subconscious. A nervous tic.

Right on the line that spiked. The cause of the test's failure.

"Do you want to do some more testing?" she asked. "I can hold my report until we're done."

"Is that, like, normal?"

"Yes. It's completely legitimate. Sometimes more testing is needed for an accurate result. For various reasons."

"Then, yes, I'll agree to more testing."

She wasn't ready to tell the truth, but she wasn't ready to leave yet, either.

It was as though she was being pulled apart from the inside out, and Heather's heart wept in response.

Sometimes, while solutions might seem obvious to those on the outside, the answers weren't as clear as they seemed.

Take Lianna and Raine... Heather had been looking out for both of them for years and had never seen that the road to their happiness had been right in front of her.

Love had had to be strong, to be diligent, to lead them to their happiness.

But the sad truth was that sometimes a woman fell in love with someone who hurt her. Badly.

CHAPTER TWENTY

CEDAR WAS IN the middle of screwing joists together late Monday morning when he felt his cell phone buzz at his waist. Still holding his drill, he walked outside the framework that would soon be a bungalow, pulling his phone from his belt as he did.

Heather.

He'd been waiting. Not completely sure she'd call, but…he'd been waiting.

"I need to do more testing," she told him as soon as he answered.

He knew her job well. "The results were inconclusive?" he surmised, feeling disappointed, and yet…encouraged, too. At least she hadn't passed.

Carin was the focus, not the fact that Heather was calling him, he reminded himself.

"I need to do some more testing," she said again. "Certain answers made me want to approach the issue from a different angle. I relayed that to Carin, and she agreed to more testing."

Not the best possible news, but still in their favor. In favor of Carin's future safety.

"I'm fully booked today," Heather was saying. "On my way to my office now. But I'd like to get this done as quickly as possible. I'm hoping to see her on Wednesday. My worry is that if we don't move quickly here, she might choose to leave the Stand. The more her injuries heal, the more we take that risk."

"What can I do?"

"I'd like some help, Cedar. You said you knew some…things. I'm sure there's something she's not telling me, and maybe some fact you know can clue me in. Help me find the right questions to ask."

He was still back at, *I'd like some help, Cedar.* Trying desperately not to take it personally. Not to care, other than for Carin's sake.

"I'm assuming you're busy, too," she was saying when he caught up. "I was hoping we could meet this evening?"

He suggested they meet for dinner.

Cedar knew that she still hadn't told her parents she'd broken up with Charles. For Charles's friends' sake, she was still wearing her engagement ring, and was still holding out hope that the two of them would marry. That he'd be able to wait until she was ready.

He listened to her response.

"I don't want to be seen alone with you in public yet. I don't think it's fair to Charles."

Yet. He honed in on the *yet.* She was right—and a lot more thoughtful than he would've been.

He was about to suggest meeting out of town when she added, "Lianna's going to be…away tonight. She's leaving right after work. She said we could use her place. So, if you don't mind eating takeout…"

He nodded. Realized she couldn't see. He noticed a couple of the guys glancing his way. Taking a break wasn't a problem. But Cedar taking one, other than a quick lunch, hadn't happened in the months he'd been with them.

"She still has the apartment on Magnolia?" he asked.

"Yep. Just can't leave that view…"

He and Heather had been there many times together. Shared more than a few bottles of wine with Lianna and Dexter on that balcony…

"Can't say I blame her," he said. "And I'm fine with takeout." He was fine with bread and water if it came to that, but offered to pick up Chinese. Didn't even have to ask what she'd want.

They set a time and hung up.

Cedar walked inside, holding back a grin. While the world was shifting beneath his feet, it was also settling into place. Heather was back. As excruciating as Friday night had been in some ways, she'd guided him into a new world, where they were…friends.

Calling each other for help.

Just like she'd said.

She'd meant it when she said they couldn't ever be a couple again.

But…she was back in his life.

WARNING BELLS WENT off in Heather's mind as she left work late and made her way to Lianna's without stopping at home first. She'd hoped to change out of the short black skirt and matching jacket, but was too eager to get to where she was going. Not because of dinner getting cold, or Cedar being locked out of her friend's apartment, but because she was seeing him again. Hence, the warning bells.

Yeah, it was great to have Cedar back in her life. To have found a way to make that happen and still preserve her heart and sanity. Putting her eagerness down to the fact that seeing him was still so new, she pulled into the complex right behind him.

When she turned to help him carry up their dinner, she caught him staring at her.

She knew that look.

Her body knew that look. And it responded to that look.

Heather turned back to double-check that she'd locked her car and headed toward Lianna's without another glance in his direction. He could bring up the food on his own.

She had to get herself under control. They were friends. They were not, and would not be, lovers.

But damn, the man looked good in black jeans. Particularly since she didn't have to imagine what was inside them.

She knew. Vividly.

Cedar's sexual prowess had never been in question. Nor had her reaction to it.

They'd been great in bed. And weren't going to be in bed again.

LIANNA, WHO'D DRIVEN down to take a class with Raine and spend the night, had texted to say she'd made a fresh jug of sun tea for them. Heather noticed her friend hadn't offered the bottle of wine that was right next to it in the fridge. But she wouldn't have opted for alcohol at the moment, anyway.

She was working.

And she was with Cedar.

Tea it was.

He'd brought a bottle of milk.

He was working, too. Heather got the message and was glad.

WINDOWS TABLET AT her side, Heather didn't ask Cedar about his day. She wasn't ready to confront that part of his life.

Truthfully, she was a bit nervous about inviting him more completely into her own work. This job in particular. Was she being a fool, trusting him not to mislead her again? Especially dealing with the same couple?

But the fact that it *was* Dominic Miller involved and that Cedar appeared to have been telling the truth about Carin, made her want to trust him.

In any event, she needed his help.

Without revealing the results of the day's polygraph, she poured her tea and sat down next to him, in the same chair she'd used the week before, sitting there, sipping wine with Lianna.

Who'd already been lovers with Raine, telling her she'd broken up with Dexter, trying to tell her about Raine, and Heather hadn't had a clue…

Because sometimes you took those you knew well at face value. Sometimes you were so used to seeing them that you didn't see anything you didn't expect.

Like the fact that Cedar had been working her when he'd set up the testing for Dominic. When he'd led her in terms of the questions she should ask.

She hadn't seen because she hadn't been expecting to. That didn't mean there was anything wrong with her. That her judgment was unreliable or untrustworthy. It didn't make her anything less than what she was.

The meal was one they'd shared dozens of times. They passed cartons back and forth, setting the extras on the little table between them, eating in unison.

She mentioned the view, the purpling of the sun setting over the ocean. He talked about a crane, with a piece of heavy-looking concrete suspended from its jaws, that was in position at a new construction site. She hadn't noticed it there. He mentioned something about torque.

While it was an odd conversation coming from him, she respected the fact that he was keeping things impersonal. It felt safer with him that way.

Did he know that?

She could have asked about his family, except that, other than the father he revered in spite of the fact that he'd never met the famous creep, he had none to speak of. There were relatives of his mother's back east whom he barely knew. He might have asked about her folks, but he'd just seen them the week before—awkward as that had been.

"Your mother's looking good," he said. "I didn't get a chance to talk to your dad, though."

Her dad had purposely kept out of Cedar's way. Hadn't wanted him there. At one time, he'd thought of Cedar as a son. Had welcomed him, openly enjoyed having him around.

"He's well," she said now. She was going to have to tell her parents that she and Cedar were friends. That she'd be seeing him from time to time.

And that she'd broken up with Charles.

Without leaving the impression that one had led to the other.

Okay, it had, but not in the way they'd think.

When had life become so complicated?

She watched the traffic below. Wondered about the lives of the people on the street. About what was going on inside them that most of the world didn't see. The hurts. The worry.

The secrets?

Ones that would hurt those they loved?

Shaking her head, she grabbed her tablet.

"Were you ever at Dominic's home?" she asked, reading her notes but double-checking because it was just that important. She'd only had an hour to spend on the case that afternoon—in lieu of lunch—and planned to put in more questions the next day. Carin's testing was scheduled for Wednesday, leaving her little time to create an accurate picture from which she could extract key elements.

Her hands were sweating as she watched him

for signs of subterfuge. Body language. Expression. Nervous movements.

Not that he had any reason she could think of to lie to her.

"No. He always came to my LA office."

Which was where she'd tested him. At Dominic's request, Cedar had asked her to bring her portable unit there, rather than having Dominic come to her. She took an easier breath. She was 98 percent sure he was telling her the truth.

That meant neither of them had any idea what Dominic and Carin's home environment was like.

"What about Carin's family? We know there's a little sister, who apparently knows Renaldo, so we'd have to assume she's also acquainted with Dominic…"

She'd already asked about Chloe White, after having her question Carin's whereabouts on Renaldo's Facebook page. She had Cedar's answer right there in her notes.

But she asked him again, so she could compare answers. But also because she'd had the very distinct impression that Carin was protecting someone or something. Dominic? Maybe she feared his power. Feared that if she left, he'd find her. Heather couldn't go into her test with several objectives. There could only be one main focal point, or she'd skew the results. She had to find that point.

"All I know about Chloe is that she wasn't involved. Dominic said something about her never coming around."

A little different from before. He'd thought Carin had no contact with her. But basically the same. She chose to believe he was telling her the truth.

"You didn't hear if there was some kind of falling out between Carin and her sister?"

He shook his head. "She had no relevance to my case…"

And his cases were pretty much all that had mattered, so his words rang true.

The next question wouldn't be so easy. And if he was trying to get back into her good graces, he could very well have reason to lie to her. She took a moment. Slowed her breathing. Focused on Carin.

"Did you ever, before bringing me into it, have any indication that Dominic was mistreating Carin?"

"None whatsoever." The answer was so quick, so sure, his tone steady, his gaze strong. Unlike her test subjects, he'd had no warning the question was coming. No time to still automatic responses, neurological tells. "I only met her twice, but I thought they were fine. I interviewed her in case she was called to the stand. She answered every question. Remained calm. He treated her with respect."

"Did she show any fear of him?"

"Not that I noticed."

That she could believe.

"Why didn't you call her as a witness?"

"Because I didn't need her. If I'd called her, I would've opened her up to cross. I didn't expect trouble there, judging by how she'd done when I'd interviewed her, but why bring up the possibility of something coming undone if I didn't need to?"

She knew he was telling her the truth that time, too. He'd told her the exact same thing eighteen months before, when he'd still been in the earlier stages of preparing for Dominic's trial.

She was shaking now. Didn't know if he could tell. She wished she hadn't eaten. Going down this road was harder than she'd realized.

"When did you first suspect Dominic of beating her?"

"When the 911 calls turned up as new evidence in the middle of the trial."

"You had absolutely no clue before then?"

He had to recognize that she'd think less of him if he'd known and hadn't said anything, but she held his gaze. Waiting for his answer.

"None. But then, I wasn't looking, Heather. I was going for my win. Not for other charges against my client."

She watched him, aware of a warmth inside her. A small space in her stomach where the tension had faded. It wasn't completely gone, that tension. Cedar hadn't been a hero. He'd been an attorney out for his win.

But she believed he hadn't known ahead of time that Dominic had been an abusive partner. That he hadn't spent months keeping quiet about that fact, purposely ignoring it.

It didn't change the choices he'd made in the end—the way he'd lied to her, used her, betrayed her. The way he'd let Carin take the stand and accept the blame for her own abuse. So he, Cedar, could get his win.

Probably hadn't stopped him from calling his ghost of a father and reporting the win, either.

She wouldn't know. She'd been gone by then…

This wasn't about her.

"Does Carin have any other family? You said her mother was killed in a car accident…"

He shook his head. "I looked at the family forms I had them fill out—any people the prosecutors could potentially find and interview. On Carin's side, there was only the one sister. Doesn't mean there isn't other family somewhere, but she just named her sister as someone prosecutors might want to interview."

"Did they get to her sister?"

"Not that I was ever told."

"Maybe they had," she said now, sitting forward, forgetting in that moment that she didn't fully trust Cedar. "Maybe that's why Chloe's looking for Carin now. Maybe she met Carin and Dominic during his trial. You know, if the prosecution came looking for her to ask questions about him…"

"It's possible." Cedar used his chopsticks to take a bite from the container of leftover fried rice. "I should've been notified if it happened, but since they chose not to use her as a witness, it's possible that I wasn't."

"At least that would explain Chloe's knowing Renaldo—or knowing about him, anyway…"

Not that the explanation helped. She just didn't like how she was feeling about the whole case. And was afraid that might be because it was too personal for her.

Were her own tangled emotions, regarding Cedar and Dominic, interfering with her training and instincts where her job was concerned?

If she backed out now, would they lose Carin? One thing was for sure—she wasn't confident Carin would be at the Stand long enough for her to take that risk.

She only had one question left for Cedar, an open-ended invitation that would allow him to give her anything he chose, true or not. And she'd have no way of disproving it.

Her tension was back. Her nausea.

"What else can you tell me, Cedar? What do you know that might help me here?"

CHAPTER TWENTY-ONE

CEDAR HAD KNOWN, from the second he'd decided to approach Heather to ask for help in saving Carin Landry, that this moment would come. He might have kidded himself that she'd choose her own questions, might have hoped it would happen that way.

But redemption didn't come that easy.

Dropping the cardboard carton on the table, he set down his chopsticks, leaned forward, elbows on his knees, and looked over at her.

"I know Dominic threatened her, maybe not with violence to herself, but he very clearly threatened her, and that's why she said what she said on the stand."

Heather's face turned white. Mouth open, she stared at him. He recognized the sheen in her blue eyes, saw she was holding back tears.

Cedar could almost physically feel when Heather, looking out toward the ocean, composed herself. When she drew every bit of her formidable strength back inside that sexy black suit and readied herself to continue.

If he'd ever doubted the depth of his love for her, he would never do so again. Not after that moment.

"How do you know?" The question didn't even hint at her stress.

"Remember when you did his polygraph?" He hadn't been allowed in the room, but as the one paying for the exam, the one requesting the exam, he'd been permitted to listen in. He'd set her up in a room with a sound system that worked next door, as well. Rooms at the high-powered firm for which he'd worked were designed for the more usual small meetings being held in-house, but also designed to work for those that were too large to fit in one room.

"Yes."

"I was with them when I said the 911 calls weren't going away and he'd have to admit to domestic violence. I explained that the incidents were in the past and that, as long as Carin didn't press charges, the admission wouldn't hurt him. Dominic asked for a few minutes alone with Carin to discuss the situation."

"And you went in the other room and listened."

"Yes." He'd been out for the win. Any action was justified.

"He doesn't know that, does he?"

"No."

"Does she?"

"No."

She had to have the truth. It wasn't pretty.

Or even palatable.

"How did he threaten her?"

"He didn't want to admit to abusing her. He was adamant about that. He said it would be with him his whole life and he wasn't going to do that to his mother. Or the rest of their family. He said if she didn't take the blame, then 'B' was going to pay."

"'B'?"

"'B,' as in the initial, I think. That's all he said, 'B.' But it was pretty clear they were referring to a person."

"You sure it wasn't 'C,' as in Chloe?"

He thought back. He hadn't questioned his understanding then. But… "I suppose it could've been. Sounded like 'B,' so that's what I wrote in my notes. I don't remember having a hard time making out anything they were saying."

"And he said 'B' was going to pay?"

"That's what he said."

"Then she just gave in?"

No. It hadn't been quite that clean. Nor was his conscience.

"She said, 'You're threatening B? You'd really hurt B?' And he said, 'You have your choice. I will not admit to hitting you.'"

There. She knew it all. Not only had he betrayed her, he'd betrayed Carin, too. He'd known far more than he'd ever shared. He'd broken no law. He'd just turned his back on the implications, the consequences, of what he knew.

Dominic Miller had used a threat to force his girlfriend to incriminate herself. Cedar had that knowledge, and he had done nothing with it.

Instead, he'd done his job. He'd won Dominic an acquittal.

He'd won.

Yeah. Right.

"So this…'B'…or possibly 'C'…that's who she's protecting." Her fingers were moving furiously along the keyboard dock holding her tablet.

He looked over at her, at the concentration on her face. The document she was working on.

"Uh…yes, that's what I wanted to tell you… earlier." She had to ask Carin who "B" was. The police could likely take it from there.

"If she'd confessed, admitted that Dominic was hitting her, it would've been quicker, easier in some ways…but I think you can still help her," he added.

Heather finished typing. Flipped the tablet case shut.

"Thank you," she said, looking at him for a second and then out at the ocean again.

"You're welcome. And Heather? If you have to tell her—when you go over the questions you'll be asking on the test—that I listened in that day and repeated to you what I heard, please do so."

"You could be up on an ethics violation if I do that."

"Possibly. If someone brings one." Her frown followed him as he stood, cleared up their trash, took his milk bottle and left the apartment.

HEATHER TOOK OFF her engagement ring. Sitting alone on Lianna's balcony, she did a couple of breathing exercises Raine had taught her. Let her thoughts slow down.

When she was ready, she cleared away the glass she'd used for her tea, washed it and put it back in the cupboard. Then, with a last look to ensure that they'd left no mark on her friend's apartment, she let herself out. She'd planned to go straight home. To ready herself for her morning appointments. Think about Carin, about the least threatening way to approach her.

Carin had been put on the defensive enough.

She called Charles and got his voice mail again. Told him she wasn't wearing the ring anymore. That she'd refrain from publicly announcing their breakup, but that she was letting everyone close to her know.

Driving by his house to drop off the ring, she saw an unfamiliar car in his driveway and passed by. She hoped he was enjoying himself.

A couple of driveways later, she turned in. It had been over a week since she'd had any real conversation with her parents. Not all that unusual, since they all lived busy lives.

But hers was changing in huge ways, and they had a right to know.

She told them first about Lianna and Raine. Lianna had asked her to, in case they were disappointed in her. She wanted to prepare for that. Heather's parents were the closest thing to real family Lianna had.

They were surprisingly supportive, considering their conservative views on a lot of issues. But then, Heather had already pushed their boundaries by living with Cedar all those years, without so much as an engagement ring. Or any kind of commitment to marriage. Her mother asked her, several times, to invite both her friends for dinner as soon as possible so they could welcome Raine more fully into the family.

Encouraged by the good mood and open minds all around, she then told them about her break from Charles—explaining that she loved him, that she'd still like to marry him someday, but wasn't ready to be committed to anyone. She talked about her doubts, her paranoia where others' motives were concerned, her inability to fully trust. Even as she said the words, she felt as though she'd already made great strides with all those issues, just in the past week. But she knew she wasn't anywhere near ready to be engaged.

Her mother gasped, of course, and her father frowned, but in the end, they were both completely supportive. Hugging her. Telling her that if it wasn't Charles, then she'd find someone else. They just wanted her to be happy.

And then she dropped the Cedar bombshell. She was working with him.

That one didn't go over so well.

CEDAR WAS JUST leaving for work in the morning when Heather's cell buzzed in. He was actually back in the house after having left, retrieving the lunch bucket he'd forgotten. Some things a guy just didn't get used to and carrying a lunch was one of his—or he'd already be on the road.

"I'm outside your gate. I see your truck in the drive. Can I come in? I just want you to take a look at something I found on the internet this morning. I'm not sure it's the right people, but I think it could be..."

Standing there in jeans and a comfortable shirt, clunking around in his work boots, a utility knife on his belt, he stared at the bucket he held. Holy hell. He should've let the ham sandwich rot. Starved.

"Um, sure, you remember the code?"

Did he have time to strip, throw on a towel and

pretend he'd just come from the shower? With dry hair.

Wasting a precious second, he glanced out the front window. Saw her car at the gate. He could be getting in the shower instead. Dropping the bucket on the table, he reached for his belt. Pulled it open and…she was heading for the drive.

Cedar did up his pants.

He watched as Heather, in a navy suit—longer skirt, short jacket with edging—got out of her car, and walked up to his front door.

Confident. Sure of herself.

As he'd once been.

Had he known who he was back then? Known that he'd lost sight of what mattered? That he was controlled by the need to win?

She knocked before he had an answer.

"Look," she said, handing him her tablet. On the screen was a listing of people by the name of Carin Landry and their possible relatives. "It's beyond my job description, but this might be our only chance to get Carin to admit the truth. So… who's 'B'? If I assume it's 'C' for Chloe, and I'm wrong, she'll answer all the questions easily, and we'll be done. If I say 'B,' and she doesn't know a 'B,' we can still be done…"

"You tell her what I overheard." She wasn't looking at him. Didn't seem to have noticed his jeans and work boots. No way she was going to see the lunch box on his coffee table.

"I did a search, Cedar. I was lying in bed this morning, awake, thinking about it all, about Chloe being on Facebook. I tried to find her friends or connections, but there's nothing. So I googled Carin, and a bunch of different people came up. I've been following them from one place to another—Whitepages, Truthlooker, Intel, findU, all of them. I finally got to some public birth records. They fit Carin's information. The woman who had her—who died of an overdose, by the way—had two other children. I found that out in her obituary. It didn't name them, or Carin, just said three children, so I looked for other records of her giving birth. I couldn't find Chloe, but I did come across one for a boy. He's ten years younger than Carin, which makes him what? About eighteen? Twenty?"

"Twenty-two. Carin's thirty-two."

"And get this—his name is Brian Bartholomew. 'B,' Cedar. This could be the 'B' we're wondering about. What do you think? Have I completely lost my mind? Am I going overboard here? I just feel so... I helped Dominic get off. I have to help Carin..."

She stopped, finally giving him a chance to speak, but the way she was staring at him kept him silent.

"Why are you dressed like that?"

He'd promised her the truth. "I'm going to work."

"Dressed like that?" Her mouth hung open as she looked him up and down and finally met his gaze.

He nodded.

"What is this? Some kind of joke?"

"No."

"A case, then? You're on a case where you have to be on-site or something?" She frowned at the utility knife on his belt.

"I'm working construction at The Lemonade Stand. Building more resident bungalows on some new land located on the other side of the swimming pool."

"You're building bungalows..." Her tone dripped disbelief.

"Yes."

She shook her head. Pointless for him to have lied. His facts would be easy enough to check. He figured she'd already come to that conclusion.

"But...why?"

"My reasons are my own." He had to tell her the truth, but he didn't have to spill his guts.

"So...you still have your office here in town, right? I called it, remember?" Now she was challenging him. He didn't blame her. Wished to hell he'd never put either of them in this situation.

"I still have my office, yes."

"And you have your license to practice?"

A fair question, considering that he'd let her believe he was willing to risk it. "I do."

"And you're taking on cases? New clients?"

"No. I use my license to help, if I can, like I'll take on Carin if it turns out she needs me to defend her against any criminal charges that might arise when she turns on Dominic. But otherwise, no." And like he was helping his father. He wanted to tell Heather about Cedar-Jones finally contacting him, but this wasn't the right time. And now that charges had been filed, he wasn't free to discuss the case, anyway. In any event, Carin had to be their focus at the moment.

"I haven't been to court since the jury acquitted Dominic." He'd turned over the rest of his pending cases to others in the firm where he'd worked. Sharks like him, who'd all gotten wins.

"Are you still with Jones and Abbey?"

His old firm.

"No."

"But…why?"

"As I said, my reasons are my own. For now. And I'm going to be late." He grabbed the tablet, looked over what she'd discovered. A familiar thrill shot through him. A successful find that could lead to a win. He'd always loved these kinds of discoveries.

"I think this is it, Heather. I think you've found 'B.'"

She nodded. Was watching him. "Did you get into some kind of trouble? Did they ask you to leave the firm?" she asked.

"No. On the contrary, they offered me a partnership if I'd stay." The truth hadn't demanded that much of an explanation, after all. And he'd wanted her to know.

But as the old saying had it, pride cometh before a fall.

"Are you…" Looking around, she saw his lunch bucket. "Are you hurting financially?" she asked him. "I mean, you must've taken an enormous loss, I know, but…working construction, Cedar? Do you need money?"

If the whole situation wasn't so damned sad, it might be comic. "No. But I do need to get to work."

Picking up his lunch, he rejoined her at the door, locked it behind them, and meant to simply say goodbye.

Instead, he called to her as she moved toward her car. "I'll do some checking on Brian," he said. "I'll see if I can find out more about him. Are you seeing Carin today?" The scheduled test wasn't until the next morning.

"No."

"Can we meet again, after work?"

She nodded. "I'd like that," she said, and Cedar knew she wasn't just talking about his help on the case.

Knew, too, that he'd overstepped a boundary he shouldn't have crossed.

His plan for redemption did not permit personal pleasure. Particularly if it involved Heather.

Perhaps he'd never be a changed man.

CHAPTER TWENTY-TWO

CEDAR WORKED HARD all day Tuesday. Worked through lunch, eating his sandwiches in bits and pieces whenever he stopped for a drink of water. He got his work done, and the second quitting time hit, he left. He'd spent the evening before, after leaving Lianna's apartment, working on the DiSalvo case. He'd filed the paperwork registering him as the attorney on the case, but there were other motions to file immediately. DiSalvo would be back in the state on Thursday and would, with Cedar by his side, turn himself in to the police for an official arrest. He'd then be released on bail.

That much was already done.

He'd also prepared a brief, moving that all charges be dropped, with substantial evidence backing up his claim that the prosecution wouldn't be able to convict his client.

His biggest concern was Carin. Who had nothing to do with DiSalvo.

And Heather.

She'd glowed that morning, when she'd stood in his doorway, showing him what she'd found.

She was so much more the woman he recognized, with hardly a trace of the ghost she'd been when he'd first seen her the week before.

Whether it was her ability to help Carin, to make up for the damage that had been done the previous year, or because she'd truly needed his friendship, he didn't know. Suspected it was a combination of both.

And as soon as Carin was safe, he had to get back to his office, to pull out the next case, and the next, until he'd undone all the damage he could.

Not all his cases needed his attention. Many didn't. But he still had a handful that he had to research—to see what came after the acquittals and the dropped charges.

At his desk by four thirty, he focused on Brian Bartholomew Landry. Opening several sites, he started searches in the town referred to in the birth record Heather had found, going back twenty-two years. He'd be able to get court records not everyone was privy to. Plus old newspaper articles. Some criminal databases. He sent off a quick email to a prosecutor in LA, a man he'd trusted, asking him to check an official criminal database.

He couldn't guarantee Heather the success she needed, but he could get her the ammunition that would give her the best chance of succeeding.

She thought she needed more than just "B" to get Carin to talk. So he'd find more.

If Carin had a brother named Brian.

And if he was the "B" Dominic had been talking about.

Equally important was disproving her theory if it *wasn't* right. She had one more shot, and she couldn't waste it on easy "no" answers that would tell them nothing. And wouldn't help Carin at all.

He'd been given his opportunity to help them both. He wasn't going to fail them again.

HEATHER WAS PACKING up for the day, getting ready to call Cedar and finalize plans for a quick meeting before she compiled her questions for Carin's test the next day, when the phone rang. She'd already checked her portable polygraph machine and had it by the door, ready to go. And...

It was Charles. Wanting to stop by her office. She couldn't tell him no.

Didn't even want to. After spending most of her evenings with him over the past six months, she missed him.

She was waiting for him in reception when he came in. They went back to her private hallway, and she led him down to her office. He'd been there before. But not often.

"You're looking good," he told her, moving

close enough to put an arm around her and kiss her forehead.

The blue suit she was wearing had been one of his favorites.

"You, too." She stepped back from him.

In dark pants and a light green golf shirt, he was clearly on his way out for his usual Tuesday-night foursome. And he did look good.

"I got your message," he told her and glanced down at her ring finger. "I was hoping to change your mind about it, but I see I'm too late."

Reaching into her purse, she pulled out the ring box he'd given her. Handed it back to him. With clenched lips and a jutting chin, he took it. He stared at it as he moved it back and forth between his hands.

"I'm sorry." She hadn't meant to cry, hadn't expected to. She hadn't wanted their engagement to end. And yet…she'd had to end it.

"So, things have changed that much in just a week," he said, finally meeting her gaze. The kindness she loved about him was still there.

Her shrug did a disservice to him. She had to find words, the right words. "You see what you expect to see," she told him. "That's what this week has been about."

He nodded, although he probably didn't have a clue what she meant. How could he?

She wanted to tell him she loved him, but didn't

think that would be fair to him. Everything was already so confusing between them.

"Are we… This is it, then? No chance for the future?"

He seemed sorry. Really sorry. But not broken up.

"Seems like we should be having a harder time with this, doesn't it?" she asked him.

His nod loosened the invisible band that had been tightening around her heart. "Don't get me wrong, I'd marry you tomorrow if you told me that was what you wanted. But I've been through one failed marriage. I don't want to enter another union, unless there's enough need, on both sides, to keep us there."

Enough need on both sides…

She hadn't thought of it that way. And yet…

"You want to marry me," she said, coming closer to him, taking his hands, looking him straight in the eye. "But do you *need* to marry me?"

Without breaking eye contact, he slowly shook his head.

Sometimes you just had to ask the right question.

CHARLES ASKED HER about Cedar as he picked up her portable case and waited outside the door while she locked up, then walked with her. Sadness hung in the air with each slow step.

"You two back together, then?"

"No." The question was fair, considering how quickly everything had fallen apart. And right when Cedar had come back into her life. "We've talked. We're going to be friends. I'm good with that."

Because she knew she had to be. At least he was in her life. She wasn't asking for any more than that.

Didn't want any more than that.

His betrayal...the devastation... She couldn't go through that again. He'd crossed a line, had shown he was capable of crossing it. Who knew when something would come up, something important enough to prompt him to do it again?

"You love him."

"Yeah." She loved Charles, too, in a very different way. But she didn't *need* to marry him.

"And he loves you."

"Probably." He did. In his own way, he did.

"Maybe you should think about giving him another chance."

They were at her car. She opened the trunk and stared at him. Charles was championing Cedar?

"Speaking as a guy who knows how it feels to lose you, I'd say if you're in love with him, you should give him a chance."

"I can't trust him."

He nodded. Gave a twisted smile and then

reached out a hand to touch her cheek. "And I'm probably talking nonsense," he told her. "I don't even know what I'm saying. The last thing I want is for him to hurt you again. I saw what it did to you."

He'd nursed her through it.

The truth dawned on her. Charles had been her rebound. The idea made her slightly sick. He deserved so much better than that.

But when she met his gaze, she realized something else. He knew. Had always known.

"I'd hoped we'd make it," he said softly.

She nodded. She'd hoped so, too.

CEDAR HAD CHANGED into shorts and a black cotton pullover before heading off to meet Heather at the pub they'd chosen. She'd called as she was leaving the office and had wanted to get together right then, if they could. She'd sounded a bit… off, so he would've met her regardless. As it was, he'd been waiting to hear from her and was ready to go.

She'd suggested the pub. It was close to the beach and had been one of their favorites when they were together. The fact that she'd chosen to meet him in public wasn't lost on him.

Was she no longer keeping up appearances for

the sake of Charles's friends? Did that mean she'd talked to him?

Gotten back with him, perhaps?

Was that what had made her sound off? She was back with her fiancé? And Charles was giving her a hard time about Cedar?

He could be completely wrong. But the possibility lingered as he walked into the pub, looking for her. He could be walking into the end of the friendship.

The idea wasn't welcome.

In the same suit she'd been wearing the week before, Heather was already at a high-top table, her long legs looking beautiful, folded over the stool, those delicate feet tucked on the stool's foot bar.

Some of the shine was gone from her eyes, though.

Running her hand across the side of her head, as though checking to make sure no strands had fallen from the blond twist, she smiled when she saw him.

He tried to make something of it, but couldn't. It was just a smile.

He made something of the bare finger on that hand, though. Her left hand.

Had the ring been there that morning?

He hadn't noticed. Wanted to ask if she'd been

with Charles, to find out what was going on. But didn't. Friendship or not, she called the shots.

He'd lost that right.

"I did some checking on Brian," he said, pulling out the stool across from her as he laid a leather portfolio on the table.

"Wait…" She was frowning. "I want to hear more about the construction work you're doing. About leaving the firm. How did you get hooked up with The Lemonade Stand? And why are you working construction? Is your license really still valid?"

Her questions were understandable. Some of the answers, he couldn't give her.

"You know I worked construction in high school and college," he told her, starting with the easy answer.

"Yeah." Her arms on the table, she leaned in closer, reminding him of the first month they'd been dating. Every single time he saw her, she'd leaned in as he spoke. Like she couldn't get enough of him. He'd felt the same way about her…

A waiter approached, took their order, beer for him, wine for her. But the interruption didn't let him off the hook. The look in her eyes made it pretty clear that she was waiting for answers. And had already told him she didn't have a lot of time.

"When you left..." No, he wasn't going to put that on her. Wasn't going to tell her how life hadn't felt worth living, how empty everything had become. As though she had some responsibility for that.

She'd done the right thing. Because he'd left her no choice.

"I saw what I'd become," he said, not sure, when it came to the closing statement of his life, that he had what it took. "Winning was like an addiction with me. I knew I had to make changes, and—" he looked around "—like someone addicted to alcohol, I wasn't going to dry out unless I left the bar. So I quit the firm."

"Just like that?"

"Yep."

"And The Lemonade Stand?"

"I wanted to make amends," he said, trying to figure out how much to say, without trying to convince her he'd changed.

He'd promised himself he'd never try to convince her of anything ever again. He had the ability to sway people, and he wasn't sure that would ever change. That *he'd* ever change. He knew he wanted to, that he'd like to use his talent for good, but he was still working on it.

And he also knew he had to do it for himself. Not for Heather.

Not to get her back.

But because he was, at his core, a man of integrity.

If he was.

He was in the process of finding that out.

"What I did in that last case—ignoring Carin's plight because it didn't have anything to do with me, with the case—made me sick. Once I stopped and looked at it. And in light of having used you to get there, knowing you and your family are huge supporters in the fight against domestic violence and that you all support The Lemonade Stand, I felt I had to contribute. It wasn't going to take away what I'd done, wasn't even going to help Carin, but it's what I chose to do."

"And she just happened to end up there? And name you as her attorney?"

"I didn't have any idea she'd name me as her attorney," he told her. He'd been honest with her about that.

"After I left the firm," he went on, "when I was still working all of this out, I paid a kid to slip Carin a card for The Lemonade Stand. I wrote on the back *If you ever need it*. The kid had to give it to her directly, when she was alone, and he'd get paid."

Tension was building inside him. He sipped his beer when it came, but slowly. He was on dangerous ground, close to crossing lines again, and he had to stop. He was sounding like a good guy. Like he was selling himself to a jury of one.

"The construction is because I have to do something while I'm on sabbatical from law, and construction is the only other thing I'm trained for. Or good at."

Her eyes were glistening again.

He took a gulp of beer. "Now…I think you're on the right track with Brian," he told her, opening his portfolio and taking out a few pages he'd printed off. "I don't know how much of this you can use. I wish there was more. I think he's definitely her younger brother. I found an article about when he won a spelling bee in first grade, and Carin's in the picture. And some other things… it's all there. What's strange is that, after their mother died, and Chloe went into the foster system, there's no mention of Brian going, too. I tried to find custody records for him, but they're not available to me."

He was a defense attorney. Not a prosecutor. Or a cop. And his friend had only been able to do so much.

"We can try to get them in the morning, but without a damned good reason to petition them, our chances are about nil."

She was still watching him. Studying him, really.

"What about after he turned eighteen?" she asked.

"Just the stuff you already found. Potential addresses where he might have lived. I checked the two that showed up, looked at tax records, and there's nothing there that ties him to Carin."

"So it's like he just disappeared?"

He shrugged as his tension started to ease. "Based on the records we have access to, there are no arrests, and he hasn't bought a house. At least in any county that reports online. He hasn't filed for bankruptcy. And if he's obtained any kind of licensing or certification, it's not showing up."

"He could be in college."

He "could be" any number of things. Fact was, they weren't going to know in time for her appointment with Carin the next day.

"You want something to eat?" he asked Heather as he saw their waiter head back to their table.

He wanted to know why she wasn't wearing her ring. If she'd seen Charles. How she was doing.

She shook her head. "I need to get home and get to work on my questions. Thank you so much for all of this..." She held up the papers, took one more sip of wine and then stood. Gave him one last long look and said she'd talk to him later.

Pulling his wallet out of his pocket, he dropped

some money on the table and got up, waited until she had time to get to her car and then got the hell out of there.

CHAPTER TWENTY-THREE

IN BEIGE PANTS and a dark brown A-line top, Heather walked into the same little conference room at The Lemonade Stand where she'd tested Carin a couple of days before. The interview would happen immediately, preceding the test, which was more typical for a polygraph session.

Carin wasn't due for another fifteen minutes, which gave her enough time to set up, and to get herself focused, as well.

Machine in place, she sat, did some yoga exercises Raine had taught her in college, and made an effort to clear her mind.

She had to see this as just a job if she was going to be able to trust her instincts. And those instincts were her strongest asset at the moment.

On the table in front of her were two completely different lists of questions. One was all about Brian and threats.

The other singled out every single injury Carin had sustained during the last instance of abuse, asking, for each one, if Renaldo had caused it.

And immediately following that, if she got a negative response, she'd ask who did cause it.

The original version of that test had made direct reference to Dominic, asking if he'd been responsible for her injuries, but she'd sensed that the question would produce a *no* answer without a "tell" indicating a lie. Carin had lied in court about the abuse. She'd most likely been lying about Dominic's abuse, her denials of it, for years.

Heather didn't feel strongly about any chance of getting the truth with either test. If Carin was going to tell them what was going on, she'd have done so already.

Which told Heather that, at this point, from Carin's perspective, a failed test would be preferable to admitting the truth.

She'd had subjects lie, knowing they were going to fail the test. Not often, but enough to know that sometimes, when people were cornered, lying seemed preferable to exposing the truth. Even if that lie meant jail time.

In Carin's case, it simply meant that the staff at The Lemonade Stand were going to keep trying to help her feel safe enough, confident enough, to be able to tell the truth. But she was free to go at any time.

The only way Heather was going to get the truth was to figure it out herself and then see when Carin lied.

So…

Brian?

She hadn't included a reference to the "B" threat in her initial questions. Hadn't yet decided if she'd mention it during the follow-up report that she'd give Carin after the test.

Wasn't sure she was capable of making that decision. Cedar was close by, at work, she could ask…

No. She couldn't think of him yet. Not until she'd done her best for Carin. Because he…

Tears stung her eyes, tightened her throat. She thought of Raine. Did a couple more exercises…

Carin knocked on the door and came in.

CEDAR WASN'T AT work Wednesday morning. He'd called the general contractor and offered to work Saturday as a makeup, but explained that he had to take the day off. Since he wasn't being paid for his work, the contractor could hardly deny him the time. Not that he tried. He did try to talk Cedar out of putting in any extra time on Saturday, though.

And thanked him again, profusely, for all his help.

They'd finish the bungalows in another month or so. Cedar was going to have to decide where he went from there.

He thought maybe one of the case files in his office would direct him.

At the moment, though, he was on his way to meet with Alvin Hines, the tax preparer. Hines didn't know about their imminent meeting. But he'd find out soon.

In a gray suit, red tie and polished shoes, he sped up the highway for an hour, and then walked into the outer office of a very swank accountant's firm. Alvin Hines, CPA, read the gold-trimmed sign in the manicured green front lawn.

He needed answers, and he was about to get them.

He wasn't sure how. But he was completely confident he would.

Hines's receptionist told him that the accountant wasn't available, that he had appointments all day. Hiding his relief that the man hadn't left the country or anything, Cedar suggested she tell him who was calling.

Two minutes later, he was shown back.

Holding out a hand, he told Hines he was glad to make his acquaintance. Smiled. Complimented the fishing trophies mounted along one wall. Thanked Hines for seeing him without notice. Said he was in the area and thought he'd stop in, hoping to catch him. Just to introduce himself.

Hines was pleasant. Offered Cedar a coffee, which he gratefully accepted.

They chatted a bit about DiSalvo. About the trumped-up charges. And the lesser ones that were probably legitimate, but that Cedar didn't expect to stand up in court.

He didn't say why.

Hines didn't ask.

"I heard a lot about you," the accountant said instead. "And, hey, if I ever get framed for something, you're the man I'm calling," he added. He'd rearranged two piles of paperwork several times during their friendly chat.

"I was just doing a favor for a friend." He dismissed his involvement in the case with a shrug. "But, you know, completely unrelated to those charges, I found the strangest thing."

It had hit him after he left the bar the night before, feeling like shit and looking for a fight. Because he was pissed at himself for the man he'd become.

One who wasn't good enough for the woman he loved. One who had to protect her from himself.

He had no one else to blame. And certainly didn't hold Hines accountable for his sour mood.

No, he was there for a much clearer purpose than that.

"When I was looking at all the files DiSalvo sent me, which included emails from you, as I'm sure you know..."

Alvin Hines nodded. His fingers stilled. The

change in his demeanor gave Cedar an adrenaline rush. He was onto something.

But then, he'd already guessed how this was going to play out.

Except for one key piece—he didn't have it yet. And didn't intend to leave without it.

"I found a curious thing…" He was sitting casually, leaning on the arm of the chair, a little smile on his face. All carefully staged. "There's a mention in your emails of HHC—how it's a win, for instance."

Hines adjusted his dark-rimmed glasses. "I don't recall," he said, shaking his head. Then adjusted his glasses again. Sweat stains were beginning to show in the armpits of his white shirt. Next he'd be loosening his tie.

"That's kind of what DiSalvo said when I asked him about it. He said he'd never heard of it, which was believable because the email was from you and it wasn't addressed to him. It went to a man named Mike Fontaine, owner of L & L Shipping, a company in which DiSalvo had invested."

Hines nodded. Tapped his thumb on one of the two piles of papers. Glanced at his watch without lifting his wrist.

Probably had an appointment. Cedar had purposely timed his arrival early, planning to interrupt the man's day until he got what he wanted.

He'd had no idea if Hines would even be in that day, but so far, things had gone as he'd hoped.

"See…then I found HHC listed as a caterer, providing food for one of DiSalvo's adventure fishing tours ship. Still made sense that he wouldn't have known about that. Rich owner like him would pay someone to take care of the details, like what his guests would be eating on their cruise."

Hines nodded again. Smiled. Then didn't.

"Anyway, it's no worry of mine, because the adventure company has nothing to do with the charges being brought against DiSalvo. I'd just been looking over all his holdings, planning for the worst, you know, in case charges were going to be brought, which they are. I'm not sure if you've heard yet or not."

Glancing down, Hines nodded. "I heard. Tough break for him, but from what I hear, he's lucky to have you. To hear him tell it, the whole thing's just going to go away."

Cedar was certain it would. As soon as he filed his motion to dismiss.

"It bothered me, though, you know?" he went on. "HHC. What is it? Because I saw it in other places, too—when I started to look more deeply into reports from some of the companies DiSalvo's been associated with over the past few years. Always in different places. Food here, cleaning supplies there. It bugged me. How could HHC be everywhere, and yet DiSalvo's never heard of it?"

Yep, there was the reach for the tie. The slight tug to loosen it.

"And it occurred to me that he was lying about it. And this was after I warned him that the one thing I couldn't tolerate was being lied to. That makes me look like a fool, and I don't like looking like a fool."

Hines nodded. Glanced at the door. And his phone.

"Now, it's not like I can do anything about any of this. But I'm thinking maybe I don't want to file that motion to dismiss, although I've already prepared it. Maybe, instead, I want to make a request to the court that I be removed as the attorney of record for Mr. DiSalvo."

"Have you talked to Mr. DiSalvo about that?" Hines asked with an awkward shrug.

Cedar shook his head. "I wouldn't be here if I had," he said, changing his tone to one of utter seriousness. "I haven't made up my mind about what I'm going to do," he added. You had to dangle a carrot to get the horse to move.

No response.

"I figured, since you clearly know what HHC stands for—since your emails directly reference it—that I'd just ask you. If I'm okay with the answer, we can shake hands and pretend to be glad we met."

"I told you—"

"And I know that as Mr. DiSalvo's tax preparer, you could be held responsible for some of his troubles," Cedar interrupted.

People hired attorneys to go after their preparers when the IRS went after them. They didn't often win—but it happened.

"He signed his own forms. My license number isn't at the bottom." Which, technically, let Hines off the hook. He couldn't be in trouble for copying numbers his client had given him. DiSalvo had said he hadn't signed his own forms. They could get an expert to compare signatures and determine who was telling the truth on that one. It wasn't his concern at the moment.

His ploy had worked. He'd made the man defensive. It was almost disappointing how little this challenge actually was.

"Right. I noticed that, of course. But there are all those companies you're associated with that are named in the charges. The ones where Mr. DiSalvo's money can't be traced to the actual dealings involved. I'm guessing, as you apparently prepared taxes for those holdings, too, there might be information worth looking at…"

Hines's phone beeped. He excused himself,

picked up the receiver. "Yes, tell him I'll only be a minute," he said. "Thank you."

As he hung up, he reached for a notepad and pencil, scribbled something on it, and handed it to Cedar.

"Call this number," he said.

That was all.

Cedar stood, took the paper and let himself out.

The truth was all he wanted.

He had no idea what he had yet.

But he was certain it was enough.

CARIN HAD BROUGHT doughnuts and coffee from the cafeteria. Her hair still wet from the shower, she looked as though she hadn't slept much in the two days since Heather had seen her. Her bruises had discolored even more, which didn't help. Heather chose to join her for coffee and doughnuts, in case she had something on her mind, other than getting the test over with.

Like just telling her the truth.

Or in case she'd decided she didn't want to take the test, after all.

They talked about The Lemonade Stand, instead. Carin was working with Sara Havens Edwin, a counselor Heather had worked with a time or two in the past, helping to provide legal assertion that victims were telling the truth. They talked about Lynn Bishop, too, the resident nurse who was seeing to Carin's injuries.

Lynn had offered her something for her pain, which she'd rejected. And she'd declined any help for sleep, as well. She didn't do drugs.

That last comment had been uttered in a tone of defensiveness—as if she was certain she was being labeled because of her dealer boyfriend.

"I never thought you did," Heather told her. She probably should have assumed the opposite— that Carin was a user—if you believed what you read in books and magazines or saw on TV. But if Carin had been on drugs, that would've been in her report. "You'd be going through withdrawal by now if you were addicted," she said. Then she added, "And we wouldn't be doing this test. Any kind of drugs, even prescription drugs, can skew results."

Which was why she'd asked Carin if Lynn had prescribed anything for her—the question that had led to that particular part of the conversation. She'd asked it first time around, too.

"You ready to get started?" she asked, when it appeared that coffee-and-doughnut time wasn't helping Carin relax.

What they were asking her to do—while it was for her own good, her safety—was the furthest thing from easy. Obviously, if she believed she could get away from the abuse, she'd do so.

Carin nodded. Sat up straighter, pulling down the hem of the short-sleeved yellow shirt she was wearing with her jeans—clothes she'd picked up from the supply room on the premises. Clothes she'd be allowed to keep and take with her.

"Before I get you hooked up, we need to go over the questions I'll be asking, just like we did last time, okay?"

Carin nodded.

Heather read the first couple of questions; they were the baseline ones and identical to what she'd asked at the beginning of the first exam.

Then, the time had come. She looked at Carin. Focused on her. And said, "Before we get any further, I want to tell you that I've struggled a lot with this. I want to help you. You're here for a reason. I know you said it was to get them to leave you alone while you take a time-out—but you could have gone to a hotel, like you did the other times."

Carin didn't say a word. She just looked back at her. It was as if Carin was challenging her. And suddenly, the choice was clear.

"I'm going to be asking you about your brother, Brian," she said, as calmly as if the name had been Dominic. She was sure now that Carin wanted to be able to swear on a lie detector test that Dominic wasn't beating her. The man had that much of a hold on her.

"I've been given some information by the people who hired me to test you. They indicated that you have a brother, and they want to know—"

Carin jumped up, her chair hitting the wall behind her. "No! I refuse to take this test." She was at the door, practically before Heather could blink. "I'm leaving," she said.

Heather didn't know if she meant the room or The Lemonade Stand.

"Wait." The word was a command, although she had no authority to command Carin to do anything. But the woman seemed to need something from her.

Maybe as badly as Heather needed to give it to her.

"Please," she said, when Carin paused with her hand on the doorknob. "Let's talk, just the two of us. I'll put the test aside for now. I'm not a counselor or an attorney."

"I have nothing to say." Carin opened the door.

"I know that Dominic threatened you, threatened to bring 'B' into it if you didn't lie on the stand last year about those 911 calls."

The woman swung around so fast, Heather barely had time to choke out the words. She'd cry later. She knew she would. But she couldn't let Carin walk back into that danger...

"Close the door," she said, when Carin seemed to be at a total loss. "Come back and sit down."

"Who told you that about B? Who else knows?" the battered woman asked, one eye swollen and sitting lower on her face than the other.

"I'm not at liberty to say." The words popped into her head. "I'm given information by the people who hire me," she explained again. "You're at liberty to refuse the test, to refuse to work with me, and then I'm out of it."

If she didn't talk to Heather now, there'd be no other chance.

Technically, anyway. Not unless Carin asked to see her again, and Cedar or Lila called her in.

Slowly, Carin moved back into the room, took her seat, shoulders hunched.

"You can't bring B into it," she said, almost begging now, although every other time they'd spoken, Carin had been filled with confidence. Odd for someone who'd been regularly beaten.

"You can't." The words were a whisper.

Carin bowed her head, started to cry. And Heather needed a call button to push. Needed Sara. Lila. Someone who'd be what this aching woman needed.

"Let me get someone," she said, moving to stand, and Carin sat up. Shook her head.

"No, please," she said. "Just give me a few minutes. I'll be fine. It's just…that story about your aunt…"

"It scared you?" she guessed.

Carin nodded. "But not for the reason you think…"

"What do I think?"

"That Dominic did this to me."

She did think that. Because she'd been told. But she wasn't completely certain.

"I think that someone besides Renaldo did that to you," she said. "And I'm right, aren't I?"

Carin stared at her, tears still dripping down her face. She shook her head again. Started to sob and then just as quickly collected herself. Took a deep breath.

"I don't know what to do anymore," she said, her voice barely a whisper now. "That's why I came here. Dominic…he actually knows where I am…"

Shocked, Heather wasn't sure whether to call Sara, Lila, Cedar or the police. The one thing she knew was that she wasn't equipped to…

She reached for her phone.

"Dom's not hurting me," Carin said. "He's helping me."

Phone in hand, Heather stopped. She was there to get the truth, and she had a very strong feeling it was about to spill all over her.

CHAPTER TWENTY-FOUR

"How is Dominic helping you?" How did an abuser convince his woman that he was helping her?

"My brother, Brian... I raised him after Mom died," Carin said. "I wanted them both, him and Chloe, but she'd been in some trouble, was in juvie at the time. When she got out, they took her into the system. But Brian was just a little guy. He'd turned eight right before Mom died and I was legally an adult. I had a place to live and a job, and they let him stay with me."

She'd been an eighteen-year-old kid, apparently alone in the world, raising an eight-year-old boy. And Dominic had helped her? Which made her feel indebted to him? To the point of taking his abuse silently? Based on the domestic violence culture, Heather could see that.

And she knew there were people at the Stand trained to help. Willing to help. Wanting to help. They just needed to know what they were helping with.

She stayed focused.

"He did great..." Her gaze was filled with

compassion as she looked up at Heather. "Kept out of trouble, graduated from high school with honors..." Lips trembling, Carin stopped, and then, after a deep breath, said, "Even got a partial scholarship to college. But Dom had said he'd pay his tuition. All Brian had to do was get a job for spending money..."

Dominic would pay the tuition, and Carin paid a different price? Brian was twenty-two. Probably graduating that coming year. If he'd already graduated, there'd be nothing to hang over Carin's head, right? Unless Dominic said she owed him for all the tuition he'd paid. Was that how he'd gained control of her? For money she couldn't pay back?

And she didn't want her little brother to know about?

Tears streamed down Carin's face, but she wasn't sobbing now. Or even struggling to breathe. She just sat there, quietly crying.

Heather reached across the table and squeezed her fingers. "Tell me, Carin. Tell me the truth. It really will help. The control is still yours, but you'll have others to share the burden with you. No one here can make you do anything, if you choose not to. But getting it out will help."

The tear-filled gaze locked on hers as Carin pulled her hand free.

"I know something has to be done." Carin's

words shocked her. They were so strong. So sure. "My time here at the Stand, the classes I've attended… I see what Dom's been telling me." She started to cry again. "I just…" Sobs shook her shoulders now. "I love him so much, and I'm all he's got…"

Wait, what *Dom* had been telling her?

The truth hit her. Hard. The question that remained was whether or not Carin was ready to express it. And try to get help.

"Who really hurt you, Carin?"

"Renaldo d-did…" Her voice trailed off, and then she reached for a tissue from the box on the table and raised it to her face. "But he wasn't going for me," she said.

The story was sounding exactly as it had since Carin had first come to the stand. But everything felt completely different.

Heather did her job; she sat and waited, reading nuances, listening for truths that hadn't yet surfaced.

And her heart ached. She could feel the threat of tears and held them back. Closed her eyes. Thought about yoga. Just yoga.

They were possibly on the brink of saving a life.

"When Brian was a freshman in college, he joined a fraternity. He'd never so much as smoked a joint, but on razz night, he kept up with the rest of them, wanting to fit in, I guess. To look cool.

He ended up in the hospital, in a coma. I'm not sure what happened. There was an investigation, but nothing came of it. He left the frat party, and no one knew what he did after that. He was found unconscious the next day, lying in his bed, in his dorm. Toxicology levels were high enough to kill him. It was like, instead of experimenting with substances in high school, he just did everything in one night."

She paused, inhaled a deep breath. "And when he came out of it, he…had the mentality of a six-year-old and…anger issues. The damage done to his brain… It was in the part that deals with emotional control. He's on meds, but they don't always work, and I won't tell his doctors about the incidents, because I know they'll try to take him away from me, lock him up someplace…"

It would all be in medical records. Which neither she nor Cedar had access to.

Lynn Bishop, the Stand's nurse, could see them if Brian was a patient here, but he wasn't. Carin was.

"He's such a sweet boy most of the time. He goes for months… He'll flare up, but I can usually calm him right down. It's only me he gets mad at, like he feels safe enough with me to let it all out or something." Carin quickly added, "It's not like he's a danger to anyone else."

Heather couldn't comment on that. Or even

begin to counsel the woman. Her undergraduate psychology degree hadn't prepared her for this.

"That day…we were at a cookout at Renaldo's. I ate the last piece of cake, not knowing Brian wanted it. He got so angry…stomped his feet, just couldn't get control of himself… I went up to him to try to take his hand, to calm him down and tell him I'd bake him a whole cake, but he was too far gone. Renaldo was trying to protect me. He was going after Brian, but I couldn't let him hit my little brother. I stepped into his punch, which gave Brian the chance to do what he does when he's upset with me. He grabbed me by the head and banged my face against whatever was closest. This time, it was an armchair. It had wooden trim. I think that's what broke my eye socket…"

The tears had slowed. Carin blew her nose. Sniffled. "He always just shoves me once, and then either I can get away or he stops. The next second, he's his usual caring and compassionate, big six-year-old self. And the few times in the past when it didn't stop…Dom made me promise if it happened and he wasn't around, I'd run next door and call the police. So I did. And then he'd make sure the reports went away. He just wanted me safe, not to press charges against B. The second B heard sirens, or saw a police car, he always ran and hid. But that last time, at Renaldo's, Dom was outside. B—that's what Dom calls him—

slammed me twice before Dom came in and got him off me. B never turns on him. Dom can always calm him down." She started to cry again. "But…he said this is the last time…"

And the year before, Carin told her, Dominic drew another line. He wasn't going to cast himself as an abuser to protect Carin's mentally impaired little brother. Because it was time to come clean about that.

And Carin wouldn't. Or couldn't.

The whole situation was filled with despair. And irony, too. That an alleged big-time drug dealer had been able to help raise a completely sober kid, and then have him go off to college and nearly die from a drug and alcohol overdose…

"Are you ready to talk to Sara now?" Heather quietly asked. She wanted so desperately to hug the other woman, but Carin needed more than hugs. Sara would know exactly what she needed, and know how to give it to her, as well.

Seeming to understand that, Carin nodded.

Heather immediately put out a call for help.

And within two minutes, help had arrived.

"WOULD YOU LIKE to schedule another appointment with Mr. Hines? Or is there anything else I can do, sir?" The receptionist's tone had changed completely since he'd entered the office earlier that morning.

What Cedar needed was for the rain to stop so he could get out to his car and make a phone call. The downpour had started while he was in with Hines, and while these storms typically passed very quickly, they didn't usually come up so early in the morning.

Only one other person, a suited man who appeared to be in his forties, waited in reception. He was sitting in the same chair he'd been in when Cedar had left the inner office. Cedar assumed the man was the appointment Hines had kept waiting...

It was curious, then, that he hadn't yet called the man back.

Cedar would've liked to eavesdrop on Hines's private sanctum right about then. Was he on the phone? Reporting Cedar's visit? To DiSalvo or Cedar-Jones? Calling his own attorney, just in case? Taking a swig from the half-empty scotch bottle that had been sitting on the wet bar in the corner of the room?

Cedar-Jones had reportedly told DiSalvo to tell Cedar about the illegal side-business—with the fish sales to a Japanese company—that he was running. DiSalvo had chosen not to, testing to see if Cedar was as good as Cedar-Jones claimed. So what else had the man not told him? What hadn't Cedar found?

Impatient to make that phone call, he said a silent "to hell with it" and darted out into the torrential downpour. By the time he was in the driver's seat of his SUV, his hair was dripping onto his forehead.

And his phone vibrated a message.

It was too early to be Heather, considering how long preinterview, the test, results and the post-interview usually took. And if it wasn't for the fact that he had a phone call to make, he would've left the cell in his pocket and worried about drying off.

It was a text message—from Heather.

We got the truth. Busy now. Will talk later. Just wanted you to know.

The one time he hadn't been waiting to hear from her, he had.

But the news was good. The best. Things seemed to be falling into place nicely. Exactly as he'd hoped. Counted on.

He had another important thing to do. He was going to find out what DiSalvo was up to and then call his father, let him know what was going on, make sure Cedar-Jones wasn't mixed up in anything with DiSalvo. He was also going to talk about taking himself off the case. If Cedar-Jones *was* involved somehow, then Cedar would do whatever was necessary to protect his father. He planned to let him know that, too. That Cedar had his back.

But first, he sent a text back to Heather.

Thank God. And thank you. Talk tonight.

He took a second to be thankful. For Carin's future safety. For Heather's success. Hoping he'd rid her of any sense of responsibility where the work she'd done on Dominic's trial and Carin Landry were concerned. Relief came and he allowed it. For Carin and Heather.

For himself, there was more to be done.

He had one less soul on his conscience.

But he was still gravely in debt.

AFTER A MEETING with Lila Mantle in her office at The Lemonade Stand, where she delivered a verbal summary of the report she'd write up later that afternoon, Heather made a dash in the rain to her car. She managed to get through the rest of the morning's work—an interview, test and post-interview all at once for a federal job application—and still be in time to have lunch with Raine and Lianna.

Her friends had called her the night before and asked if she wanted to meet them. Raine had spent the night and wasn't heading back until after lunch, and the three of them were getting together at a highly popular restaurant not far from the hospital where Lianna worked. While it was odd having Raine spend the night in town—and not visit with her—it was kind of nice, too, having the two of them close.

Still, she had to admit she felt left out. And yet...she didn't. They were each so vital to her, and it was as if two parts of her inner being had been separated and were now finally together. As if she was more whole because of their partnership.

The rain had long since stopped, the sun was out, and she hurried into the restaurant just a minute late. She'd seen Raine's car outside—hadn't seen Lianna's, but she'd only given a cursory glance. They were both there. Sitting side by side at a table with two chairs on either side.

They looked...cute.

As usual, she hugged them both hello, and then sat down across from them. Their waitress was there immediately—she'd obviously been watching for their third to arrive—and all three ordered Cobb salads with tea.

"What's wrong?" Lianna asked before she'd even set her purse on the seat next to her.

"Nothing's wrong. It's just been an emotional day..."

"You aren't wearing your ring."

She nodded. Had such a lot to tell them. But

she wanted to hear about them, too. "Charles and I broke things off for good last night." She told them about his visit to her office. "We realized we didn't *need* to get married. I didn't *need* to marry him," she finished.

Raine and Lianna exchanged glances, something she was going to have to get used to, apparently.

"We do," Raine said. "Not yet, of course. This is all still so new for both of us. We haven't even told my mom about us yet. But we've already talked about marriage someday. It's like she's what I've been looking for all this time." She smiled at Lianna. "I'm still struggling to wrap my mind around it all, but it feels so...right."

"She's my fireworks," Lianna added. "No more warm-bath sex."

While she was a bit uncomfortable with that last remark, she was also truly relieved. And happy. "This is what I've been waiting for with both of you. Too bad I didn't figure it out ..."

Raine shrugged. "Who knows if either of us would've been ready before now. Like, what if we'd tried this a few years ago and she hadn't figured out that while she was comfortable with Dex, he didn't bring passion to her life. And me... I don't think I was ready to admit I wasn't looking for a guy. I had to look and not find him to know that."

She made perfect sense, as usual.

Heather wondered whether it was possible that she and Cedar had been the right love at the wrong time. What if they'd met now, after he'd discovered his "win" addiction? After she'd realized that she'd set impossible expectations for anyone to live up to?

"Cedar didn't use my work to send an abuser back to hurt his girlfriend." She was still reeling from the news. Had actually told Lila about the whole thing when she'd gone in to give her report. Only because she'd been unable to hold back the tears that were threatening to fall under Lila's discerning stare.

"What?" Both girls leaned forward, focusing on her. Lianna in scrubs, Raine in black leggings and a crop top, both so beautiful to her in their constant support.

"I know," she said. "I mean, don't get me wrong... He thought he did. It's even worse than we believed it was, because he heard Dominic threaten her to get her to take the blame on the stand. Dominic wanted Carin to come clean about Brian. She wouldn't. She was protecting him at all cost. But Dominic wasn't going to take the blame. Cedar didn't know it was because of Brian, though. He just heard the threat and chose to ignore that part because it didn't have anything to do with his case. It just didn't turn out that his client was the abuser."

"Cedar heard him threaten her and did nothing?"

"I know," she said again. The man she'd loved, maybe still loved, had been acting so out of character, and she hadn't paid enough attention to know. "He was addicted to winning," she said now. "It doesn't excuse what he did—at all—but if your partner is suffering from substance abuse, you notice, right? So why didn't I notice?"

"I think you did," Raine told her. Raine had been there when she'd met Cedar. She'd been the one who'd been most involved in their lives. "You got on him more than ever when he didn't call, didn't show up at a function or showed up late. Didn't answer your calls. It was like you were the partner police, always watching to see if he'd fail. But you were doing it because he *was* failing, and you didn't know what to do about it."

"I guess we failed each other, huh?" she asked.

"He crossed a moral line," Lianna said.

"I know." And she did. She just wished... "He quit the firm," she said.

"He did not!" Raine's voice, normally so quiet, rose, and the people at the next table stared over at them.

"He quit?" Even Lianna seemed shocked by the announcement. "As in...took some time off, or walked away?"

"He walked away. They offered him a partnership to keep him, and he walked away."

"You're still in love with him," Raine's words, much softer now, fell between them.

"I might be. I think I probably am. That case, the one where he used me, was his last one. When he saw what he'd done, he quit. Cold turkey. Just quit. Passed all his open cases on to other lawyers and just walked out." She still couldn't believe it. Had awakened during the night and lain awake, thinking about it. "He donated a bunch of money to The Lemonade Stand because that was the shelter my family supported, and I was the one he'd done wrong."

She teared up again, as she said that part out loud.

"What's he doing now? If he's not practicing law?" Lianna didn't sound as cold as usual when Cedar was the topic of conversation, but she didn't sound warm and fuzzy, either.

Their salads arrived, but they sat on the table, untouched.

"He's working construction at the Stand right now. They're putting up more resident bungalows."

"Construction?" Lianna's voice oozed sarcasm. "Cedar? This is the same guy who left Christmas morning, before presents and breakfast, because a client of his had something he wanted to show him? Because his clients, his law world, was more important than family and… Christmas?"

She'd forgotten that and felt her heart tighten as the memory came flooding back. "He worked construction all through high school and college. He says, other than law, that's all he knows."

"And you're sure he's not telling you this to get you back? Or to sleep with him?" Raine stopped, her eyes wide. "You haven't slept with him, have you?"

"Of course not." She couldn't. Not with the past still such a sore spot between them. But she wanted to.

"You're sure he's really working construction? Not just giving you a load of bull?" Lianna's approach was more blunt.

"He wasn't actually going to tell me." She looked from one to the other. Was she being crazy here? Letting her feelings for Cedar come to life again? Letting him in at all—even as a friend? She'd learned her lesson. Paid dearly. Should she cut and run now that Carin's truth was out, and she and Cedar didn't need to be in contact anymore? "I stopped by his house to show him some files regarding the woman I told you about, and he was walking out the door in full garb. Knife on the belt. Work boots. Everything."

"Wow."

"I'll bet he was hot, huh?" Raine asked, but she wasn't smiling. Instead she looked concerned.

"Yeah. And I know. I'm in dangerous territory here." Again she glanced between the two of them. "But what if he's *my* fireworks? I don't want to spend the rest of my life with a man I don't need to marry."

"People make mistakes," Raine said. "Sometimes they're unfaithful, and it's horrible and painful, but it doesn't always mean the relationship ends. Sometimes the love is so strong that the couple finds a way to put it back together, and it's even stronger."

Probably not the words she needed to hear right then. But she soaked them in, clear to her soul.

"You think I should give him a chance?"

"No!" Lianna butted in. "At least…" Then she shook her head. "No. So he's working construction and he donated a chunk of money to the Stand. He has to see that what he did crossed a line, that it was horribly wrong. He has to want to change because he doesn't want to be that guy. Not because he misses you and wants you back."

Heather realized that. All of it. She nodded. And asked, "But how do you know? How do you know if he's changing because he sincerely has to, or because he misses me and sees quitting law as the only way to have another chance with me?"

"If a guy quits law for you, especially one who

was as addicted to it as Cedar was, I'd say that's a pretty strong avowal of love right there. Not many people get that kind of love in a lifetime," Raine said.

Lianna looked at her new partner. And then, with a tilt of her head, agreed. "Okay, so it's possible he's the good guy you fell in love with, deep down inside his dirty self somewhere. But he has to earn your trust back, Heather. Please...please... please...be careful?"

"I second that, sweetie," Raine added. "Cedar's a fire in your life, I'll give you that. Just make sure he doesn't get a chance to burn you again, okay?"

How did she do that? Except by cutting him out of her life?

Was that really what she should do?

Was her breakup with Charles, as well as Lianna and Raine's good but still shocking news, getting to her? Making her turn to Cedar because he felt so good at the moment?

Because she'd missed him so much?

Or *was* he her soul mate? One who'd screwed up and needed her support and forgiveness to find his redemption?

"But wait a sec," Lianna said, swallowing a bite of salad. "At the beginning, you started this whole thing today saying your work *didn't* help an abuser go free? The guy's been caught, then?"

She shook her head. Told her friends what she

could about Carin, about Dominic's support, as opposed to abuse, through the years.

"So what happens now?"

"Who knows?" Waving her fork in the air, she said, "Hopefully, the people at the Stand will help Carin get help for her brother, and for herself, in a way that's acceptable to her. Dominic's behind her. He just isn't behind her doing nothing anymore. They had a fight and she left, taking care to make sure he didn't know where she was. But then she got scared he'd ship her brother out and called him to tell him she was at a shelter doing what he asked. Getting help. And it's not like he's squeaky clean," she said. "The feds know what he's doing, and you have to believe that, at some point, they're going to get enough solid evidence to make a conviction stick. He has a lot of men in between him and the drugs, but from what I understand, everyone pretty much knows…"

She took a bite of lettuce. Chewed. Thought about Carin and Dominic. "I mean, I guess he could love Carin enough to get out of the business, if that's even possible—getting out, that is—but realistically, you think he's ever going to?"

"Not sure. But it sounds like Cedar loves *you* enough." Raine looked thoughtful.

Oh, God, she wanted to believe that, wanted to listen to her heart, give in to it, run with it straight into Cedar's arms.

But...what if...

"You ever hear of a big-time drug dealer just 'getting out'?" she asked.

She had to be realistic. About Dominic and Carin, and about Cedar and her. To have realistic expectations. She wasn't seeing life as a fairy tale anymore.

"Still, it's cool that he stood by her, took in her brother, took care of them both..."

"Just because a guy does a bad thing doesn't mean he can't do good ones, too," Lianna pointed out in her usual matter-of-fact manner. And she was right.

Too right.

These good things Cedar was doing didn't mean he wouldn't also repeat the bad.

"Think of all of the people he hurts, keeping drugs out on our streets..." Lianna continued, but Heather didn't need to hear any more. She'd already gotten the point.

CHAPTER TWENTY-FIVE

No one picked up when Cedar called the number he'd been given by Hines. Three times before lunch he'd tried, and three times there'd been no answer. And no voice mail.

He was clearly calling a burner phone.

Or a number that he'd been given as a ploy to get rid of him while Hines figured out what to do?

Like skip the country?

While the thought was drastic, not like him at all, he wondered if what he'd learned could be reason for someone to want him to go away. The tax fraud was a relatively small issue compared to the mentions of HHC and the shell companies that wove in and out of each other with no apparent explanation. And HHC being billed as a service, a cleaning supplier, a food provider. Even, at one point, a passenger on a tiger-hunting expedition. Disgusting as that was.

He'd really started to focus on the whole HHC thing, which had been the night before, after realizing that DiSalvo had lied to him about it—and because he hadn't wanted to think about Heather.

He texted Heather, letting her know he could talk when she was available. He was anxious to hear about her morning with Carin. Wanted to know where things stood now.

Was Carin pressing charges against Dominic?

Would Cedar be getting a call?

Telling Dominic he wouldn't represent him would give him a second's pleasure.

Trying to figure out whether DiSalvo's lies were worth taking himself off his case, Cedar made himself a sandwich and sat down with it and a glass of milk. He went over what he knew and studied his flow charts one more time, to see if he could sort out what he was missing.

And every half hour, he called the number he'd been given. Hines had until two o'clock that afternoon. If Cedar's call hadn't been answered by then, he was going back up north.

At one o'clock, his call was picked up. A text buzzed, too, but when he heard the voice at the other end of the line, he didn't look to see who'd texted.

"Cedar, I'm sorry I missed your earlier calls. I was in a recording session."

"Mr. Cedar-Jones?"

"Really, you don't need to call me that. Randy works fine. Hold on a sec, I have another call coming in."

Cedar was confused as hell. Hines had him call Cedar-Jones? On a burner phone?

At the moment, those facts faded as he realized he'd just sounded foolish, a grown man of thirty-four, who'd never actually met his father, calling him by his last name. He'd just been so shocked to hear Cedar-Jones answer the phone.

He'd always thought of the man as his father. His mother had always referred to him as "your father."

"Sorry about that!" His father was back, sounding relatively cheerful, considering the fact that his son had just called him on a burner phone.

The thought kept repeating itself to Cedar, as though his normal intelligence was on a break.

"What's going on?" he asked. Now that they were finally in touch, he didn't want Cedar-Jones to think his son was some kind of geek. Or anything other than the intelligent, capable man he was.

He'd won acquittals for some of the biggest players in the California money world, and for others, including Dominic, a suspected drug lord, whom the FBI had been after for years and been certain they'd finally gotten. Certain they'd had an airtight case.

Until Cedar had been able to turn a couple of witnesses, putting doubts in their minds, which left doubts with the jury. He'd put a new twist on the timeline, as well, showing that Dominic had been on vacation in Italy when a major deal he was supposed to have been involved with went down. Dominic *had* been in Italy; he'd just left late one night and returned the next morning by private plane. No one knew he'd been on that plane except Cedar and the drug dealers involved. There'd been other things. He couldn't think about all that now.

"Alvin Hines called me today with his panties in a wad," Cedar-Jones said, a note of amusement in his tone. "You must be a helluva convincing guy, because Hines doesn't get rattled. Makes him good at what he does."

Cedar hadn't found the man the least bit impressive. Hines had been quaking in his shoes before Cedar even got started. Still off his game, he refrained from saying so.

"You're even better at your job than I realized," Cedar-Jones was saying. "I'm real proud you're my son and I had you out there to call..."

His father had just acknowledged their genetic ties? The same month Heather had said she needed him in her life?

And that Carin Landry was going to be safe?

Had he died and gone to heaven instead of hell?

Or...could it be possible that he'd earned his way out of purgatory? At least enough to experience moments of good will again?

"So, here's what I need you to do now. Hold on again." Randy's voice had changed, become more like that of a general ordering his troops. Cedar figured that was par for the course for a man as rich and famous as Randy. Probably had an entire staff at his beck and call, every minute of every day.

When he was a kid, he used to imagine what it would be like, visiting his father. Being waited on, rather than having to set the table and do dishes for him and his mom every night. Having anything he wanted.

He almost chuckled aloud. He'd forgotten he'd ever thought that. Must've been when he was around eight or nine. After that, he'd been happy to help out his mother, who'd sacrificed everything for him and had done it cheerfully. Lovingly.

She'd been at every game he'd ever played. Supported every choice he'd made for his future, even the ones that had failed—like the time he'd figured he'd be a professional surfer. And the summer he'd said he was going to be a truck driver. She'd helped him do the research. Had talked excitedly about the possibilities he'd have on the open road.

She'd left him to decide if that was the kind of life he wanted. And she'd been so pleased when he'd decided he should go to college instead.

"Cedar, you there?" Cedar-Jones was back, still sounding brusque.

"Yes." Didn't Randy get it yet? He'd always be there. He loved the guy. Cedar knew him through the internet. But mostly through his mother. And Randy's music.

He knew every word to every song his father had ever written.

He knew him through their shared genes.

"Here's what you're going to do," Cedar-Jones said. "You show up at the airport tomorrow to meet DiSalvo as planned. You act shocked that he's not there. You plead ignorance to the officials there to arrest him, and you go on your way."

Wait. What? "I'm sorry, I—"

"It's not going any further than DiSalvo," Randy said. "He's the fall guy."

The fall guy?

The *fall* guy?

"What?"

"Don't worry about him," Randy said with a chuckle, lightening his tone again. If Cedar had been in a courtroom, he'd have suspected he was being played.

"He volunteered for the position. Between you and me, I think he was hoping things would work out this way. He's set for life without ever lifting another finger…"

"Wait. I don't—"

"Your trip to Egypt, Cedar. Think."

He'd gone to meet with a guy who'd skipped the country to avoid serious federal charges that most likely would have put him in jail for life. He hadn't been Cedar's client, though. Cedar's client was a man who'd been able to stay out of prison with evidence the man in Egypt had given him. As planned. All evidence would point to the "witness" in Egypt who would never be found...

"DiSalvo's already gone, Cedar. It'll be all over the news in the morning. You found HHC. Went for Hines. You weren't giving up. You can't be the only good attorney out there, and we just couldn't take a chance that someone else would make the same connections. It would've been good to keep DiSalvo here. We're going to have to find someone else who's willing to play his part, but for now...this works."

What worked? He wasn't...

All over the news? With Cedar right there, on record, involved in the scheme?

"Just go to the airport. Act shocked. Leave. And you're done."

Done? What about...

He'd thought he was at least going to meet his father somewhere in this process. And...

On the news. Him, part of a plot to help someone escape charges? A successful plot. Heather would read about it. And while he could talk until he was dead, there was no way she'd believe him. The proof pointed in another direction.

She already knew he was unreliable. Knew he'd managed to fool her.

She knew him to be capable of bending the law to keep moneyed people out of jail.

Done?

He wasn't done. Not by a long shot.

Randy underestimated him if he thought Cedar was just going to do what he was told. He was there to help. Could do a helluva lot more than act shocked and disappear.

He could protect Randy and let DiSalvo rot. Randy had to give him a chance to get DiSalvo back in town for his arraignment and trust Cedar to take care of the rest.

He told him so.

"Believe me, you're at the top of my list," Randy said. "If something comes up again, you're the first one I'm calling."

"You already called. Let me help. Tell me what's going on. If you're in some tax trouble with DiSalvo... Is it something to do with his Asian fish interests?"

Randy didn't reply.

It wasn't until that moment, until that silence, that it hit him. He'd asked about HHC, and they'd sent DiSalvo out of the country.

For such a sharp man, a killer defense attorney, Cedar had been embarrassingly slow on the uptake.

He'd asked about HHC, and he'd been given the number to a burner phone. With his father on the other end of it.

HHC.

Harold Horatio Cedar. His father's real name. He'd forgotten until then…because he hadn't been looking in that direction. He'd been out to protect his father. Not to suspect him.

Harold Horatio Cedar. He'd never thought of him that way. It wasn't public knowledge. Not even on Wikipedia. Cedar-Jones had his name legally changed decades ago and the records sealed. In a drunken stupor, the night Cedar had been conceived, he'd told Cedar's mom what it was.

And when Cedar had been complaining as a kid about being made fun of for his name, asking her why she couldn't have picked the Randy or the Jones part, she'd told him she'd named him Cedar, instead of Randy or Jones, because Cedar had been the only part of his father's birth name that he'd kept.

"HHC is code for things being shipped to or from you," he said now. Once he'd opened his eyes to the possibility that his father was using him, that Cedar-Jones wasn't just an incredibly talented singer but a conman, it was right there. Plain as day.

Maybe it wouldn't have been for some. But Cedar had his own special talent.

He'd followed all the smallest line items, hunted out all the buried pieces…and then failed to put the puzzle together.

"I'm a bit of a collector of rare, mostly illegal, items," Cedar-Jones bragged. "And I like to hunt illegal game. But I dare you to prove any of that." It was the smugness that got to him.

Really got to him. Cedar could easily have been recording the call. But Cedar-Jones was shrewd, and knew enough about Cedar to trust that he was such a pansy for his dad that he wasn't recording him. You didn't secretly record someone you were protecting.

Randy knew Cedar well because Cedar had been calling him and reporting in for all those years. The more brutal the win, the more eager he was to call…

All those years, when there'd been no response, his father had been listening.

Randy wouldn't have worried about a recording anyway. In California, recorded calls were only admissible if both parties agreed to the recording. Even phone conversations. It was the two-party consent law.

Cedar remembered the rare bronze instrument, more than a thousand years old, he'd read about in the DiSalvo report—it had had the HHC label.

He thought about DiSalvo saying Cedar was being tested. And the whole truth came crashing in.

DiSalvo hadn't been testing him; Cedar-Jones had. DiSalvo had been ready to skip the country all along, if he had to. Cedar-Jones had been trying to find out what else, from DiSalvo's tax troubles, would be discoverable by prosecutors if DiSalvo stayed.

He'd wanted to know if their operation could remain intact.

"Just do as you're told, Cedar, eh? Do it for me," Randy added. "There's another call coming...we'll talk..."

A click followed, and Cedar was left sitting in his office, feeling like the world's biggest fool.

His phone rang almost immediately afterward, and he grabbed it up off the table, looking to the screen with some inane thought that it would be Cedar-Jones calling back, making things right.

It was Heather.

He didn't answer.

THANKFUL FOR A job that completely consumed her, Heather left work with a mind cleared of all personal stuff. She'd done a couple more employment tests; the local police force was hiring, and while polygraph tests weren't proven accurate enough for some uses, even the federal government still used them for select applications—Border Patrol, CIA, FBI. So did the Santa Raquel Police Force.

And she'd had an interview with a couple, Jenny and Tom Silverman, who'd wanted her to administer the test to the husband—his offer—to prove to his wife that he wasn't cheating on her.

Tom had been caught in a hotel room with another woman, both fully clothed, and claimed that, yes, while she was a prostitute, he had neither hired her nor availed himself of her services. Someone had sent the woman to his room. Probably the same someone who'd alerted the police to illegal activity in a hotel that did not support soliciting of that nature.

He'd been arrested, but immediately released, with no charges filed.

Jenny was having difficulty believing that he hadn't hired the woman.

Although she hadn't been in the room while Heather administered the test, Jenny had approved all the questions and could hear her husband's responses. And she was present as Heather told her that when her husband stated that he loved his wife, that he'd never been unfaithful to her and that he'd never hired a prostitute, there'd been no tells, not even a little blip. Nothing indicating that he might be stretching the truth. Tom had passed the test.

They'd left her office hand in hand.

She was still smiling as she walked out soon after them. So nice to see love work out. To know that couples could be honest with each other—and that even if a couple had doubts between them, there were ways to deal with that.

Doubts were normal. Add extenuating circumstances and...

She stopped a few feet short of her car, feeling a whoosh of heat that had nothing to do with the late-afternoon California heat radiating from the blacktop.

Doubts were normal. And when you added in circumstances that gave real cause for doubt, it didn't have to mean the love had died. It meant the relationship had a problem that had to be tended to.

Together, if the couple wanted to stay together. Tom had understood Jenny's doubts. She'd had cause, although he hadn't had anything to do with the cause.

And Jenny had given him the benefit of the doubt and agreed to the testing.

She unlocked her car and got inside.

She'd been thinking, just before she'd gotten involved with her work, that she'd call Cedar as soon as she was done. Thinking they could meet for dinner someplace.

Maybe even at her place.

If nothing else, they had Carin's breakthrough to celebrate. To talk about.

She used speed dial to call him. No answer. She left a voice mail and thoughts continued to consume her.

Dominic hadn't been guilty.

But Cedar had.

He'd done something really wrong.

And so had she.

Because she'd never given him a chance to repair the damage. She'd never given their love a chance to heal the breach he'd caused.

Instead of facing the challenge together with him, she'd walked out.

There was no guarantee they would've made it through the challenge. But even without her standing beside him, giving him that chance, he'd set forth to repair his damage.

With her, but with others, too. And not just recently, not just since she'd invited him to her engagement party, but before that.

Way back when he'd done the damage. He'd paid someone to get that Lemonade Stand card to Carin. Even before any soul-searching he might have done after Heather's desertion.

It was that card that had ultimately allowed Carin to seek the help she needed. Where Carin, Dominic and Brian went from there, she didn't know, but she trusted the great people at The Lemonade Stand to do everything they possibly could to provide a solution that not only kept Carin safe, but helped Brian, too. Cedar had also trusted them, way back, when she'd thought his moral compass was skewed and his heart corrupt.

He'd made a choice, out of the goodness of that same heart, to pay a man to get the card to Carin.

Which meant his heart wasn't totally corrupt.

Driving now, aimlessly following the coast road, Heather started to cry. Had to pull over until much of the pent-up misery inside her spent itself. She'd missed him so much.

She'd been so devastated by his betrayal and in denial that it was even possible for her Cedar to do that to her.

But things happened.

People weren't perfect.

Good people got caught up in bad things.

And sometimes love was strong enough to heal damage caused by the mistakes people made.

Oh, God, she was so confused.

Wanted Cedar so badly.

Wanted to be there for him, to support him, if he was truly the man she'd believed him to be, and had just swung off course. If he was honestly trying to make his way back, she *had* to be there for him.

There was no other option.

She put her car in gear and slowly headed back into town.

CHAPTER TWENTY-SIX

CEDAR STOPPED BY his office to pick up some files, and then went to LA for the night. He was due to meet with DiSalvo in the morning, according to his plans with his client, and since he hadn't yet heard from him, he was going to be in town and available.

Maybe.

Mostly he didn't trust himself to be close to Heather. Suspecting that he'd end up trying to pour his heart out and beg her to believe him.

To what end? To serve himself? Grab what he most wanted and needed—her?

Be the selfish bastard he'd somehow become?

Yesterday, he'd wanted to believe redemption could be his. Less than twenty-four hours later, he was no longer sure it was possible.

He'd made his bed, and all that. Defined himself by his choices.

And while he hadn't knowingly agreed to be part of Cedar-Jones's grand scheme, the circumstances that had led him to that point had been his own fault. He'd become the man Cedar-Jones could use.

Which had been his goal pretty much his whole life.

So there'd been no way he could have known that turning into a shady defense attorney would be exactly what the man needed... He'd been out to show his father, his *famous* father, that he could be the best at what he did. That he could be talented and rich, too. Have powerful people vying for him.

Well he'd done that. And become what he'd become.

He'd done all he could for Carin. She'd called him late that afternoon. She was going to look at some possible homes for Brian—ones with male caregivers who were trained to deal with occasional bouts of violence in a nonthreatening manner. She saw now that this was for Brian's own good, as well. If he seriously hurt Carin, killed her, he'd end up in jail. She hadn't made the decision to commit him to a home yet, but she knew that something had to be done and was finally committed to finding that something. She couldn't protect him anymore. She thanked Cedar, somewhat tearfully. Dominic had been there and added his thanks, as well. Cedar didn't want the man's gratitude. He just wanted that part of his life to be done.

And the future?

Glancing at the files on the seat beside him, he figured he'd find his answer there. Since he'd sold the apartment he and Heather had shared in LA, he checked into a hotel he'd never been to with her—not for any function, or even a meal— and threw his overnight bag on the luggage rack. Pulled a two-shot bottle of scotch out of the mini-bar, and then spread his folders on the desk.

His laptop was next. Uncapping the bottle, he poured a shot's worth in a glass, without bothering to get the ice. Took a sip. Stood there, hand on his hip, looking at his work space.

He moved over to the window, glanced out at the magnificently sparkling signs and vehicles that reflected the last of the sun's light. Soon he'd be staring at miles of lights, as far as he could see.

Cedar-Jones had said "it" would be all over the news in the morning. A man as powerful as he was could certainly arrange such a thing. Through someone who went to someone else, who went to someone else. In the end, Cedar-Jones wouldn't know how the piece actually got on the news, or through whom. It didn't matter to him.

Cedar got that now.

He could almost write the piece himself. Something about a tax audit that led to the un-covering of one of the state's largest fraud and money-laundering cases in years. All of DiSalvo's business dealings would come to light—and he'd be connected to the mess that wasn't really his, through the companies Cedar had just spent a week sorting out. His adventure company would be used as the cover for everything, since that was the one holding that hadn't been connected to anything else.

Except HHC, providing food for a boat.

His illegal selling of tuna in Asia would probably be exposed, as well. And other things of which Cedar had no knowledge. He knew how this worked. Cedar-Jones and his group were on the verge of being caught, so they were going to dump everything and blame it all on DiSalvo.

Paper trails had been carefully established all along to do so.

According to Cedar-Jones, the man had volunteered for the job. And he'd bet that hadn't happened just that week.

Cedar would bet it had happened three years ago—at the point he'd found where the roots of the entangled crime tree started. He could almost see it...rich, bored men on an illegal fishing adventure, getting drunk and concocting a way to keep the adventure going, while making a shitload of money. Or to keep Cedar-Jones's adrenaline running high and making a shitload of money.

And Cedar had walked right into the plan. Had

probably been their safety net for most of those three years without even knowing it.

He'd been his father's protection. Just as he'd wanted to be.

Glass in hand, Cedar watched the sun lower over a city that, with Hollywood, probably held more dreams than any other in the nation.

And had the filth and crime and devastation that went hand in hand with broken dreams.

His among them. If he'd ever been fool enough to believe in dreams.

He was the attorney of record for DiSalvo. His name would be on the internet, too, along with DiSalvo's. And on news stations, if he'd pegged his father right. They'd probably flash up some stock photo of him, looking menacing as he gave closing statements to a jury.

Being on the news wasn't new to him. In the past, he'd made an event out of watching himself. Critiquing himself.

It was going to look like he was representing a known criminal.

Emptying his glass, he stood there, still in dress pants, a hand in his pocket.

He knew exactly how it was all going to look to Heather. He'd told her that he didn't have any clients. Wasn't taking on cases.

But he had. Technically. As DiSalvo's attorney. That would be the proof. The rest was his word against...whose? Cedar-Jones's? It wasn't like she'd be able to reach DiSalvo.

Not that it would've come to that.

She'd see the news, and it would be all over. She'd figure everything he'd said the past week had been lies.

Cedar poured the other shot. Returned to the window.

He could call Heather. Give her a heads-up.

But again, what for? To serve his own ends?

He had nothing solid to offer her—other than assets that had meant so little to her, she'd walked away without taking a single thing. He couldn't swear that he was the man he wished he was. That he'd ever be that man.

He was working on it.

But he might fail.

"Ha!" His sarcastic chortle sounded weak in that elegant room. "The great Cedar Wilson, a man addicted to the win, fails at life."

Shaking his head, he tried to imagine a scenario in which he explained his current situation to the woman he loved. How far-fetched it would seem. After all these years, with no contact whatsoever, Cedar-Jones suddenly calls him? Getting her to believe that would be about as likely as her believing he was no longer working as a defense attorney. Especially with his name down as attorney of record on a case with charges so new, the defendant hadn't yet been arrested or formally arraigned...

Heather had watched him call Cedar-Jones after each trial. She knew the man never picked up. Never returned his calls.

He'd seen the compassion in her eyes slowly turn into pity over the years. She'd never bad-mouthed the man who'd sired him, but her low opinion of Cedar-Jones had come through in other ways. Like the fact that she wouldn't listen to his music.

Cedar didn't want her pity.

Didn't want anyone's pity.

Including his own.

The morning would come. Either DiSalvo would call as planned to arrange an airport meet, or he wouldn't. The news would happen, or it wouldn't.

And Heather would want to speak with him, or she wouldn't.

He couldn't control others. And even if he could, he'd made the choice not to. Not anymore.

He would only attempt to control his own destiny.

So the question was...did he do as his father asked and show up at the airport? He was already cooked with Heather. He couldn't influence the news media. He'd show up there—either in a stock photo or a photo of him standing alone at the airport, waiting for a client who wasn't going to appear.

The real question, the only question was…did he continue to protect his father? Did he stay in Cedar-Jones's good graces?

He had until morning to decide.

With that last thought, Cedar emptied the contents of the glass down his throat, pulled out the desk chair and sat down to plan his future.

One old case at a time.

HEATHER WAITED MOST of the night for Cedar's call. She'd left a voice mail. Had even driven by his house, but hadn't let herself in the gate.

She'd heard from Carin…and knew she'd spoken with Cedar earlier—right about the time Heather had been with Jenny and Tom. Carin was staying at the Stand for a little while longer, because going home to Brian might persuade her to keep him, interfere with her ability to think clearly where he was concerned, and because she needed the counseling they offered there. But Dominic had come in to see her—at a place not far from the Stand. An arranged visit. He'd already been and gone, and she'd been back at the Stand before Heather left work.

She'd heard from Raine, too, who'd wanted to follow up with her after their lunch conversation, afraid she'd thrown Heather right back into Cedar's arms.

Along with the unwitting help from Jenny and Tom, that might have been the case—if Cedar had been around.

As it was, he was showing her that not everything had changed. They'd been back in each other's lives less than two weeks, and he was already failing to call.

And to return her calls.

If he hadn't answered Carin's call, she'd have worried that something had happened to him. Instead, she spent the evening working on her own mind control. Her expectations were too high. She'd made relatively small things much bigger than they'd needed to be.

Her job was to keep herself occupied. Be a friend to Cedar, rather than needing a friend. So she cleaned the bungalow, blaring songs from her high school days and singing along to them. Not a single Cedar-Jones hit among them.

She lit a candle and, with a glass of wine, took a hot bath.

All the while keeping her phone close by.

They weren't a couple. Didn't have to talk every night.

But they'd been on an intense quest to save a woman's life. Together. They'd been on the quest together.

Their work had led to an incredibly emotional culmination.

Surely she could expect to at least have a debriefing about that.

On and off through those long, dragging hours, she got more and more annoyed. The least he could do was acknowledge that his text that morning had said "talk tonight."

But if something *had* come up, she had to be reasonable, give him a chance. Trust that he'd be in touch soon…

By midnight, without so much as a text message, she was just plain worried.

In her lightest-weight, spaghetti-strap nightie, she sat up in the queen-size bed she'd purchased along with the bungalow, stared at her phone, and then, after more than a minute had passed, tapped her messaging app. Started typing. You okay?

The response came immediately.

Yes. And I apologize. Did it again, didn't I? Didn't think about the fact that you'd worry.

He had no reason to expect her to worry about him right now. Not based on one call he hadn't made. The realization had been there all night, as she'd tried to slow herself down. Calm her pounding heart.

No expectations. She typed. Deleted. Then she typed again.

Just because of Carin, I expected you'd call. Got worried when you didn't.

His response came.

And I should have called. Once again, I apologize.

She was relieved that he was fine. And engaging with her. But Heather still didn't feel satisfied. Or ready to lie down and sleep. She stared at the phone again. Wanting to say something else, not knowing what it should be. Or if it should be at all.

If he was truly working on becoming the person she'd always believed he was inside, if he had just slipped up, made mistakes, then she wanted to be there for him. Needed to be there for him.

Just as Jenny and Tom had stood by each other. Not because she and Cedar were necessarily going to get married, but because that was the kind of love she believed in.

And she loved Cedar.

Lianna and Raine had recognized what she couldn't see in herself. Which was why they'd been so worried. And refused to believe her when she'd insisted she was over him.

You in bed? His question buzzed in before she could decide what to do.

Yeah. Should she ask him if he was, too? So they could be in bed together?

She got warm and wet just thinking about it. Thought about phone sex. They'd done it once when he'd been away, interviewing an expert witness for a case. While not nearly as satisfying as having him right there with her, in her...it had been...pretty damned good.

Sleep well. He texted.

Disappointment surged. You, too.

She wanted phone sex. As a prelude to being back in his arms. She needed Cedar. Needed to marry him.

He wasn't asking. Hadn't ever asked, but at the moment, that wasn't the point. The point was that he was the man she *needed* to marry. As opposed to one she only wanted to marry.

She could phone him. He'd been waiting for her to call the shots ever since he'd come back into her life. Even that, his return, had been prompted by her when she'd invited him to her engagement party.

Their work with Carin was finished. They no longer had an excuse to speak. If she didn't prompt something, it very probably wouldn't happen...

But he hadn't called all night. Never mind that

she'd phoned and left a message. By his own admission, he hadn't thought about the fact that she might be worried. Clearly he'd moved on to something else.

Or *someone* else.

The idea hit her like a ton of bricks. What if he'd been with someone?

Not that she blamed him. He was gorgeous and free.

And even if he was…he'd texted her right back.

Yes. That was true. He'd texted her right back.

And told her to sleep well.

They didn't need to rush things. Absolutely shouldn't rush things.

Cedar wasn't pressuring her. Wasn't going to pressure her. Because he felt the need to back off, let her make the decisions.

And maybe…just maybe…he didn't trust her completely, either. Because she'd let him down, too.

She'd run out when he'd made his big blunder, instead of giving him a chance to see the error of his ways, try to correct himself and give their love, their relationship, a chance to heal.

The truth was hard to see sometimes. And even harder to face. Particularly when you didn't have any emotional distance.

She wanted to be more than friends with Cedar. Much more. It was only fair to tell him that. But not tonight.

And maybe not the next.

Maybe they just needed to spend some time together. To heal slowly.

Sleep well. She read his words once more.

She lay down, gave sleep a try.

And thought about him instead.

CHAPTER TWENTY-SEVEN

THE PHONE WAS RINGING. Pulling herself out of a sound sleep, Heather reached an arm from under the comforter and felt for the phone charger on her nightstand. Then she opened her eyes.

It was light.

That was the first shock. She usually woke up before dawn. Before her alarm.

Lianna was calling. At—she checked—six in the morning.

"Can you put on some coffee and spare a minute? I need to talk."

Out of bed, and on her way to the kitchen already, she said, "Of course," and wasn't surprised when she heard a click instead of goodbye.

It wasn't the first time her friend had shown up at her door first thing in the morning. That had happened in grade school. And then again, a couple of times in junior high and high school. But now, with Raine in the picture...

The second shock came when Lianna's knock sounded on the door before Heather had even had a chance to get a K-Cup in the holder. Her friend must've been right outside.

With her heart pounding, she hurried to the door. If Lianna and Raine had had a fight...or, God forbid, something had happened to Raine...

Nothing had happened to Raine. She was standing there with Lianna, looking more worried than Heather had seen her in a long time.

Nauseous and ready-to-cry worried.

"What?" she asked, reaching out a hand as she opened the door. Raine took it, and Lianna ushered all three of them into Heather's living room.

"I...the coffee..." She knew the words were inane as she heard them. It was as if her subconscious was trying to put off the inevitable.

Raine sank to the couch, pulling Heather with her.

Standing in front of them, Lianna had the TV remote in her hand, pointing it at the flat screen.

Heather wanted to ask what was going on, but didn't want to know the answer any sooner than she had to. It was going to be bad.

Her brigade was there, ready to hold her up. She knew the ropes. Had been on the other side of brigade duty many times. For both of them.

Was it her parents? Had there been an accident?

Wouldn't the police have come and told her? Before they put it on the news?

Had there been another terrorist attack? Was

that it? Lianna had spent the night with her the night before the 9/11 attack. It had been early morning on the West Coast, when the first plane had hit. They'd still been asleep until her mother had knocked on their door to tell them what was going on. They'd lain there together, watching the news with horror…

Lianna chose a local news station. The announcer was discussing something plebian about an expected electric company rate hike. She didn't care about her electric bill at the moment, so she sat, clutching Raine's hand, feeling the warmth of Lianna's body on her other side, wishing she had a glass of water.

Her mouth was dry. Her throat was dry.

Wanting the damned electric story to end, she looked down at the scroll, at the bottom of the screen, testing herself to see if she could get the words read before they went past. Whatever it was didn't matter; it was just to help her remain calm.

Raine wasn't giving her the usual yoga instructions.

It had to be terrorists.

But if it was…wouldn't that be the only thing on TV?

On 9/11, the news had taken over everything else.

With minute-to-minute updates scrolling at the bottom of the screen.

Cedar Wilson…

The name caught her eye. On her television screen. Scrolling past.

And everything inside her stopped. Just stopped. She couldn't breathe. Wasn't even sure her heart was beating.

Had *Cedar* been in an accident? There'd be no reason for police to call *her*.

Lianna always turned on the news the second she woke up in the morning. She must have seen it.

Waiting for the scroll to come around again, she sat there stiffly. Squeezing Raine's hand.

"Breathe, sweetie." Raine's words reached her from a long way off. "Deep breath in…deep breath out…"

Raine kept repeating the words. Taking note of the instructional tone, Heather did as she was told. Took a deep breath. Let it out. Took in another. Slowly.

Started to focus again. The words on the screen were about some huge fraud scheme that had been exposed…a warrant having been issued…and the suspect skipping the country before he could be arrested and charged…

She tried to pay attention. To be ready for Cedar's name.

Her friends were there. She was aware of them. But couldn't take her gaze off that screen.

The announcer had finished the electricity story, but seemed to be echoing the scroll, talking about the Dean DiSalvo character who'd apparently disappeared from the country on a private jet in the black of the night…

And then—a picture of Cedar was on the screen. It was one she recognized. It'd been taken in court, a couple of years before.

But…what did he have to do with this DiSalvo guy?

Another second or two, and she had her answer.

And knew why her friends had rushed right over.

The television went blank, Lianna dropped beside her, and her two best friends became the bread to her lifeless sandwich.

CEDAR DIDN'T GET a call from DiSalvo. In his heart of hearts, he'd known he wouldn't. Up most of the night, looking through cases, he'd faced dawn with a new direction.

He'd specialized in white-collar crime. He'd helped a lot of cheaters not only get away with having cheated, but had basically taught them how to be better at it.

He could take the cases one at a time. Try to find a way to expose the guilty without risking his license or doing anything illegal.

Not that he wasn't willing to risk it in terms of himself, but if he didn't mind his p's and q's, those who were doing wrong could get away with it because of his interference. The good cases he'd won could suffer, could be reopened, if he stepped too far wrong.

But what if he looked at the larger picture? What if, instead of somehow righting each individual wrong, he turned away from those cases, and offered his services to those who were fighting the same fight?

The plan was still more jelly than anything else, but he could put together a proposal, visit with a higher-up he knew at the FBI. Run it by the District Attorney's office. He could be the guy behind the scenes, following every single thread of evidence, putting together the flowcharts, finding the gaps—basically everything he'd always done, but doing it for the good guys.

He'd still be helping those who were innocent, because he could prove their innocence before they ever went to court. And once charges were filed, he'd use his skills to help the prosecutor make them stick.

There were kinks in the plan. Logistics. Things he'd have to figure out.

But it could work.

That was his bottom line.

He'd be using his talent, doing what he loved, but he'd stay in the background. He wouldn't get credit for the win.

He showered, packed his bag and was just leaving the room when his phone rang.

He hadn't turned on the news. But he was sure the story had broken.

Expecting to see Heather's number—to get his final kiss-off—he reached for his cell, but paused. He was prepared.

Had been preparing himself all night.

He was paying for the choices he'd made.

He'd had a week with her...a few days of friend's status.

He'd been able to help her heal.

And maybe even saved her from a passionless marriage.

So the wound in his heart was raw all over again. It wasn't like he was ever going to recover. Heather was his forever woman. He'd blown it.

Four rings. Six and it would go to voice mail. He pulled out the phone. Took a look.

The screen showed *unknown number*.

Someone from the press, wanting a statement, most likely. He'd already figured he'd find the voice mail on his office phone overloaded. Hadn't bothered to check messages. Or delete any to make room for more.

His cell number was private, but there were ways to find pretty much anything if you were diligent enough. There were reporters in LA who were that diligent...

Five rings.

"Yeah." He'd cut things off at the start. "No comment" was the only answer anyone would be getting out of him.

"You disappointed me."

Not a reporter.

Not Heather, either.

But he knew the voice.

Harold Horatio Cedar.

He hadn't done as his father had ordered. He hadn't gone to the airport.

"You've been disappointing *me* since the day I was old enough to understand that my father didn't have time to meet me."

Randy Cedar-Jones was a player. He played instruments—and people.

No more, as far as Cedar was concerned.

"I'd insist on a paternity test, in the hope that it might come out negative, but I'm not going to take a chance that it would be positive and the news would get out." He might have the man's name. His genes. Even his drive to succeed. But that didn't mean he had to be him.

He wasn't going to live in a shady world. The win wasn't worth it.

"Then I guess we have no more to say to each other," Cedar-Jones said.

"Not at the moment we don't."

And if they met again, it might not be to Cedar-

Jones's liking. Certainly it wouldn't be at his bidding. It was possible that Cedar would never be able to connect enough dots to make a solid line, one that would see the man prosecuted, but he had a pretty damned good start. Because Cedar-Jones hadn't hired him. He'd been DiSalvo's attorney of record. Only DiSalvo had attorney-client privilege.

"Don't bother calling the number you have for me again," Cedar-Jones said. "It's been changed."

Cedar had already deleted it from his contacts, glad his mother hadn't lived to see the day her hero fell.

Cedar was the one to disconnect the call.

If he'd ever pictured a moment such as this, he'd have thought he'd be dying under the weight of it.

Instead, he actually felt kind of...free. His mother had idolized Randy Cedar-Jones. She'd lived inside his music during her teen years, filling emotional voids with his intense lyrics, his promises of a love that reached beyond the disappointments and healed all hurts. She'd thought him akin to a preacher. Spreading love and hope in the world.

She'd raised Cedar on his rhetoric, giving him a preconceived notion of who he was as Cedar-Jones's son. Of the legacy he carried. Teaching him respect for the incredibly gifted man who had important work to do.

She'd overcome tough times with the help of his lyrics. Over and over, she'd tell Cedar about things that had happened and how his father's lyrics had given her the strength to endure. From dealing with her own parents' unending fights, a high school group that bullied her for being a bookworm, an angry parent in the classroom when she was teaching, to the time she was almost mugged and had been afraid to go out at night. Cedar-Jones's songs always seemed to have a message for her. Which had been her sign that her reverence wasn't misplaced.

As he thought about it all, Cedar figured it could seem like she was half off her rocker, but the truth was, his mother was one of the kindest, strongest, most grounded women he'd ever known. And that was probably why Cedar had placed such emphasis on his father's importance.

She'd always understood, so much better than he had, that Cedar couldn't be acknowledged as Cedar-Jones's son. First, for his own sake, because growing up in the shadow of fame would give him an unrealistic view of himself, his world, his responsibility.

And second, because it would've brought scandal to Cedar-Jones.

As if a love child would have mattered to his fans.

Of course, it could have brought out more piranhas than normal for someone in his position. And the fact that he'd paid for Cedar's care could have strengthened other people's chances of getting money out of him.

Who knew what the man thought, or why he'd made the choices he had? He sure as hell wasn't sharing.

Cedar's mother had died, still idolizing Cedar-Jones. Still loving him.

Funny, it wasn't Cedar or his beautiful mother who'd tarnished what Harold Horatio could have been. He'd done that all by himself.

CEDAR HAD TO rush home to make it to the construction site at the Stand on time. Welcomed the chance to work off steam. To pound out the pain that seemed to be oozing from his pores, along with the sweat.

If any guys on the crew had seen the early-morning news or recognized him from it, they didn't say. But then, as little as he looked up, they could've been gossiping about him all morning, and he wouldn't have known.

Or cared.

Heather would have heard by now. If she hadn't seen the news, Lianna would have. She was one of those people who always had to be in the know.

He'd always respected that about her. Until this morning, when he'd been certain she'd see the news and rush over to "comfort" Heather and commiserate with her about how lucky she was to have escaped the likes of him.

Problem was, of course, that he agreed with Li-anna. And Raine. They had good cause to worry. Not because of the DiSalvo case, but because he was a man who couldn't trust himself to make the right choices. How could he possibly ask anyone else to trust him?

He'd done the right thing that morning—not going to the airport—but it had been touch and go up until the last minute. He'd known when DiSalvo's flight was due to land. His father had told him to be there. He'd been dressed in a suit and ready to go. Had watched the clock, still back and forth on whether or not he'd do it.

He hadn't gone.

God, this whole redemption thing was killing him. He pounded. Lifted beams that were meant for two-man crews and got them into place. He could take a break, pull his phone out of the case hooked to his belt and call her. He could explain.

This time.

And to what end? His own reprieve. If he truth-fully felt that Heather was better off with him, he'd call.

But he didn't feel that way.

So he pounded.

And pounded.

And pounded.

CHAPTER TWENTY-EIGHT

HEATHER DIDN'T GO to the office that day. It was a first, her canceling work. Rescheduling appointments had been a mess, since most polygraph tests were time-specific, with people waiting on results. She'd have to work late the rest of the week and go in on Saturday morning, too, but she'd managed to cover her workload with time to meet all her clients' deadlines.

And then she went to the beach. Lianna and Raine had both offered to stay with her. Raine could call in other instructors, she'd said. Lianna had "personal time off" hours she could use. She'd sent them both away. No one was dying here, after all.

Not literally.

She was a big girl, and it was time she wore her big-girl panties, as Lianna liked to say.

Heather's time off was meant to serve as her attempt to do just that. She didn't expect to line up the rest of her life in one day, but she knew she had to get back on track. Move forward.

Charles called. He'd seen the news. Offered to

take her out to dinner that evening, if she wanted to talk.

She hadn't even been tempted to accept.

Still, it was nice to know that they could be friends.

Her parents had called, too, on speakerphone. Of course they'd seen the news. Wanted to make sure she was okay. And they didn't know the half of it. They just thought Cedar had reached a new low. They had no idea that he'd told her he'd quit his job. That he was no longer working as a defense attorney. That he hadn't taken on any new cases since the one during which he'd betrayed her.

She wanted to delete his contact from her phone. To change her number so he could never call her again. At the very least, when she came off the beach, she could block his number so he couldn't bother her anytime soon.

Because she hadn't slept much, she dozed on her blanket in the sand, sounds of the beach all around her. A sense of comfort and security, a sense of fun and normal, in the midst of her heart shattering.

And she sat and watched the waves lap the shore, too. In and out. In and out. No matter what happened out on that ocean. Whatever tragedy—from hurricanes to war—those waves kept flowing in to shore. Sometimes with more force. Sometimes bearing dead bodies. But they always flowed.

It was a constant.

Like love was a constant.

Even now, with her heart breaking so badly she couldn't even cry, she loved Cedar. Truly loved him.

She needed to be there for him. Whether he was a changed man or not. That was what she'd learned about herself through all of this. She couldn't just turn her back and run. She had to stay long enough to find a way to let love win.

But try as she might, she couldn't figure out how to do that.

THE LAST THING in the world Cedar wanted Thursday night was to have a face-off with Heather's best friends. He'd have avoided it at all costs, but they weren't about to be avoided. They were waiting for him, just outside the gate of his home, when he pulled in after work.

He could have thrown the SUV into reverse. Maybe should have.

But they weren't going to leave until they'd given him a piece of their mind. He knew them. He'd found them somewhat formidable as individuals. Now, as a couple...

He lowered his window, asked them what they wanted.

He wasn't inviting them inside that gate.

Jerk he might be, but even assholes had rights. His home was his space. It was where he could be completely honest with himself. Where he was totally open about making amends. It was his healing place.

"We'd like you to come with us." Surprisingly, Raine was the one who spoke. From the passenger seat of Lianna's white Chevy Equinox.

"I'm not getting in that car with you." He wasn't a back seat rider.

And he refused to be trapped. He'd listen to them. Maybe. But he didn't owe them.

"That's fair," Lianna said, her tone, while certainly not conveying respect, was lacking in sarcasm at least. "Follow us."

Backing up, letting them lead the way, he did. He didn't have to stop when they stopped. Didn't have to get out if he didn't like the spot they chose for this showdown.

Personally, though, he hoped the place was acceptable to him, as he really just wanted to get this over with.

They had a valid complaint—on Heather's behalf. They were her protectors, the same way she was theirs. It was a system that worked.

One he would've liked to have.

But didn't.

Because, other than Heather and his mom, he'd never felt connected enough to anyone to be open to such an arrangement.

He'd had buds. But nothing that got personal. Because a guy who had to hide his real identity learned early on that he could never be completely honest with anyone.

That was how he'd known that Heather was The One. He'd told her the truth about his identity, his father, on their second date.

After a ten-minute drive, they ended up, of all places, at Lianna's apartment. He liked it well enough. Could insist that they have the conversation on her balcony. He could take a jump off it if it came to that...

The thought, while not serious, amused him as he got out of his SUV, minus the knife on his belt, and sauntered toward them.

He'd give them their pound of his flesh. And then he'd tell them how very much he loved the friend they were right to defend. He'd ask them, in confidence, to come to him, no matter what, if she was ever in trouble. If she ever needed anything...

It was the solution he'd worked out that day. One that would let him live with himself—live without Heather. He could do it as long as he knew she'd come to him if she was ever in a crisis and he could help.

That was family.

That was love.

It was why he'd agreed to Cedar-Jones's request.

HEATHER HAD NO idea why her friends had invited her over for dinner and then left her sitting on Raine's balcony, without so much as a glass of wine. They'd said they forgot something. That they'd be right back.

She didn't buy it.

But she was too tired, sun-weary, cried-out and emotionally spent to care. They'd invited her over. Wine would be involved when they got back. And she could sleep on their couch.

She just had to be up in time in the morning to get home, shower and get to work.

Truthfully, she'd welcomed their call—for more than escapism or coddling purposes. She needed to talk to both of them. Together. They had to help her figure out how she could stand by Cedar, support him, give love a chance, without losing herself to his downfall in the process.

She believed he was really trying to change. That he'd seen the error of his ways and wished they weren't there.

She just wasn't sure he had an internal compass that would allow him to change. He hadn't even called the night before—they'd fought so hard for Carin's sake, and he hadn't taken a single moment to discuss the outcome.

She knew why, now. He'd been involved in a case.

Which meant he hadn't changed all that much.

But it had only been a year...

In the dark gray pants and white formfitting short blouse she'd intended to wear to work that morning, she was leaning over, elbows on her knees, and happened to look down to the floor, instead of out at the view.

Just inside the sliding glass door behind her was a leather case.

Hers.

The one that held her portable polygraph. She'd left it in her car.

Hadn't she?

Was she that out of it? Had she brought up the case instead of her purse?

Before she could go investigate, try to find the purse she thought she'd dropped on the couch when she had come in, the front door of the tiny apartment opened, and Lianna was there, half blocking Raine from her view.

"Finally," Heather said, standing, moving into the doorway from the balcony. "Wine time."

They'd said they'd forgotten something, but Lianna wasn't carrying a bag. Neither was Raine.

And...neither was the man who came in behind them.

"Cedar?" What the hell was going on? Had he kidnapped her two friends on their way to the store? Made them bring him to her?

All day long, even after the news came out, he hadn't bothered to call...

"Heather?" The way he said her name, almost reverently, hit clear to her broken heart.

Lodging there. Salve or sting, she didn't know. It just lingered.

"So…" Lianna, all business-like, moved into the room. Grabbed Heather's case and opened it.

As though she'd known right where it was. As though she'd put it there.

They'd picked her up at her bungalow, saying Raine would drive her home in the morning. Apparently they'd picked up more than just her.

"You two have the kind of love that lasts forever," Raine said, looking from Heather to Cedar, while Lianna was busy setting up Heather's machine on her table.

Which amounted to taking it out with the monitors already attached and plugging it in.

"And you have problems." Lianna took over. "Real problems. The kind that can kill a girl slowly…over time…"

"And a guy, too, when the girl doesn't trust him," Raine added.

"So…we figure, before everyone gets hurt beyond repair, let's just hook Cedar up here and find out the truth."

Heather shook her head. The idea was brilliant, really. She thought of Jenny and Tom.

But she couldn't do this. She didn't have questions. Was way, way too personally involved.

"I don't need a test to tell you the truth you

need to hear," Cedar said. "I can't ask Heather to trust me, because I can't trust myself."

"We saw the news," Heather blurted. He'd come. He was standing there, facing her firing squad.

He'd gone to work at the construction site that day. Its dust was all over him.

He looked...even more delicious than wine.

But he'd lied to her again...

"You don't have to hook me up to get the truth about that, either," he said, standing there, his expression open, his arms down at his sides, not crossed. Meeting them all eye to eye as he looked back and forth among the three of them. "Of course, you might need it to be able to believe me..."

"You took a case, Cedar. But not everything you told me was a lie. You went to work at the construction site today." She had to support him. To at least try.

Because her heart was giving her no other choice.

He just stood there. "Cedar-Jones called me."

She stared at him. Could hardly believe she was hearing right. She'd really thought the man was little more than a ghost. That maybe even the phone number his mother had given him had been fake.

"Who's Cedar-Jones?" Lianna asked the question. "Not that singer—"

"My father," Cedar broke in, telling the secret that had never been hers to share. "And yes, the singer."

"Your father's Cedar-Jones? I thought you never met your dad." Lianna clearly wasn't liking the turn of the conversation.

"My father is Randy Cedar-Jones. I've never met him. He won't formally acknowledge me, but he fathered me. And sent my mother child support until I reached eighteen. He also paid for my college. And last week, he called me."

"Randy Cedar-Jones?" Raine squealed. *"Really?"*

Heather nodded, but was still staring at Cedar. Unsure what to think. Had he lost his mind?

Or were miracles happening?

There was no hint of a twinkle in his eye. Nothing but dead seriousness.

If his father had called, after all those years, wouldn't he be...happy?

"Yes, Randy Cedar-Jones. Whose real name, by the way, is Harold Horatio Cedar."

"You're saying that *the* Randy Cedar-Jones called you?" Lianna asked.

"I am."

"Heather?" Lianna's tone brooked no argument, and she looked over to where Heather and

Raine were standing by her polygraph machine, at the table.

She nodded again. "He told me. On our second date."

"And you never said a word?" Raine's voice was breathless. She'd always been a fan.

Probably not much of one anymore, though, when Cedar finished his story about his association with the man. Starting from the first call, more than a week ago, to that very morning.

It took everything Heather had not to run to him, to take him in her arms, wrap them tightly around him and never let him go.

But she wasn't strong enough to stop the tears. They dripped down her cheeks as she stood there, frozen in place.

"I can't believe he did that to you," Raine said.

Cedar shrugged.

Lianna was surprisingly quiet.

Cedar was the first to move. "I'd like to take your test," he said.

"But...I don't have any questions." Heather couldn't do this to him. Put him through such a humiliating exercise and in front of others, too. She couldn't do her part, either.

"You hook me up," Cedar said, looking at Heather. "Then the three of you ask away. Whatever comes to mind. As many questions as you like. Then we'll see where we are."

"No way." She was shaking her head so hard she was almost dizzy. "It's not fair, Cedar. You don't have to do this. I won't let you do this."

"See...that's the funny thing," Cedar said, rolling the sleeve of his T-shirt up to his shoulder. "Because while you have complete say over your choices and your life, I have say over mine. And I want to take your test." He was looking her straight in the eye, his gaze narrowed. Intense. "I'll take it for me, Heather. For my own sake," he said. "I want to know as badly as your friends do."

In one sentence, he'd given her all the truth she'd ever needed. He loved her at least as much as her best friends did—probably more.

As she did him.

But...he needed this. He needed to know what she knew. What she'd so recently discovered—about herself. And him.

Her job was to show the truth, to get her clients to express their truth.

She was good at it.

She nodded. Hooked him up, her fingers burning everywhere she touched his skin. At one point, she actually jolted, and he looked at her. His raised eyebrow was also very Cedar, and she stepped back. "I...haven't touched you in a long time."

He wanted his test. He could flirt with the tester.

"Okay," she announced. "We're ready."

"I'll go first," Lianna, not surprisingly, spoke up. Heather nodded.

"Did you knowingly betray Heather?"

"Yes. I did." No hesitation. No "tells." The machine, while she had no base marks for her read, indicated no change in his bodily reactions.

"My turn." Raine stepped forward, and Cedar gave her his attention. "Do you love Heather more than you love your own life?"

"Yes. I do."

Absolutely no change.

Lianna and Raine studied Heather carefully. "Your turn," Lianna said when she remained speechless. There was only one question she wanted to ask. Didn't need to anymore, but wanted to.

"Are you really trying to fight your addiction to winning?"

"Yes. I am."

There was a blip. A small one.

And he said, "But to be honest, I think I have a solution on that one, so maybe *fighting* isn't the right word."

"What's the solution?"

"Wait a minute," Lianna said, "this isn't part of the test. You can't start to have a conversation here."

Lianna knew how it worked. *Yes* and *no* questions. Heather had, at Lianna's request, tested her years ago. She'd been trying to figure herself out, and the test had failed miserably. They'd both ended up in tears and hugging each other.

"I want to know the solution," Heather said.

"I do, too," Raine added, and Lianna waved a hand in Cedar's direction.

He told them about an idea he'd had to use his skills to help put away the very types of criminals he'd excelled at setting free. Said he had a proposal already written up, and that he had an appointment with his contact at the FBI, as well as a legal specialist who could actually make a decision on the matter, early the following week.

As backup, he had appointments with the Santa Raquel county district attorney and the LA county attorney, as well.

The entire time he talked, the machine showed no changed reactions. None.

This test could be over. There were no more questions.

"My turn again," Lianna said. Cedar nodded, his chin slightly raised, taking her on. Heather didn't have the heart to stop whatever was going on between him and Lianna.

"Do you want to marry Heather?"

Oh, God. Just because she and Raine had talked about marriage already... Cedar didn't have to marry her if marriage wasn't for him...

"I do. More than anything else in the world."

She stared at the machine. Waiting for the spikes to fly. Waiting. Still waiting.

No spikes.

Maybe because of the tears in her eyes.

She blinked.

Still no spikes.

She looked at him. His eyes were glistening. Something she had never, ever seen before.

And she ended the exam.

THEY STAYED WITH Heather's friends long enough to drink one glass of wine, and then Cedar took her home. Because it was what he wanted to do.

Needed to do.

She'd asked, and that had been his answer.

He needed to take her home.

To make love to her.

To eat dinner with her.

To marry her.

To spend the rest of his life with her.

He needed it all.

And still...

"I know what I want," he told her, lying naked in her arms, later that night. They'd done it all. Except the marrying part. They'd gone home—to his house, by her choice. After stopping at hers to pick up a few things. They'd made love. Had dinner. Made love again. "But I can't promise that I can deliver..."

He hadn't called the night before, because he'd wanted to so badly, but he'd wanted to concentrate on her, not himself. But he'd been so busy thinking about his own wants and needs, he'd failed to consider that she'd be worried. And hurt by his lack of a call.

She put a finger to his lips. And then her tongue. And then her lips. She kissed him in a way she'd never kissed him before. As if she was leading them on a brand-new dance floor.

His penis got hard for a third time that night. Painfully hard. He was ready to pull her on top of him, to sink inside her, when she said, "I'm probably always going to be sensitive to you not picking up the phone, Cedar. I don't know why I am. I'm working on it. I don't want to expect things that aren't reasonable, and then get hurt by them. But I probably will sometimes. You're going to forget to call, too. Or get focused on a case, on the job right in front of you, and end up missing our anniversary dinner."

He'd done that once.

"But the thing is, our promise to each other, the only promise…because it's the only one we can both make with total honesty…is that we will always come back together. No matter what happens, we will let our love fight for us, and trust it to repair the damage."

There. She'd said—

He sat up so quickly, she almost fell off him. Not quite. He held her in place, still ready to make love for a third time. But he was, as she'd said, focused on what was right in front of him.

"We don't trust each other as much as we trust the love we share…"

"Exactly." She smiled. "You see how that works? We aren't perfect. We're going to make mistakes. But our love… Now, that's way up there on the perfection scale."

"I don't have to trust myself," Cedar said. "I trust that my love for you, and your love for me, will keep me on the right path as much as possible, and allow you to stand by me if I screw up."

"Yes. And vice versa."

She moved. He moved, too.

And when she slid down on top of him, he knew that, although they were imperfect people, they'd found their own piece of perfection on earth.

Heather had given him, shown him, the ultimate truth.

* * * * *